Malevolent

E. H. Reinhard

AUTHOR'S NOTE

This book is a work of fiction by E. H. Reinhard. Names, characters, and incidents are products of the author's imagination or are used fictitiously. Any resemblance to actual events or persons, living or dead, is entirely coincidental. Locations used vary from real streets, locations, and public buildings to fictitious residences and businesses.

E.H. Reinhard
http://ehreinhard.com/

Malevolent: Cases of Lieutenant Kane Series, Book 1

Tampa homicide lieutenant Carl Kane has a tough job. His day to day consists of decomposing dead bodies and removing murderers from the general public. But when two women's bodies are found under similar circumstances, it quickly turns into more than your average case. The killer is clearly looking to make a name for himself, and his plans for these women go far beyond death.

When the media runs with the story, the killer's moment in the spotlight arrives.

It's up to Lieutenant Kane to bring the man the press has dubbed the Psycho Surgeon to justice. However, being the lead on the case has its drawbacks—like becoming the focus of the killer yourself.

As Lieutenant Kane closes in on his suspect, he soon realizes the case has become far more personal than he could have ever imagined.

The Lieutenant Kane series:

Malevolent

Requite

Determinant

Perilous

Progeny

Denouement

Want to make sure you don't miss my next book?
Sign up for my VIP email list at:

http://ehreinhard.com/newsletter/

ma·lev·o·lent

adjective /muh-lev-uh-luhnt/

: having or showing a desire to cause harm
to another person

Chapter 1

The phone rang and rang.

On the seventh or eighth ring, I answered. I already knew who it was. "This is Kane."

"Kane, we have one."

I let out a puff of air in disappointment. I hadn't gotten a decent night's sleep in weeks. "You really need me there?"

"Yeah."

"Fine. Where?"

The captain rattled off the address. "Right away," he said and hung up.

The address was the Manchester office building a couple miles from my condo.

While my schedule said I had Sundays and Mondays off, I couldn't recall the last time I didn't work a Sunday. Mondays were the only days I could somewhat count on not being bothered—murderers weren't as active on Sunday nights and Monday mornings. However, as a department lead, I was always on call. That led to a lot of overtime. The clock on my nightstand read 7:33 a.m. I rolled out of bed.

I rummaged through my closet and selected my day's attire. The pants, shirt, and tie tucked under my arm were somewhat clean. The walls of the hallway guided me toward my bathroom. I splashed water across my face and ran my hands across my couple-day-old stubble. Though I'd just turned thirty-eight, the color of my beard was becoming more salt than pepper every day. I was positive my hair would match if I'd had any. For the past fifteen years, I'd been sticking with the Mr. Clean look. I kicked on the shower and rinsed off the lingering smell of bar from the night before. Dressed, I grabbed my badge from the gun safe in my closet and pulled on my shoulder holster.

In the kitchen, I picked up the bag of coffee from the counter and gave it a shake. A few stray grounds remained at the bottom. I remembered my to-do list from the day before. The third task from the top was *get coffee*. My caffeine fix would have to wait until I found a gas station.

Butch looked up at me from the couch. He meowed and dug his head back into his pillow. I walked over and gave him a pat on the head. My keys jingled as I scooped them from the kitchen counter. I locked up and left.

My Mustang's thermometer read seventy-nine degrees—the temperature would flirt with a hundred by midday. I liked the heat. Only a handful of years had passed since I moved from Wisconsin. I still enjoyed the fact that it was always some form of summer.

Bumper-to-bumper traffic lay before me as I headed down Kennedy. Tampa's entire first-shift workforce had apparently decided to avoid the freeway on their work commutes. After a quick stop for what gas stations called coffee, I made a right off of Kennedy into the Manchester building's parking lot.

The office building was a large tan high-rise with mirrored glass windows. It stood over twenty stories tall. Two smaller outbuildings, five stories each, sat to the sides. Impeccable landscaping surrounded the entire complex. The building's courtyard was home to a pyramid shaped water fountain. Water bubbled from the apex and cascaded down the sides. Benches lined the front entryway. On a towering pole in the center of the courtyard, an American flag flicked in the morning breeze. As I pulled through the employee parking lot, I caught flashing red-and-blues at the side of the building. I found my way around to where four squad cars sat. The flashing lights and police cars were drawing employees from every office in the complex. I pulled the Mustang into the first vacant spot I found, grabbed my coffee from the cup holder and got out. I hung my badge from my neck and started over to the scene.

The crime scene spread out before me as I rounded the back of the building. The rear parking lot butted up against the freeway. More parking for the employees and a bank of dumpsters lined the back. A handful of uniforms stood at the police tape surrounding an area twenty feet from the building's back entry. They were keeping the building's employees at bay. I stepped over the barrier and headed for the first familiar face I saw, Sergeant Hank Rawlings.

Rawlings was a tall, thin, forty-something-year-old cop,

complete with police-issue mustache and buzz cut. I was his superior, yet through all the homicides we'd worked together, I considered him my partner. He stood talking with a uniformed officer twenty feet inside the yellow tape. His designer suit didn't have a wrinkle on it. His tie was crisp. The sun shone off the toes of his shoes. A set of aviator sunglasses hid his eyes. His wife had been doing his shopping again.

"Go out last night?" he asked.

"For a little. Got in around midnight."

Hank raised his sunglasses so they rested on his forehead. "Did you make it to the gun show after you left yesterday?"

"Yeah, I caught the last hour. The place was packed. I scooped up a few things and left." I guzzled down a swig of the coffee. "What's with the outfit, Slick?"

"Karen says I should present myself better at work. She picked me up a couple of new suits."

I smiled and nodded, making a mental note to bust his chops later about his wife dressing him. "Give me the short version."

He motioned for me to follow him as he walked toward the gray, fenced-in area where the dumpsters sat. "D.B., female—employee found her by the dumpsters over here."

Inside the fence, a yellow tarp covered a body lying on the ground. Ed Dockett, the county's chief medical examiner, knelt next to the tarp. I caught a view of the body over his short gray hair and thin shoulders.

"What are we looking at, Ed?"

He ran the back of his hand across his bushy gray

eyebrows. "Female, blond, thirties." Ed folded back the corner of the tarp, exposing the victim's face. Her eyes were open, foggy, and fixed on the morning sky.

"Smells like bleach," I said.

Ed nodded. "Body was cleaned."

He pulled the tarp back farther. The woman lay dressed in green lingerie. He pointed to some purple marks around her wrists. "We have ligature marks on her wrists—same on her ankles. Someone had her tied up. She's got a wound on the side of her head here. It may have penetrated into the skull cavity."

"Bullet?" I asked.

"I'm not so sure. I'll have to wait to give you the cause of death until after I do the autopsy." He pointed at the area over her right ear. "More damage to the skin around the wound. It's weird looking." Ed moved his face closer. "It almost looks like a burn. I'll have to take a peek at it under magnification back at the office." He turned the woman's hand over, showing me the back side. "She has a fresh brand here. Not more than a day old would be my guess."

I cocked my head. The brand was a circle divided into fourths. Four small triangles sat to each side of the center circle.

"Kind of looks like a reticle in the center," Hank said.

"Guess it could be." I had a bad feeling bubbling deep in my gut. Women didn't voluntarily get their hands branded. I jotted it down in my notepad. "You have an approximate time of death, Ed?"

"Three to six hours. Eyes are cloudy. Rigor has started

to set in." He laid the tarp back over the body, removed his latex gloves, and pushed his glasses back up his nose. "The forensics guys are done with the body, so we're going to get her loaded up."

A few guys from Ed's team approached with a stretcher and a body bag. Hank and I gave them space to bag the body and load it into the coroner's van.

"Stop by later this afternoon. I'll have a full report by then," Ed said.

"Thanks." I surveyed the scene and spotted a nervous-looking office worker. He was standing with one of our detectives against the building. "Is that the guy who found her?" I nodded toward him.

"That's him. I guess he works in one of the offices upstairs."

"You don't say?"

"He was taking out the trash when he spotted the body. Jones is getting his statement. He was first on the scene."

"Let's go have a chat."

Hank and I walked over to Detective Maxwell Jones. He'd gotten promoted to our homicide division a year prior. He was speaking with the man leaning against the wall. While I wasn't small, standing over six feet and having spent a decent amount of time in the gym, Jones was a mountain of a man. He was at least six-foot-six and had to be over three hundred pounds. He should have been a professional wrestler.

"Jones," I said.

"Lieutenant." He nodded at me then at Hank.

"Sergeant."

I turned to the man standing to his side. "I understand you're the one who found the body?"

He nodded. The guy was clean shaven and in his later twenties. Two creases ran down the front of his khakis. He wore a white short-sleeved button-down shirt. A yellow tie hung around his neck. The apparel appeared to be that of a stereotypical office worker. I imagined he had himself a nice cubicle inside somewhere.

"I'm Lieutenant Carl Kane. This is Sergeant Hank Rawlings. Can you give us the run-through on how you found the body?"

"I came out to dump the trash and saw her lying on the ground back behind the dumpster. That's about it. I walked over and could tell she was dead."

"How could you tell?"

He pulled his head back. "Did you look at her?"

"And then you dialed 9-1-1?" I asked.

"That's right."

"Recognize the woman?" Hank asked.

"No."

"Touch her at all?" Hank asked.

The guy wrinkled his face. "Why would I touch a dead body?"

"What time did you call?" I asked.

Jones flipped a page on his clipboard. "The call came in at 7:18 a.m."

I wrote the time down. "And you're sure you haven't seen the woman before?"

He shook his head.

"Thanks." I motioned toward Jones. "Detective, can we get a quick word?"

He followed Hank and me out of earshot from the guy.

"What can you tell us, Jones?" I asked.

"Not a lot. No identification on the body—no purse, no cell phone. We have a body by a dumpster. That's about the extent of it."

I glanced at the fence. "Is the dumpster area supposed to be locked?"

"I don't think so," Jones said.

"Witnesses? Did anyone see anything?" Hank asked.

"We didn't find anyone. The other officers went through the crowd that gathered. It seems everyone here now is just gawking." He gestured at the ever-growing mob of people standing at the edge of the parking lot. They crowded the police tape.

I choked down another sip of the black swill in my Styrofoam cup. "Doesn't this kind of seem like an odd place for a body dump?"

My question didn't receive a response.

Like clockwork, news vans arrived on the scene. Reporters jumped out. The news crews began running cables and setting lights, preparing to broadcast. I surveyed the rest of the parking lot and spotted Rick Daniels, from our forensics department, leaning against the coroner's van. A cigarette hung under his mustache. The buttons on his burgundy shirt were straining, as usual. He was talking with someone in a white jumpsuit. We left Jones to finish with the man who'd called it in and walked over to Rick.

"Hey, Rick," I said. "What's the word?"

"I thought you had today off."

"Guess someone had other plans. I thought you were quitting smoking."

He pulled the cigarette from his mouth and flicked the ash. "I cut back."

"Who's this?" I jerked my chin at the white-suited guy.

"I'm breaking in our newest edition."

The kid was about five-foot-five and had a baby face. A faint trace of a peach-fuzz beard sat beneath his chin. He looked fresh out of high school at best.

The kid held out his hand. "I'm Pax."

Hank accepted the handshake. "I'm Sergeant Rawlings. So, Pax? Is that a first or last name?"

"It's my first name, sir. Pax McLain."

I shook the kid's hand. "Is that short for something?"

"Nope. Just Pax. It's going to be great working with you guys."

He was too chipper to be dealing with a D.B. at eight-something in the morning. As I looked at him, a single thought ran through my head: *Who the hell names their kid Pax?*

"Any evidence from the lot? Prints on the fence here?" Hank asked.

Rick ran his hand through his short brown-and-gray hair. He shook his head. "Nothing. It looks like it was wiped down. We were just about to dig through the dumpsters to see if we can find any of her belongings."

"See any video cameras on the building back here?" I asked.

"First thing we looked for." He shook his head. "I talked with a guy inside. They have cameras in the lobby. Nothing outside, though."

"All right, let me know," I said.

We left Rick and Pax to do their dumpster diving. Hank and I headed for the gawkers at the police tape. Maybe some questioning with the building's employees would shake something loose.

"What are you thinking, Kane?"

"Women don't get brands on their hands."

Hank nodded.

At the police barricade, reporters shouldered each other for position, each one trying to get the best footage of the scene.

I gulped down the last bit of coffee from my cup. "I'll go deal with the press."

Hank flashed me a look of surprise. "You sure you don't want me to handle that?" He knew my disdain for the media.

"Nah, I got it." I walked over to the group of reporters lined up outside the police tape. They went into a frenzy as soon as I approached.

Rich Martin, from Channel 11, waved at me. "Lieutenant Kane! Kane, over here! Can you tell us what happened?"

I knew to keep my answers succinct. The local media had a habit of embellishing. "We found a body."

"Male or female?"

"Female."

"Lieutenant, is this a murder?" a reporter from a local paper asked.

"We just started our investigation."

"Do you have anyone in custody?" another reporter asked.

"As I just said, we just started the investigation."

J.R. Steele, from Channel 6, pushed through the other reporters to get to the police tape. "We have information that the woman was held captive. Can you comment on that?" He held out his microphone for my response.

I eyeballed him. He looked like a Ken doll with his hair combed and styled to perfection. His face didn't show a hint of stubble. He wore makeup. His suit looked like it cost a minimum of four figures. Physical attributes aside, the guy was a jerk. His voice dripped with arrogance. Every time I heard it, I became angry.

"That will be all. We will schedule a full press release when we have more information."

I grabbed a uniformed officer and instructed him to move the police tape farther back to get the press out of our hair. The reporters had all the information they needed to concoct their headlines.

Chapter 2

He stood just beyond the police tape, trying to get a view over the heads of the gathered crowd. The woman was nowhere in sight. In a matter of seconds, disappointment set in. The coroner's van came into view between the people.

Damn, she died.

A few cops wandered around, interviewing and talking with people. He spotted a bald, bigger man wearing a suit. Another thin man, dressed similarly, followed him. They walked from group to group, taking notes. Both men showed noticeable bulges from shoulder-holstered firearms under their suit coats. They looked like detectives. The bigger one held a cup of coffee. His body language was casual. He looked to be in charge. That could have been the officer whose job it was to catch him—but not yet.

He had big plans.

They walked toward him in the crowd. He caught a glimpse of their badges, swinging from lanyards on their necks as they approached.

Damn. She was alive when I left her here.

The two cops got closer. He coughed into his fist. He needed to leave—quickly.

Chapter 3

We spoke with a few more people at the scene. None of the office workers could shed any light on what we'd found. I left and returned to the station a little after nine o'clock. I walked in and headed straight for the lunch room. A cup of coffee was in order, one that didn't taste like burnt motor oil. A few minutes later, I sulked back toward my office, empty handed. The station's coffee machine had been on the fritz again.

I walked through the bullpen—a large rectangular room with twenty-plus desks separated into cubicles by low walls. In the morning, the bullpen was quiet, but by the afternoon, it bustled with activity and noise. The crew that made up the graveyard shift had just headed home. Their nights consisted of dealing with the city's drunks and domestic disputes. The day shifters were just starting their day.

Offices of department heads and detectives lined the perimeter of the bullpen. The two larger offices in the back left of the room were mine and Captain Bostok's. I headed into my office. The interior of my glass box rode the line between order and mayhem. I made an effort to keep things inside my office organized, but the never-ending paperwork that funneled through my office made it a losing battle. File cabinets lined my back wall. They had been full for so long I didn't remember the contents. The rest of my office was pretty standard—a small couch, two guest chairs, a couple tables, some miscellaneous books, and a computer. Service awards and photos of my nephew filled the shelves behind my desk.

I walked around and took a seat in my extra-large office chair. I'd picked it up a couple days prior—real leather, built solid, and made in the USA. The chair cost over a thousand bucks. It was worth every penny. My job could involve long nights of desk time. A good chair was a necessity.

I grabbed the phone and called Steinberg in missing persons. I ran the woman's description by him. He had no one similar who'd been reported missing. He said he would call around and get back to me.

Hank walked into my office, holding two tall cups of coffee. He took a seat across from me and slid one of the cups over. "I stopped at a coffee shop on the way back. I didn't want to roll the dice with the machine."

"You would have lost." I grabbed the cup and took a drink. The coffee was far better than the gas station swill I'd drunk earlier.

"That's what I figured. Are you staying or going?" Hank

dunked his mustache into the coffee cup and took a sip off the top. He squirmed in my guest chair.

The fact that it was my day off had escaped my mind. I kicked the idea around in my head. While the thought of going home was nice, I had no plans. I would just think about the case between reruns of whatever was on television. "Think I'm going to keep looking into the brand on the woman's hand until I hear back from Ed at the M.E.'s office."

"New photo?" He nodded at the picture on the shelf behind my desk.

"Yeah, it's this week's addition."

Hank set his cup of coffee down and walked over to the edge of my desk. He picked the frame up from the shelf.

The photo was of my nephew, Tommy. Melissa, my sister, younger by seven years, managed to take, package, and send at least a dozen photos of my nephew to me each month. That was aside from the daily e-mails, which included more photos and videos. When I told her I didn't have frames for all the pictures she sent, she started sending them in little photo albums. I'd only been back up to Wisconsin to visit a few times since moving. My sister reminded me of this with each conversation and e-mail.

"Little guy is getting big. When are you going back up to see him?"

"Well, I planned to this spring, but we had that spurt of gang shootings. The fourth of July would have been nice, but it's too late to request off now. I don't know—maybe fall. The thought of going up there in winter doesn't do too much for me. My old man and stepmom have been laying on the guilt trips nice and thick as of late. I'll have to go up there soon."

"How are they doing?"

"Same as always. Living the retired life."

Hank set the photo back on the shelf and retook his seat across from me. He squirmed again. "Did you get new guest chairs?"

"Yeah, why?"

"These things are awful."

I tapped the armrest of my chair. "Most of the office budget is under my ass. They aren't that bad."

"You aren't sitting here. This might be the most uncomfortable chair I've ever sat in."

"Try the other one."

"It's the same thing."

I shrugged.

He let out a long sigh as he rearranged himself and looked for a more comfortable position. "Don't put off seeing your family for this job. It comes with vacation time for a reason."

"Yeah, I know. I'll get something set to go up there."

He took another sip from his cup. "You need me for anything? I can't sit in this torture device any longer."

I shook my head. "Not yet. Finish up whatever you have on your desk. Check back with me in a couple hours."

"Sounds good." He got up and walked out.

I walked over to the guest chair and tried it out. He was right—it was pretty damn uncomfortable.

For the rest of the morning and early afternoon, I tried to find a reference to the brand on the woman. I looked online, which netted me nothing. I called over to the team that worked cold cases. They had nothing in their files that involved branding or lingerie. I went down the list of local tattoo shops to see which ones did branding. No one would admit to branding a woman's hand in the last twenty-four hours. Rick called to tell me they'd come up empty with their dumpster diving. We were getting nowhere. My stomach rumbled and told me I'd missed lunch. It rumbled again and told me I'd missed breakfast as well. I dialed Hank's desk.

"Sergeant Rawlings."

"It's Kane. Come to my office." I set the phone back on the receiver.

He walked in a few seconds later. "What's going on? You hear anything back from Ed yet?"

I rattled my fingertips across my desk. "I'm about to call him. He should have the autopsy report done by now. Want to grab lunch and go pick it up?"

"Works for me."

I pulled myself closer to my desk and grabbed the phone. I dialed the medical examiner's office.

Within a ring or two, the receptionist answered. "County Medical Examiner's Office."

"Hi, it's Lieutenant Kane. Is Ed in?"

"Sure. Let me get him for you."

I spun a pen between my fingers as the hold music played in my ear.

"Medical examiner."

"Hey, Ed. It's Kane."

"Hey, Lieutenant. I was just going to call you. I got your report ready. Want me to send it over?"

"We were just leaving for lunch. We'll stop in by you and scoop it up. Should be there within the hour." I hung up the phone. "Ed says it's ready. Take out from Dotana's?"

"Sounds good. Real food will be a nice change. Karen has been packing me these microwave meals for lunch all week. She says they are good for me. You wouldn't know it by the flavor. They are really bad. You ever taste a microwaved veggie burger?"

"Can't say I have."

"It's not good. Not good at all."

"Ever think of telling her you don't like them?"

"I don't know. I guess they're not that bad."

I shook my head. "So you're afraid to tell her is what you're saying?"

"Whatever. It's not worth getting into it with her."

I smirked.

We let Captain Bostok know we were taking off and walked to the parking garage. I grabbed the keys to one of the station's gray, unmarked, Dodge Chargers for the trip. We popped into Dotana's on the way. It was a little greasy spoon down the street from us. Most of their customer base was people from our station. I had a hunch they would be out of business if we all stopped going. I made a point to stop there often. We grabbed a few burgers and ate in the car.

Ten minutes later, we drove through the gated entrance of the county medical examiner's office. Hank and I walked up to the front doors of the complex—a long, tan building with green-tinted windows. Our county opened the multimillion dollar facility in 2009. From what I heard, you would gag from the smell of the old place on Morgan before you ever got out of the car. I was thankful I hadn't gotten to experience it. Hank and I pushed open the front doors.

Ed stood at the front desk, chatting up the receptionist. He cut his story short when we approached. "Kane, Rawlings, how we doing?"

"As well as could be expected. Tell us what we got," I said.

"Cause of death was a brain injury."

I nodded. "That wound on her head?"

"Yup. I have to say, it's a new one for me."

"New one?" I asked.

"Yeah, it's new, all right. You guys want the office version or the look-and-see?"

I glanced at Hank, who shrugged. I figured the look-and-see option couldn't hurt. Maybe we could learn something from Ed's presentation. "Look-and-see," I said.

"All right. Follow me on back." Ed turned and started down the hall.

We trailed after Ed, past the refrigerated storage area of the morgue. They conducted the autopsies in the room ahead. The thick odor of death grew stronger as we walked. Ed pushed opened the swinging doors, and we entered the room. Stainless steel covered the walls while, for some reason, red was the color of choice for the floors. Ed continued past a row of covered bodies, stopping at the second from the last. He laid the folder he was carrying on a shelf and grabbed a set of latex gloves from a push cart. He pulled the gloves onto his hands. "This is her." He drew back the white sheet.

Hank and I stepped in closer.

"Here's our cause of death." Ed pointed above her right ear. Red damaged skin was visible through the stubble of her shaved head. "Her hair was doing a good job of covering the extent of the damage," Ed said.

"What are we looking at here? Small-caliber bullet?" I asked.

Ed shook his head. "Nope. X-ray showed nothing inside. I'm about ninety-nine percent sure it's from a drill."

"Someone drilled into her head?" Hank asked.

"That's not all. They poured boiling water in the hole. The damaged skin around the hole is from scalding. Brain was, for lack of better words, cooked by boiling water."

I rubbed at my eyes.

"Anything that suggested she fought back?" Hank asked.

Ed shook his head. "We scraped her nails and looked her knuckles over for any signs of bruising—nothing. We checked in her mouth—no flesh from biting or anything like that. I found faint traces of bruising around her chest and waist. I think she was tied down. She couldn't fight back."

"Was she dead before any of this happened to her?" I asked.

Ed shook his head. "No. She was alive."

"Any signs of sexual abuse?" I asked.

"Negative." He paused. "I just got the tox report back before you guys showed up. We got a little something there."

"What's the something?" I asked.

"She tested positive for Xylazine."

Hank shrugged. "And that is?"

"It's a horse anesthesia and tranquilizer."

"Spelling?" I asked.

Ed gave it to me.

I jotted the word *Xylazine* in my notepad. "Is that something that's injected?"

Ed nodded in confirmation.

"That stuff is all regulated, right?" I asked.

"Yeah, if you want to call it that. Every vet, zoo, Department of Natural Resources, and game farm in the state should have it. There is a black market for it as well. They have a big problem with it in Puerto Rico. I saw a show on it. Guess they mix it with heroin—turns people into walking zombies."

"Don't zombies normally walk?" Hank asked.

Ed didn't respond.

"Any more highlights?"

"Small clover tattoo on her hip. It could help with an ID."

I made a note of the tattoo. "Can you tell us anything about the brand she had on her hand?"

"It was early in the healing process, so my guess of not more than a day old should be pretty accurate."

"Any idea what it means?" Hank asked.

Ed shrugged. "I took some close-up photos of it and placed them in the file."

"Where is the lingerie she was wearing?" I asked.

"I have the clothing bagged for your forensics guys. You want to take it with you?"

"That's fine. I'll drop it off with Rick when we get back," I said.

"Okay, her clothes are right over here." He pulled the sheet back over her head and walked to a row of slotted shelves at the side of the room. Ed took a bag from the shelf and handed it to Hank.

I jerked my head toward the folder he'd brought in. "Is that our report there?"

"Yup." He grabbed it and passed it over.

I thumbed it open. Photos of her injuries and photos from the scene and the autopsy report filled the file. "So animal tranquilizers, tied up, branded, and dressed in lingerie?"

"Death by drill and boiling water," Hank interjected.

Ed nodded. "Looks like you gentlemen have your work cut out for you."

"Yeah." I flipped the file closed and put it under my arm.

"That's about all I have for you. I need to get started with these other autopsies. Everything else is in the file there. Good luck on the investigation, guys."

"Okay, Ed. We'll see you," I said.

He raised his eyebrows. "Not too soon, I hope."

We headed back toward the station.

Chapter 4

He'd experienced many ways of taking women's lives. The first, second, and third he'd overdosed. Beating, strangulation, and drowning befell his next victims. He had shot a woman a few years back, but it had left him unfulfilled. 2013 marked his twenty-third year—he was an old pro at his trade. His changing methods and locations kept him out of the spotlight.

His last year had been filled with hospitals, doctors, and an inevitable death sentence. Before he went, he planned to achieve something he'd never had in his forty years—his fifteen minutes of fame. The plan for the women wasn't death though it was always a possibility. He had something more in mind—something more dramatic.

He pulled his baseball hat low on his head—his dark, thinning, stringy hair curled out from beneath it. A thick, black-and-gray beard covered most of his sunken face. He peered out of the windshield at cars and people. They came and went, some quicker than others. He was keeping a watchful eye on a loading zone. His car was third in line. His cell phone rested on his stomach—a stomach that had once fallen over his belt line. It was now flat. The phone sat on a light-yellow polo shirt tucked into a pair of jeans. He tapped the button to play his video, which loaded and began. On the screen was a close-up of a woman's face— the woman that had died by the dumpsters of the Manchester building. Tears ran from her cheeks into the pillow below her head.

Her voice trembled through the small speaker of the phone. "I have money. Please, don't do this." Her words came slow and slurred. She was drugged.

The camera blurred, zoomed out, and then focused on the female, bound to a bed. Two tie-down straps, over her chest and midsection, kept her movements at a minimum. The sheets covered her legs. She wore a green teddy—a lacy piece of lingerie with a low, plunging neckline. She wore a matching green thong bottom. Rope wrapped her wrists.

She wiggled against the straps. "What are you doing? Please. Please."

The same man watching the video walked on screen. He held a syringe and a glass vial. The tip of the needle drew a measured dose of Xylazine from inside. He gave it a squirt into the air and then plunged it into her arm. The fluid inside the needle disappeared into her vein.

"That should do for now," he said.

"Please don't. Let me go." Her pleading faded off as the drug made its way through her bloodstream.

His attention focused outside the car's windshield, and

he pulled up one car length. Then his eyes reverted back to the phone's small screen.

The woman's head lay facing the camera. Her blond hair fell against her shoulders and covered her right eye. He walked back on screen holding a blowtorch in one hand and a branding iron in the other. He fired up the blowtorch and held the flame over the iron until it glowed a fiery orange. Her skin sizzled as the iron sank into the flesh of her hand.

He looked up from the video playing on his cell phone and smiled. The branding was his calling card. The press, police and world would know who was responsible.

He walked off screen and returned with a small pull cart on casters. The little wheels squeaked as it moved. A cordless drill and miscellaneous tools sat on the right side of the cart, an assortment of books and syringes covering the rest.

He picked up a tape measure and a marker. With the tip of the marker, he made a circle at his desired entry point. He loaded a bit into the drill's chuck, spun it closed, and tightened it with his hand. The Xylazine he'd pushed into her arm rendered her unconscious. His knees rubbed her sides while he straddled her. With a handful of her blond hair to pull against, he put the tip of the drill bit on the marked area of her skin.

The motor of the drill whirred as he squeezed the trigger. Her hair wrapped around the bit and pulled from her scalp. The metal twisted into her flesh. Blood flowed from her head, ran down her face, and began to pool on the sheets. Small droplets of blood from the rotating bit spattered around the room. More blood hit him in the chest and face. The drill bit spun through her skin and hit skull. He held it steady against the side of her head and applied pressure. Thirty seconds later, he still hadn't penetrated the bone. The bit, dull from earlier use, began to smoke. He swapped it out with a new bit and went back into the hole he'd started. He pulled the trigger again. His pressure was steady. The tip needed to just penetrate the skull so he could pour in the boiling water. With one more squeeze of the trigger, he removed the drill to examine the entry point. Between pumps of blood, he could see that he was through.

The video went black before resuming with the man holding a tea kettle over her head. Steam rose as he thumbed the kettle's flapper. He began. A faint trickle of water came from the kettle into the funnel. The water steamed as it fell into the drilled hole. He pulled himself off of her and went to the camera. It went black.

When the video started again, it showed a close-up of the woman. Her mouth hung half open, her right eye remained closed. Her left eye floated up and down. A man's voice could be heard on the video—his voice. "Let's go drop you off and start my rise to fame."

The camera zoomed closer to her face. Drool ran from her mouth. The video went black again.

"Dammit!" He clicked the garbage can button on his phone to delete the video. "She was alive when I left her there. She was perfect!"

One car still remained in front of him. He clicked the button on his phone for the Internet. He pulled up the

Tampa Police's website and thumbed through the tabs of the different departments. Each department listed a handful of the higher-ranked officers with photos of them in uniform—captains, lieutenants and sergeants. His thumb scrolled through the photos and stopped when a face looked familiar. He raised his phone to eye level for a closer look. The man on the screen was Lieutenant Carl Kane from the homicide division. He was the bigger cop in command of the scene at the Manchester building.

A smile crept across his face. The identity of his adversary was in front of him. The car waiting ahead of him moved. He pulled his cab forward for his fare.

Chapter 5

I dropped off the lingerie in the forensics lab on the first floor. Rick said he would let me know if they got anything from it. The clock inched toward 7:00 p.m. Until we got an ID on the woman, we were dead in the water. We'd put together a description of the deceased and sent it out to the media, hoping someone would come forward. Aside from the crime scene of the morning and the presentation at the medical examiner's office, I spent the rest of my day off wrapping up Luis Alonso's case from the prior week. He was a low-level pusher that got robbed and murdered during a drug deal. The girlfriend of one Jose Lapsey had phoned us after Jose came back to their apartment with blood on his clothes and a handful of bloody cash. The investigation didn't take long. Jose would enjoy our jail facilities until his trial. The paperwork was just about ready to be filed when Hank knocked on the sill of my office door.

"You're still here?"

I didn't look up from the paperwork. "About to bug out."

"What's on the agenda tonight?"

I signed off the bottom of the report, closed the file folder, and gave him my attention. "Head home. Maybe go grab a beer."

A smile crept across his face. "You ask that bartender out yet?"

Callie was the name of the bartender he referred to. She had long black hair and striking eyes and was a solid ten years too young for me. She worked at a little hole-in-the-wall bar a few blocks away from the station. The place reminded me of the corner bars in Wisconsin that I grew up in—small, dark, and smoky with an endless supply of cheap beer. I popped in there a few times a week for dinner. The bar had a great steak sandwich. Hank had tagged along a couple weeks prior. He caught the back and forth between Callie and me. He did his best to bring her up whenever he could.

I rocked back in my big leather office chair. "No, I haven't asked her out yet."

"Why not? I don't think that girl could make her interest in you clearer."

I shook my head and shrugged. I didn't need relationship advice from Hank. "Don't know."

"How long has it been since Samantha left?"

That wasn't a conversation I wanted to have. If there was ever a hot-button issue that I would lose my cool on, it was my ex-wife. "Two years."

He slapped the edge of my doorway. "It's time to move on, partner. I don't think she's coming back."

I furrowed my brow and tried not to let the topic send me into a rant. "Not looking for her to come back. I wouldn't take her back if she tried. Besides, she's enjoying her new dentist husband and family." I stood from my desk and motioned for Hank to leave. "I'm heading out."

He rolled himself out of the doorway. "All right, see you tomorrow."

I locked up my office and left the station. My condo was just a couple-minute drive from work. It kept the mileage on my car low. I pulled into the underground parking and put the Shelby Mustang away for the night. It had been a spur-of-the-moment purchase a year back. Hank referred to it as an early midlife crisis. After a year of ownership, the car had a touch over a thousand miles on it. I took the stairs up and headed to my place, unit 502B. I turned the key in the lock and cracked the front door.

"Butch!" I called.

With the jingle of a bell, Butch the cat bounded down the hall toward my feet. He wasn't coming to greet me. I jammed my foot in the space between the door and wall to block his escape. I squeezed myself inside. Eighteen pounds of feline fury attacked my foot upon entry. He bit at my shoe and flopped onto his side to scratch at my foot with his back legs. That was his typical welcome-home greeting. Butch thrashed at my foot for another few seconds before running back into the living room and taking his place on the couch.

"I should have bought a dog."

I'd never been a cat person. Between sending me photos

of my nephew, my sister had caught a daytime talk show about all the benefits of pet ownership. She claimed that owning a dog or cat would help me relieve stress, which she said I had too much of. A dog was out of the question, due to my work schedule. Through continuous prodding and e-mails of different designer cats, she'd convinced me that I should buy a savannah cat. It was a hybrid between a domestic and wild cat; however, I think they forgot Butch's domestic genes. At least he was a good-looking animal.

I kicked off my shoes and tossed my keys, badge, and pocket notepad onto the breakfast bar. I hung my shoulder holster over one of the breakfast bar's stools and pulled a beer from the refrigerator. The sound of the refrigerator door perked Butch up from the couch. He ran over and did a few circles around my feet, trying his best to get a treat. I pulled the bag of cat treats from the cupboard and dropped a few in his dish. He didn't deserve them—they were a distraction so I could get out onto the patio without having to block him and get my shoeless feet torn to shreds. My condo overlooked Hillsborough Bay, the eastern section of the Tampa Bay. The beer snapped and hissed as I popped the top. I sat outside and slid the glass patio door closed.

I took a sip. Hank's mention of my ex-wife from earlier was still stewing in the back of my head. We'd moved to Tampa from Milwaukee in the spring of 2009. Her parents had retired to Florida, and she couldn't deal with the separation. Samantha and her mother were close. She started looking into jobs as a dental hygienist in the Tampa area, and I looked into transfers. When a job became available, I put in my paperwork, and we headed south. I used half my inheritance from my mother to buy Samantha her dream house in the suburbs. We had plans to start a family, but those plans dwindled. I suspected her of cheating on me with her boss. She denied it. Her denial of it did nothing to ease my mind. Trying to deceive someone whose sole job is to sniff out that sort of thing was her downfall. I attended one of their dental conferences at a resort without her knowing. Her and her boss sat poolside, kissing and hugging. They shared a room. Divorce papers were filed the next day. Two months later, she moved in with the guy, and they married. I sold the house and got rid of every last scrap that reminded me of her. I wished it was that easy to remove her from my life. Samantha and my sister became close and still talked. I got frequent updates from Melissa about my ex-wife's life, new husband, and children.

I ran a hand over my bald head and crushed the empty beer can in my other hand. I slipped back into the condo fast enough to not have to deal with Butch. In my bedroom, I tossed on a pair of old jeans, a T-shirt, and a ball cap. It was my normal *out on the town* attire. I dialed the cab company from memory to pick me up. I wasn't in the mood for walking and being alone with my thoughts. Ten minutes later, a cabbie honked out front. After five more minutes, plus seven dollars, the driver dumped me off in front of Lefty's.

I pushed the front door open and took my usual spot at the end of the bar. Classic rock music blared from the single speaker in the jukebox. At most, ten people spread throughout the place. A few regulars sat at the other end of the bar, a group played pool, and a foursome sat at one of the tables by the dartboard. I spotted Callie coming from the back. In our flirting across the bar, I'd learned she was from southern Florida, but moved to Tampa a few months back for the proverbial fresh start. It didn't take too many of my detective skills to tell me she was living beyond the means of a bartender—she owned a sixty thousand dollar car, and a house, by herself. I figured she had wealthy parents. She walked over. I noticed something was different about her.

"Hi, Kane. Two nights in a row, huh? You come to sweep me off my feet tonight? Take me out of this place?"

"Yup, let's go."

"Oh, you're all talk. What can I get you, sweetie? The usual?"

I smiled. "Yeah, you know what I like."

"Eating too?"

I nodded.

She wrote out a ticket for the food, walked it back to the little window, and handed it to Bill, who worked the kitchen. When she got back to the bar, she grabbed two shot glasses, poured them to the top with Jägermeister, and set them in front of me.

"There you go, hon. Let me get your beer."

She poured a frosted mug full and tossed down a coaster, setting the beer on top. She scooped up one of the shots from the bar. "Food should be up in about ten minutes. Long day?"

I picked up the other shot glass. "Kind of."

She held her shot glass up for a toast. "Booze will help. Down the hatch."

We knocked them back.

She used the bar to pull herself closer and spoke quietly. "You're not very observant for a cop."

I took a drink from my beer and set it back down on the coaster. "What do you mean?"

She rocked back from the bar and twirled around. "I got my hair cut earlier. They took off almost three inches. You like it?"

Her black hair was still well past her shoulders. It fell to rest over a number of shoulder tattoos as she put her hands back up on the bar and leaned in again.

"Yeah, I was going to say something. I noticed it right away. It looks good."

"You're such a liar. You didn't notice, but thanks for pretending to."

"Seriously, I noticed."

She smiled wide. "Smell it."

I raised my eyebrows. "Smell it?"

"Yeah, smell it." She leaned in and stuck a handful of her hair under my nose. "Smells good, huh?"

She was right. Her hair smelled like magnolias. It would stick with me the rest of the evening.

She leaned her head toward mine and talked through her hair. "Are you ready for another shot? It's on me."

"If you're buying, I'm drinking."

Callie bounced back behind the bar and poured two

more shots to the top of the glasses. "I'm going to try to get you drunk and see if I can take advantage of you."

I laughed. "Good plan."

We tapped the glasses together and drank the shots. Callie went to make a round through the bar, seeing if any of the other people needed drinks. She was upping her flirting to a new level. Bill came from the back and dropped off my steak sandwich, utensils, and a couple napkins. His white apron had grease stains from the day on it. His brown hair was damp from sweat.

"There you go, Lieutenant. Do you need ketchup, steak sauce, or anything?"

"I should be good, Bill. Thanks."

He turned to head back to the kitchen. "No problem. Enjoy."

I dug into the steak sandwich, remembering I hadn't had a bite of food since the burger before visiting the morgue. Within five minutes, a wadded-up napkin and a few drips that had escaped my mouth were all that remained on the plate.

"Was it good?" Callie asked.

"Perfect."

She tossed the silverware onto my plate and took it away. *One more beer, and I'll head out, call it a wrap.*

Callie walked back to me at the bar and smiled. "You want another beer?"

"You read my mind."

She filled another mug and set it front of me then headed to the end of the bar to grab drinks for a few others.

The small television hanging back behind the bar was playing sports highlights. I tried to make out the scores scrolling at the bottom of the screen, but my eyes wouldn't focus. The yawning started. I was beat. I dialed up the cab company for a pickup. The beer went down in four big swigs. I stood from the bar stool and motioned to Callie as though I were writing in the air.

She walked back over. "Leaving me so soon?"

"Yeah, have to. Can you close me out?"

She pulled my tab from back by the register and laid it in front of me. It was twenty-two bucks and change. I tossed thirty dollars on the bar.

"When are you stopping back in?" she asked.

"Tail end of the week."

"Good. I'm here every night. Don't stand me up."

I smiled and headed out front to wait for my cab.

Chapter 6

Hank poked his head through the doorway of my office. "Captain wants us. We may have an ID on our vic."

I'd just walked in and didn't even get a chance to sit down. The clock on my office wall read a couple minutes after eight. I tossed my keys on my desk and followed him next door, to Captain Bostok's office. The door was open.

The captain sat with his elbows on his desk and his fists jammed into his jowls, leaning over a file. Bostok had been leading our homicide division since I transferred. He was in his late fifties, overweight by fifty pounds, and sported a snow-white mustache that finished at the bottom of his chin. His reading glasses sat at the bottom of his nose as he looked over some paperwork. He flipped the folder closed, leaned back, and took off his glasses. "Kane, Rawlings."

"Morning, Cap. We have a possible ID?" I asked.

He pointed to the guest chairs. "Grab a seat."

We did.

"Steinberg put a call through to me a couple minutes

ago. A man named Ken McMillian from Chicago is down here looking for his wife. She flew in on business. I guess she was supposed to put on a presentation for an ad agency in town here. She never showed. When he didn't hear from her the entire next day, he contacted the hotel. After some back and forth, they told him that she never checked in. He caught the first flight out."

"Does the description match the guy's wife?" Hank asked.

"He saw the release we gave to the media on the news this morning—matches down to the clover tattoo. I sent him over to the medical examiner's office to make a positive. Should be hearing back soon."

"Do we have the guy's contact info?"

The captain nodded. "He's going to give me a call when he is through with Ed. I'll set something up for an interview. I'll let you know."

I stood. "Thanks, Cap."

Hank and I left his office and headed back toward mine.

I didn't enjoy that part of my job. Working homicides was one thing, but dealing with grieving family members was something else. Interviewing them required a delicate balance of providing empathy mixed with a line of questioning to see if they had any part in the crime. Husbands and wives were the worst, provided they weren't the perpetrators. The loss of a significant other brought forth a range of every emotion, and I often had a front row seat for each one. What happened to this man's wife was something different altogether. Her death wasn't a botched robbery or a drug deal gone wrong. That woman had been held captive and had a drill bit driven into her head. I didn't look forward to the conversation. I stopped just short of my office door and turned to Hank. "Grab a cup of coffee?"

He cocked his head. "Is it working today?"

"One way to find out."

Hank followed me to the lunch room. A few detectives were sitting around one of the tables, shoveling down a quick breakfast.

I pointed to the coffee machine. "Working?"

John King, a detective from our drug task force, answered. "Not sure, Lieutenant. I gave up on that thing weeks ago."

Our station had acquired the finicky coffee machine a few months back as a gift from the mayor. My guess was that he was looking for the department's support for his next election bid. Three feet tall and made of stainless steel, the Deluxe Coffee Station looked as though it would be more at home in a coffee shop than in our dingy lunchroom. An LCD screen covered the front. Miscellaneous buttons and windows sat below it. The machine ground the beans on demand, allowing choices between a single cup and a carafe, as well as different strengths. It did make one hell of a cup of coffee when it functioned. The problem was that the thing didn't work most of the time.

Hank and I walked over to the machine.

"It says 'ready' on the screen. That's good," I said. I grabbed a foam cup from the rack and placed it at the base of the machine. I thumbed the button for a large. "Okay, so far so good."

I pressed Columbian Roast, the strongest offered, and hit the big blue Start button. Beans dropped into another window and bounced up and down until they were ground to perfection. The machine whirred and hummed. Noise from the machine working drew the detectives from their table to come over and watch.

"That thing making coffee?" Detective King asked.

Hank watched the process over my shoulder. "Looks like it."

I heard a rush of water. "Someone must have fixed it."

We looked on in awe as the machine went through its process and released caffeinated goodness into my waiting cup. A bell dinged, and the blue light under the cup flashed. I snatched up my coffee and went to the counter to add two creamers. Hank and the detectives shouldered each other for position to be the next to get a cup. Hank won, sticking his cup in and hitting the buttons. The machine dropped the beans and whirred again.

"About damn time," Hank said.

The sound of water rushed again, and steam rose from Hank's cup as the liquid flowed into it. *Ding!*

Hank pulled the cup from the machine. "Ha!" He brought the cup to his mouth, blew on the top, and took a sip. "What the hell?" He gargled his words around the mouthful of hot liquid. Hank ran over to the sink and spat out the contents of his mouth. "It's filled with grounds!" He grabbed a few handfuls of water to rinse his mouth.

The detectives chuckled.

"Let's see if I have better luck," King said.

He stuck his cup into the machine and let it go through the process. Twenty seconds later, disappointment crossed his face as he pulled his cup from the machine. "It poured me a cup of water." He stuck his finger into it. "It's not even hot."

I smiled and leaned against the counter, taking a sip of my perfect coffee. "Maybe you can add some of Hank's hot grounds?"

The crowd didn't find the humor in my joke. I turned to leave.

Hank poured his cup of wet grounds into the sink, tossed the cup in the garbage can, and followed me back toward the bullpen. He headed off to his desk. I headed back to my office.

I spread the contents of the file across my desk to go over it again. We needed to put a line of questioning together that would hit the points we needed to discuss. We needed to know what she was doing in town and who she knew in the area, and we needed to confirm her husband's whereabouts over the last few days. My office phone rang a couple minutes later. I picked up the receiver. "Lieutenant Kane."

"We have a positive. Her name is Sarah McMillian. Her husband will be here within the hour."

"Thanks, Cap."

Chapter 7

His eyes locked on the pickup area, watching the people come and go. He'd been working straight through the night with no hint of what he sought. Then, up ahead, he spotted a potential candidate. She waved for a taxi. The car in front of him started to creep forward. He wouldn't let her take another cab—not after waiting a full night. He yanked the wheel, pulled out, and cut off the cab in front of him. The cabbie next in line slammed on his brakes to avoid the collision. The guy honked and flashed him the bird out his window. He dismissed the angered driver and pulled his taxi up to the woman on the curb. He opened the door and pulled himself out. "Need a ride, ma'am?"

"Yes, thank you."

From the curb, he carried her two bags to the trunk. His excitement spurred a coughing attack. Flecks of blood covered his fingers—he wiped it away on the back of his faded jeans before she could see it. He moved quickly to the cab's back door and opened it for her. She ducked inside.

He took his seat behind the wheel and looked over his shoulder to see her. "Where to?"

"Channelside Towers, downtown."

"It should be ten minutes or so." He stared at her and waited for a response.

She nodded and went about looking at a paper.

His eyes covered every inch of her in the rearview mirror. He thought of her in his room—in the bed. Then he focused his attention forward as he pulled out into traffic.

"Here on business?" he asked.

"No, just got back. I'm finally headed home."

"What do you do? If you don't mind me asking."

"No, I don't mind. I'm a defense attorney for Stanley and Wallace."

"That's over on West Cypress, right?"

She looked up from her newspaper, nodded, and smiled.

A few minutes later, he pulled to the front of her building. "Hold on one second. I'll be right there for the door."

"Oh, okay." She folded her paper and slid it under her arm.

She was tossing her purse over her shoulder as he slid himself out of the driver's side and took off his hat. His hand ran through his sweaty, stringy hair. A clump of hair stuck to his fingers. He flipped it away and pulled the hat back over his head. He reached into the pocket of the driver's side door and pulled out a syringe. The index and middle finger of his right hand held the collar of the needle, and the tip of his thumb rested on the plunger. He opened her door. As she slid across the seat to exit, he leaned into the doorway and sank the syringe into her thigh.

She tried to scream, so he covered her mouth. Her hands pried against his fingers. She'd just been filled with enough of the drug to knock her out for the rest of the day. Her grip on his hand became weak. He pushed her back into the car by the face and closed the door. The child locks prevented her single attempt to get out. Back in the driver's seat, he turned the mirror on himself. His thin face was red. A bead of sweat rolled down his forehead and got lost in his beard. He checked his mirrors and pulled away from the front of her building. She was his.

Chapter 8

The husband had a few hours to process that he'd lost his wife. Although that was just a short while, we had enough time to move past the initial emotional outbursts. Hank and I stood on the back side of the observation mirror, looking into interview room one or, as we called it, the Box. A uniform from the front had placed Ken McMillian in the room ten minutes prior. The amount of gray in his black hair told me he was in his late thirties, maybe early forties. He wore a blue polo shirt and light khakis. His glasses didn't hide the fact that his eyes were red and swollen from crying. Rick had brought the lingerie she'd worn back up to me earlier. I wanted to see if the husband recognized the outfit. We hadn't found any trace evidence on it. Hank and I had our line of questioning set. I set the equipment to record the interview. We walked inside.

I greeted him as I entered. "Mr. McMillian, I'm Carl Kane. This is Hank Rawlings."

He nodded.

"Can I get you anything before we get started?" Hank asked.

"Maybe water?" His voice crackled.

"Sure."

"Hank, can you grab him something from the lunchroom too?"

"Sure." Hank left the room.

I sat across from McMillian and set the bag of clothes by my leg. I got my file ready. Hank returned a minute later with a bottle of water and a bag of potato chips. He placed them on the table in front of him and took up a seat next to me.

"We want to give you our condolences before we start here today. We realize you have a lot to process. I know that this has to be unbelievably difficult for you. At the same time, the sooner we can compile information, the better the chances are of us getting to the bottom of this," I said.

He stared at his hands, folded in front of him. He looked up at me. "I'll do anything to help."

"Thank you. Just so you are aware, we are recording this interview. While we do our best to take notes, being human, sometimes we can miss small details. We don't want to miss anything. Sometimes the smallest, most insignificant things can turn into big leads. By having the interview recorded, we can go back if there's ever anything in question. Are you okay with that?"

He nodded.

"Let's begin. Do you have any children?"

I started with a baseline question. It was a question that

would fetch a truthful answer.

"No." His answer was quick, direct, and truthful.

"When did you see Sarah last?"

"The morning she left to come here. Her flight didn't leave until the afternoon. She planned to take care of her errands before she left."

"Was that the last time you spoke?" I asked.

"No. She called me when she arrived at the Tampa airport."

"Anything odd about the conversation? Did she mention anyone from the flight or airport?"

He shook his head. "No. She said the flight was fine. We just talked for a couple minutes, and then she said she would call me when she got settled into her hotel room." He took off his glasses and rubbed his eyes. "When I didn't get a phone call, I just figured she went to bed."

"What time did her flight arrive?"

"It was a little after nine. I have a copy of her itinerary that I printed out."

He pulled a folded-up paper from his pocket, unfolded it, and handed it to me.

I looked over the travel arrangements and made a note of the flight time and number. "Can we keep this?"

He nodded. I slid it into the file.

"And the hotel confirmed that she had never checked in?" Hank asked.

"That's what the woman told me when I called."

"Mr. McMillian, how did she plan to get to the hotel? Did she have a business colleague picking her up from the airport? Did she plan to take a hotel shuttle? Cab?"

He put his glasses back on and took a deep breath. "I'm not sure. She didn't mention that anyone from the company was picking her up, so I would think a shuttle or a cab."

I made a note to check it out. "What company?" I asked.

He sat quietly for a moment before speaking. "I think this one was called Ace Marketing. She did sales training for marketing firms all over the country. The places hire her company, and then her company sends her to whatever city."

The information got written in my notes. "So, Ace Marketing?"

"I believe so."

"Do you know where the place is located?"

"Sorry, I don't know."

"That's fine. What hotel did she have a room at?" I asked.

"Imperial Suites. I believe the hotel is downtown here somewhere."

I was familiar with the hotel. It was a few blocks away. "How long did your wife plan to be in town for?"

"All week. Her flight back was on Saturday morning."

"Okay. Now, what can you tell us about her job? Is there an element of competition? Did she have rivals at work? Enemies?"

He coughed and took a sip of the water. "Her job wasn't like that. She's a sales trainer. Traveled to different companies and put on presentations. She didn't have coworkers that she worked alongside. It was a different city and different employees that she presented to every few weeks. When she didn't travel for work, she was at home. She loved her job."

"What about the places she did her presentations? Did she ever mention problems with any of the company's staff?" I asked.

He shook his head.

"And these presentations she did. None of the employees attending were at risk of losing their jobs for underperforming or anything like that?" Hank asked.

"No. The trainings were for new hires."

"All right. Now, our forensics team has looked over the clothes she wore when she was found." I pulled the translucent bag with its orange adhesive evidence strip up onto the table and slid it toward him. "I just wanted to see if you recognized the outfit."

He began to cry when he saw it. "She didn't own anything like that. She wasn't—"

I held up my hand and shook my head to interrupt him. I knew what his question was, and I didn't want him to have to ask it. "No."

He nodded.

We would keep the outfit as evidence. We had all we needed about his wife and the day she arrived. I dug through the file and removed the photo of the brand.

"Do you have any idea what this represents?" I turned the picture and slid it toward him.

He choked on his tears, shook his head, and slid the photo away.

I slipped it back into the file. The next line of questioning would be the difficult part. We started by digging into their marriage and his whereabouts during the time she went missing. He claimed they were happy. There was never any adultery or any reasons to even let it cross his mind, he said. He claimed he had still been in Chicago when she went missing, which would be easy enough to confirm. We brought up their financial situation, as well as life insurance policies. Through tears, he discussed everything at length. He didn't seem evasive on any of the questioning. The same held true when we discussed the rest of the couple's friends and family. We asked him if she took any recreational drugs. He claimed she'd never taken anything, never even smoked as much as a cigarette her whole life. After another hour, we concluded the interview. We told him that we'd be in contact with any developments.

I stopped by the captain to give him the highlights of the interview. I put Hank on checking into McMillian's alibi and calling Nick Waterman. Waterman was the head of security at the airport. We needed to take a look at any video footage they had. I found my desk and hit the phones, starting with the hotel.

"Thank you for calling Imperial Suites, This is Sandy. How can I help you?"

"Hello, this is Lieutenant Kane with the TPD homicide division. Could I speak with a manager?"

"I'm the manager on duty. What can I help you with?"

"I wanted to see if you can confirm or deny a check-in

from a few days back?"

"Oh, we're not supposed to give out that information."

"Sandy, I don't want to go through the trouble of getting a subpoena for the registry, when you can just give me a yea or nay on the phone. I would consider it a personal favor to the TPD."

"Hold on."

I tapped my fingers across my desk as I listened to rummaging and whispering from the other end of the phone.

"The guest name and date?"

"Sarah McMillian. The check-in would have been Sunday evening."

"I have it here as booked, but she never checked in."

"Thank you." I jotted it down as confirmed on my sheet. "Do you guys have video surveillance out front of the hotel?"

"Yes, we do. Would you like me to transfer you over to someone in security?"

"If you could, that would be great."

"Sure, no problem. Hold on."

I sat on hold for a few seconds before the music stopped and someone picked up.

"This is Ralph." The man's voice sounded as though he was a heavy smoker.

"Hi, Ralph. Are you in security there?"

"Yes sir, what can I do for you?"

"This is Lieutenant Kane with the TPD. I wanted to see if you had surveillance in front of the hotel?"

"Three cameras. One faces straight out the front doors. One shoots east, and one shoots west off the top of the car port. What are you looking for?" A muffled coughing attack followed his question.

I waited for him to finish before I continued. "I wanted to see if you caught a person of interest on video the other night. Think I could send someone by to look at your footage?"

"Well, I guess that would be fine. I'm here until eight."

"Thanks, I'll send a detective over. Should I just have him ask for you?"

"Yup. Ralph in security."

I was ready to hang up when a note on my sheet caught my eye.

"Hey Ralph, one more thing, and I'll let you get back to work."

"Shoot."

"Do you guys run a shuttle back and forth to the airport?"

"No. We used to but quit a few years ago."

"Thanks, I'll send someone by."

"Glad to help." He went back to coughing.

I hung up and wrote everything he told me down. If no one from the ad agency had picked her up, she had to have taken a cab. Locating Ace Marketing and getting in contact with them was next on my list to do. I woke up my computer and plugged the ad agency's name into a search engine. It came up right away with a phone number. The address listed sounded familiar. Figuring out why took me only a second. The address came back as the same place we'd found her body—the Manchester office building. Whoever killed her knew why she was in town. Some face-to-face with the folks at the ad agency was in order. I sent Detective Jones to go have a look at the hotel's video footage and stopped at Hank's desk on my way out.

"Alibi?" I asked.

"It checked out. He was in Chicago."

I nodded. "Did you hear anything on the airport surveillance?"

"I just got off the phone. Waterman wasn't in his office. I left a message for him to call me back."

"Transfer your desk phone to your cell and take a ride with me."

He picked up his phone, punched in the code to forward his calls, and stood. "Where we headed?"

"Ace Marketing. Want to guess where it's located?"

Hank flashed me a puzzled look.

"Manchester building."

"Where we found the body?" he asked.

"Bingo."

We grabbed a cruiser from the parking lot. The lunch-hour traffic was backing up Kennedy. We pulled into the Manchester office building a few minutes after noon.

The elevator took us up to Ace Marketing on the eighth floor. I checked the sign on the wall, and we proceeded down to the double glass doors at the end. Hank pulled open the door.

The girl working the front desk looked up from her

computer. "Can I help you, gentlemen?"

"Hi. I'm Lieutenant Kane with the TPD. This is Sergeant Rawlings." Hank gave her a nod. "Can we speak with a manager or whoever is in charge here?"

"That would be Brenda White. She's out at lunch right now. Just about everyone is."

"What time are you expecting her back?" I asked.

"She should be back in a half hour or so."

I pointed to the handful of guest chairs. "Okay if we just wait here?"

"Sure. That's fine."

"Thanks."

We took seats in the waiting area, and I picked up an issue of *Road & Track*. Hank chose *Field and Stream* though I doubted he'd ever seen a field or a stream in his life.

I'd forgone making fun of him about his wife on a couple occasions, and I was due. I tossed him a copy of *Good Housekeeping*. "Here you go, Hank. You don't want your wife to find out you're reading about guy stuff."

He grabbed the magazine and glanced at the cover. He shook his head. "I already have this issue at home. Karen got me a subscription. They have a nice recipe for scones in this one though."

I looked for a crack of a smile. It wasn't there. He may have been serious. I thumbed through my magazine and stopped to read an article on the new Corvette. After that article and another, plus two more magazines, I heard some women talking in the hall. Two women walked through the door of the ad agency. They both carried bags of what I assumed to be leftovers from whatever place they'd stopped at for lunch.

The receptionist got the attention of one of the women and pointed toward Hank and me. That woman handed the bag to her companion and approached.

"Hello, I'm Brenda White. How can I help you?"

I stood. "Hello, Miss White. We would like to ask some questions regarding the deceased that was found outside of the building."

"Oh, okay. It's all anyone has been talking about. I have a few minutes. Do you want to come back to my office?"

"That would be fine, thanks."

Hank and I followed her back and sat across from her at her desk. Miscellaneous sales awards and posters covered the back wall of her office.

She scooted herself close to her desk and folded her hands. "How can we help?"

"Miss White, the deceased woman was scheduled to do a sales training for your company."

She leaned back from the desk but didn't speak.

"Her name was Sarah McMillian. Did you know her?" Hank asked.

She shook her head. "No, I didn't know her. We had a sales training scheduled, but the presenter never showed up. We had almost thirty people booked for the training there."

I flashed her a perplexed look. "There? You don't do the trainings here?"

She shook her head. "No. We book out a conference room over at the Helix hotel. It's where we do all of our sales trainings."

"Was someone from the office supposed to pick the woman up at the airport?" I asked.

"No, no. We send our trainees to the hotel. They send the trainer. That's the extent of our relationship."

"Just to be clear, no one from your company had any direct contact with Sarah McMillian?" Hank asked.

She shook her head again. "Sorry, no. The company that we booked the sales trainer through was out of Chicago. I gave them the date I needed, the location, and what time we would like to start the training. They gave me the name of the trainer they would be sending. That was it."

We ran more questions past her before we wrapped up the interview. She seemed truthful about the fact that she didn't know and had never met the woman. However, the fact remained that someone had known what company she was there to do the training for and dumped her at their building. We thanked her for her time and headed back to the station.

Chapter 9

Hank's phone rang on our way back. The head of security at the airport was ready for us. We parked in the structure and navigated our way through the airport. We made our way to the TSA's security office on the second level and walked in. An obese man in his midfifties was holding down the front counter. He wore a blue long-sleeved collared shirt and a black tie. A TSA badge sat clipped to his breast pocket. Sewn insignias decorated his shoulders. His name badge read Bates. We approached.

"Can I help you?" he asked.

"Lieutenant Kane and Sergeant Rawlings to see Nick Waterman."

"One moment." He stood and waddled toward the back. Bates poked his head into one of the offices at the end of the hall.

Waterman appeared and walked toward us. Over a year had passed since I'd seen him last. He was a touch heavier, and his hair was grayer than I remembered. He was a good friend of the TPD. Waterman worked a lot with our drug task force. He was our eyes and ears at the airport. His position didn't require the standard TSA uniform. He wore a dark-gray suit and a blue tie.

"Gentlemen."

I reached out for a handshake. "Hey, Nick."

A handshake with Hank followed.

"So we need to find a certain woman on video, I understand?"

I nodded. "We have a name, flight number, and description. Can we work with that?"

"Should be all we need. Let's head back to the surveillance room." He turned and gave us a wave over his shoulder. "Follow me back."

Down the hall and to the left, we walked into the airport's surveillance center, a long rectangular room with a wall of forty-two-inch monitors, all displaying different camera views. Each of the six agents monitoring the screens had a work area with three more monitors. We followed him to an empty station at the back of the room.

Waterman took a seat. "This is going to be us here."

Hank and I pulled over two free chairs and sat.

Waterman punched away at the keyboard to access the system. "What's the name, date, flight number?"

"Sarah McMillian." I pulled my notepad from my pocket and flipped to where I'd entered the information from her itinerary. "Flight 1187, Sunday night."

He plugged it into the computer. "I'm going to bring up the video from the gate and see if we can spot her coming off of the flight. From there, we can follow her through the airport."

"You can do that?" Hank asked.

Waterman nodded in confirmation. "We have cameras everywhere. We don't miss a thing. Here we go. The flight came in at 9:03 p.m. Do you know what her seat number was? I should be able to get us a pretty good starting point that way."

I shook my head. "We have a copy of her itinerary at the station in her file, but I don't have the seat number here."

"That's fine. I'll start us at 9:06 p.m., and we'll work from there. Know what she was wearing?"

I shook my head again. I doubted she'd come off the plane in lingerie.

"Rough description?" Waterman asked.

"We're looking for a blond about five foot six and in her thirties. If I had to guess, I'd say dressed in business attire."

"We should be able to find her. Let's have a look."

He started to roll the footage on the desk monitor. We watched as the travelers started to come from the jetway into the airport. Two men in suits walked out first. Both dragged carry-ons and chatted with each other. An overweight man in a yellow polo shirt followed next. A twenty-something year old in a hooded sweatshirt and backpack appeared from the doorway into the airport. He wore a flat-brimmed hat and a pair of white headphones. A blond followed him out. Oversize sunglasses rested on her forehead. She wore a white blouse and navy blue skirt. A laptop bag hung over the handle of the carry-on she wheeled out. The woman on the screen matched everything we had for Sarah McMillian.

"Is that her?" Waterman asked.

"Pretty sure," I said.

We watched as she walked through the frame and disappeared off camera. Waterman clicked a few buttons, and a different view came on the screen. The camera focused down the length of the walkway in the concourse. She entered the frame at the top. We followed her on the screen until she disappeared heading past the security checkpoint. He pulled up another view that caught her making a right toward the escalators.

"She's headed down the escalators—either picking up checked luggage or going out to street level. Let me pull up the view from the baggage area. We should be able to catch her coming off the escalators there." He punched at his keyboard.

She hadn't spoken with anyone in the airport. She was heading from point A to point B. She didn't even stop at the bathroom. From what we could tell, nobody was following her. We watched the monitor, waiting for her to come down the escalator. She appeared on the screen and made a right toward the baggage carousel. She waited for her luggage. Through ten minutes of video, she stood there waiting on her bag. No one approached her. At the thirteenth minute, she removed her phone from her bag and made a call. It must have been the call to her husband. The call didn't last much more than a minute. She put the phone away. The carousel began to spin, and bags started sliding down. She pulled a black suitcase off and made for the doors leading outside.

"Do you have video out there?" Hank asked.

"Absolutely. One second."

Waterman pulled up the footage of the curbside loading zone for the arriving flights. We spotted her walking toward the taxi station. She entered the line for a cab.

"Do you have a camera closer?" I asked.

Waterman shook his head. "I think this is as close as we got."

We watched as she advanced in line and got into a taxi. A cab driver loaded her bags. The distance of the camera was too far away for us to get anything usable. The cab driver appeared as a half-inch blur on the screen. He reentered the cab and pulled to the far left lane to avoid the other cars at the curb. The cab drove from the frame. I dialed up Jones. He picked up right away.

"Jones, it's Kane."

"Hey, Kane. I'm just finishing up looking at the hotel's security footage now."

"Anything?"

"Nothing that matches the woman's description."

"Okay. We got her getting into a taxi at the airport about nine-thirty. I would guess that she would have to have been there before ten at the latest."

"I didn't see anything like that. I'll give the footage another once over."

"Thanks, Jones. Let me know." I hung up.

Waterman switched cameras and followed the cab on the screen until it disappeared from the arriving flights area. He rewound the footage to the point where she entered the taxi. We went frame by frame, trying to get anything we could from the cab: a company, tag number, car number, something we could use. We came up empty, aside from the car being yellow and having a taxi light on top.

"There's just not a lot to work with, guys. The cab being blocked from the other cars and the distance doesn't give us much," Waterman said.

"Think we could get a copy of the footage from when she entered the cab? Maybe our tech department at the station can do their magic and get something from it."

"Sure, let me grab a disc."

Waterman had our copy of the footage burned to DVD a few minutes later. Hank and I wrapped up at the airport and headed back to the station. I dropped off the video with Terry Murphy in our tech department and headed for my office. The time neared five o'clock. My voicemail light on my phone was flashing. I clicked the button to play the message. It was Jones letting me know the hotel's footage showed no cabs and no one matching her description throughout the night. I erased the message and took a seat behind my desk.

The captain rang my phone a few minutes later, looking for an update. I filled him in on the details from the interview at the ad agency as well as the footage we'd brought back from the airport. I had the chain of events nailed down. We had her getting picked up but not arriving. What we needed to do was find that cab. The captain wrapped up the conversation by telling me to go home. I had been working fifteen days straight. I grabbed the case file and keys from my desk and headed out.

Chapter 10

She lay unconscious and bound to the bed. He'd branded her, just like the last. He'd had her for a total of seven hours. No longer wearing her business attire, she wore the same green teddy and thong as Sarah McMillian. He had twelve identical outfits, courtesy of the department store he'd stolen them from a few months back. Her driver's license told him her name was Diane Robins. She was thirty-six and one hundred twenty-three pounds. She was a blond with blue eyes—a perfect candidate. He took a seat a couple feet away from where she lay. His victim didn't move aside from the slow, rhythmic motion of her breathing. He put one leg over his other knee and watched her chest moving in and out with each breath. A coughing attack ensued. His eyes watered. Blood puddled in his hand. His illness was progressing.

He pulled himself from the chair and went to her. With the back of his hand, he smacked her face. She didn't respond. He had his new work area set. Xylazine was circulating through Diane's bloodstream, just enough to keep her out. He waited another ten minutes to be sure and then untied her. Her body lay limp in his arms as he carried her through the kitchen to the garage. A pesky fly buzzed around his ear, and he shook his head to shoo it away.

A rectangular dining room table sat center stage in the garage—no chairs. Plastic from rafters to floor separated his work area from the other sections of the three-car garage. The yellow of the taxi cab could be seen beyond the makeshift plastic wall. Plastic sheeting covered the surface of the table and floor to catch any spatter of blood. His cleanup after the last had been far too time-consuming. He laid Diane's body on the table and positioned her for the procedure. He went to his rolling work cart, which held his tools.

Earlier in the day, he'd made a trip a few towns over to steal a lobotomy book from the library. He needed to get more structured with his attempts. The results from the previous methods were too hit or miss. He opened it to the first dog-eared page. His head nodded as he read it over for the umpteenth time. He headed back inside to change.

Dressed in white coveralls and latex gloves, he walked back into the garage. He plugged electric hair clippers into the extension cord hanging from the ceiling and buzzed her right temple. A razor from the tool cart shaved away the stubble that remained. He finished prepping the area with a swab from an alcohol pad.

Measuring out three centimeters back and six centimeters up from her orbital socket, he marked the area with a felt-tip pen. He took a scalpel from his tool cart and cut the skin from the area. He placed the flap in a small dish of saline solution to reattach later. A squirt bottle of the same solution flushed away the running blood. A postage-stamp-sized area of white skull shone through the blood with each squirt of saline. The drill came next. He secured a half-inch hole saw to the chuck. He'd modified a bit with a collar that wouldn't allow it to cut deeper than 7.1 millimeters. From his recent research, that was the correct thickness of an adult female skull. He placed the drill bit against the bone and squeezed the trigger. He flushed the area with water while he worked and kept a mindful eye on the depth. From the collar on the outside of the bit, he could see he was close. He slowed the drill's revolutions until the collar bottomed out. He set the drill on the cart and flushed the opening with saline. The bone moved freely when he touched it with his forceps. He pried the piece of skull away and exposed the inside of her head.

With a scalpel, he cut away the casing to reveal her brain. He then slipped the blade between the white matter in the prefrontal lobe. He made a number of small slices, as shown in his book. Even with his reading and searching online, he hadn't found a solid reference on how to reattach the bit of skull he removed. Doctors used a thin wire that became permanent, to reattach pieces of removed skull. He didn't have the capacity or materials to complete that part of the procedure. The removed bit of skull found the hole it had come from. It would have to do. He used the forceps to place the removed flap of skin back over the area and sutured her up.

He stepped back from his patient and looked over his work. In a few hours, he would see how successful his new procedure was.

Chapter 11

My list of cab companies that worked the airport was getting shorter. I gave our victim's description and time of pickup to each dispatcher. A few companies were checking with their drivers and had agreed to call me back. While I wouldn't get paid for my efforts, I wasn't comfortable leaving a murderer on the streets any longer than I had to. If it took a few off-the-clock hours to make some headway, I'd damn sure work them. The clock on my cable box read a quarter after eight when my phone rang. I figured it was someone from one of the cab companies.

I caught the number on the phone's caller ID. It was my sister, Melissa.

"Hi, Mel."

"Hey, bro. What are you doing?"

I plopped down on the couch and let out a deep breath. Butch stared at me. He didn't look pleased that I was encroaching on his living space. "I'm working from the house."

"It's after eight. Why are you working from home?"

I didn't feel like getting into the case with her on the phone. "I'm making phone calls and checking up on a few things."

"Oh. Are you done?"

"I guess. What's up?" My nephew chattering and making noise in the background came through the earpiece.

"We need to talk about Dad."

"What about Dad?"

"He came over last week. It seemed like he was having a hard time remembering things."

I looked at the ceiling. My sister had a flair for the dramatic. "Like?" I asked.

"Well, he called Scrambles, Oscar. Oscar has been dead for years."

"Really?" I asked it in the most sarcastic tone I could muster.

"Why do you say it like that?"

"It's the same damn dog. They are the same breed, same color, and same size. Oscar lived to be fifteen. Fifteen years of Dad calling your brown fluffy dog Oscar. Now you have a new one that's—again—identical, and you think Dad is getting senile because he called it by the old one's name. I can pretty much guarantee you that I'd do the same thing. I didn't even remember the new one's name until you just said it."

"That's because you're never around. Besides that, he's having problems remembering other things too."

"Like?" I asked.

"A lot of little things."

"Mmm hmm."

"Fine, if you don't care... You know he's going to be sixty-eight this year."

"Sixty-eight isn't that old, Mel."

"He's starting to slow down. It's been a while since you've seen him."

Her last sentence made me lean back and rub my eyes. My sister was about to take the conversation to her normal guilt-trip territory. I didn't have the energy.

"Hey, I have a work call I'm expecting in a couple minutes. Let me talk to Tommy quick before I have to go."

She didn't respond, but I could hear her call him. A rattling on the other end of the phone followed.

"Hello?"

I put on my best talking-with-little-kids voice. It was a touch higher pitched and upbeat. "Hey, buddy. It's Uncle Carl. How's it going?"

"Hi, Uncle Carl."

"How are you doing, pal?"

"I'm good. I got a new car."

"You got a new car? You're driving already?"

He giggled into the phone. "A toy car."

"A toy car? What's it look like?"

"It's red and big. It has fire on the sides. When I pull it, it takes off real fast."

"Sounds cool."

"Yeah."

Static and thumping came through the phone. He

talked to someone in the room—my brother in law, Jeff, maybe. I had exhausted the attention span of a child on the phone.

"Okay, buddy. Love you. Be good."

"Okay."

"All right, Tommy, give the phone back to Mom."

I heard more thumping through the earpiece. He ran the phone back to my sister. She came back on.

"You need to come up here, Carl."

"I know. I'll get something scheduled. I'm getting that call any minute, and I need to get some paperwork arranged first. I'll call you soon."

"Fine. I just e-mailed you some pictures of Tommy. Call me tomorrow."

"Okay. Tell Jeff I said hi."

"All right, I'll talk to you tomorrow."

"Yup. Bye."

I hung up and blew a giant breath from my mouth. Every conversation with her went that way. A *nephew sandwich on guilt trip bread* was what I liked to call it. She laid on the guilt, I had a quick talk with my nephew, and she finished with a touch more guilt. When the sandwich was finished, I made up an excuse to get off the phone. The call did make me wonder about my dad's state of mind. I made a mental note to call him in the morning.

I went through the cabinets and refrigerator for anything resembling food. No luck. The search reminded me that I was still out of coffee. I had zero interest in leaving my condo and going to the grocery store. A magnet on the refrigerator from a pizza joint down the street caught my eye. I called and put in an order. Some pizza, combined with the couple stray beers I had left in the refrigerator, would hold me over until breakfast. Sarah McMillian's file lay spread out across my table. I dug back into it until the food arrived.

My pizza showed up a half hour later. I tossed the box on the coffee table and flipped open the lid. Butch perked up and came to investigate. He bridged himself between the couch and the table.

"No, Butch! People food. Not for cats."

He cocked his head, looked at me, and then leaned in closer to the pizza.

"Butch!" I tried to put a tone of authority in my voice.

He dismissed my scolding and stuck his nose into a piece of the pepperoni.

"Get out of there! Bad cat!"

I was just about to shoo him away when he followed up his sniff with an exploratory lick. The piece was his. I'd seen what he licked in his free time.

"Fine, you want some pizza?" I took the slice from the box and stood. He hopped from the couch to follow. His collar bell jingled as he bounded along at my feet. I tossed the slice into his dish. He gave it a sniff, looked at me, and then walked back to the couch.

I shook my head. "Stupid cat." I would have been surprised if he'd eaten it. The only cat food he would eat was forty dollars a bag. He had a taste for the finer things in life. Greasy pizza wasn't on the menu.

Two cab companies returned my call as the night progressed. Both had had fares coming from the airport around the time Sarah McMillian went missing, but neither went to the Imperial Suites, and neither was a female. I read over her entire file and all my notes again. My eyes began to strain. I decided they needed a little resting and leaned back into the couch.

A little after one in the morning, I woke up. The case would have to resume later. I was beat. A sleeping, purring ball of cat lay on my lap. I gave Butch a few pets on the head and then slipped him off my lap onto his couch pillow. He was a good cat when he wasn't awake.

Sarah McMillian's file was spread across my couch and coffee table. I gathered the papers up, tossed the file onto the kitchen table, and went to my bedroom. My shift wouldn't start until nine, and I needed to get a good night's sleep.

Chapter 12

It had been an hour and a half since he'd checked on her—he'd inserted an IV into her arm. Buprenorphine, a synthetic opiate, filled the drip bag. He had picked it up when he acquired the Xylazine to deal with his illness, but it was too strong for his tastes. Watered down, it could work to keep her docile when she awoke.

The lever to engage the deadbolt was on the outside of the door. He flipped it open and entered the bedroom. In his arms were fresh bandages. He closed the door behind him as he walked into the room. Diane Robins lay motionless. Straps across her chest and thighs secured her to the bed. He approached her from the side. She was still out. He grabbed her by the jaw and rocked her head back and forth to wake her. "You alive?"

She blinked her eyelids while she stared at the ceiling. Her face was blank.

He sat at the edge of the bed and shook her by the head again. "Can you hear me in there?"

She didn't respond. A line of drool rolled from the side of her mouth.

He leaned over her and removed the bandages around her head. He examined his work. A small amount of blood was still seeping from the bottom of the sutures. He dabbed the blood away. She didn't make any movement. He wrapped fresh dressings around her head and tossed the old ones out. He sat next to her on the bed. Her eyes rolled to the side. They stared at the wall.

"We're going to do the other side in a bit."

Her eyes shot to the right and focused on him. Unanticipated rage filled her face.

He glanced at her arm. The IV wasn't there. He looked further down to see that the straps holding her to the bed were no longer attached to the bed frame. Her left arm flew up from her side, wielding the IV needle. She plunged it into his neck as he tried to spring up from the bed. He stumbled across the room and crashed into the closet doors before falling to the ground. His hands went to the side of his throat. He fumbled at the needle embedded in his neck. Blood was running from the open end.

Diane scrambled from the bed and got herself to her feet. She ran for the door. As she flung it open and attempted to flee, he caught her by the ankle. She kicked him in the face and rushed through the doorway.

He pulled the needle from his neck and tossed it on the bedroom carpet beside him. He was lucky it had missed everything vital. A half inch farther forward, and it would have punctured his jugular—two inches farther forward, and it would have hit his windpipe. He pulled himself to his feet and burst from the room after Diane. He could hear her running through the house. He found her at the glass patio door leading outside. She was fumbling with the door's lock.

When she saw him, she ran to the kitchen and pulled a knife from the knife block. She had her back to the sink. A wild look filled her face. The knife was at her side, the blade pointed out, ready to strike. A granite-topped kitchen island separated the two. He rounded the side. She headed two steps in the other direction.

She poked the knife at the air in front of her. "What did you do to me, you son of a bitch?"

He took two quick steps toward her. "Give me the knife."

She mirrored his movement, taking two steps to the side, still holding the knife out in front of her. She glanced toward the living room. A look of horror crossed her face.

He rounded the side of the kitchen island to flush her out. He thought she would make a run for it. She didn't. Instead, she held her ground and stabbed at him. He dodged to the right as soon as he saw she wasn't fleeing. The knife tore a hole through his shirt and sliced against the skin of his side.

"Now you're just going to die, you stupid bitch." He grabbed her blade-wielding hand and slammed it into the granite countertop. After only two strikes, the knife flew to the floor and skidded across the kitchen tile. He grabbed her other hand as she tried to claw at his face. With both her hands in his control, he reared back and head butted her in the nose with all the force he could muster. He saw a flash of colors on impact and felt her body go limp. The blow left his vision blurred as he opened his eyes. Blood covered her face, her nose broken. The head butt had knocked her out. He let her go. Her body fell to the floor.

He rested against the kitchen island. He shook his head and squinted his eyes in an attempt to clear out the cobwebs. A violent cough from the physical excursion sent blood from his lungs spattering across the granite of the island. He was dizzy, more than likely concussed from the impact. He wiped his mouth and took in deep breaths from his nose—he exhaled. The sound of metal scraping against tile filled his ears. Before he could see where the sound was coming from, he felt an explosion of pain jolt up his leg. He screamed and looked toward his feet.

Diane was lying on the kitchen floor, holding the handle of a knife. The two-inch-wide blade was lodged into his calf. She pulled the blade out, causing him to scream in pain again. She yanked her hand back and went for another stab. He pulled his leg away. The blade missed and stuck into the cabinet door of the island.

He balanced on his injured leg and pulled his right foot up. He stomped her head. It bounced off the tile and back up into the sole of his shoe. He stomped down again and again. Her head became soft. Blood splashed with each blow. She was dead. She lay at his feet. He stomped her again.

"You could have been famous."

He stumbled out to the garage. Fresh plastic was covering the table and floor. Gone was the blood spatter from Diane's first operation. He dropped his pants and slid off his bloody shoes. In his blue boxer shorts, he turned his back at the edge of the table and slid himself up onto it. He crossed his injured leg over the other knee to get a better view of the wound. She had plunged the knife into the middle of his calf. With the saline bottle, he flushed away the blood so he could see the extent of the damage. The stab wound was a couple inches across and hung open a quarter inch. His blood flowed from the cut. It needed to be stitched. He took his materials for suturing and a bottle of alcohol from the cart.

His teeth ground together as he splashed alcohol across the wound. He splashed more alcohol across his stitching needle. He looped the thread through the needle and tied it. Though he had drugs to ease the pain, he would take nothing. He wanted to be clear headed. He inserted the curved suture needle into his flesh. His skin bulged and turned white before the tip broke the surface. He pulled the thread through, sank the needle into the other side, and then pulled the thread tight. The stitching went slowly and, for the first few minutes, rivaled the pain from the wound itself. Numbness took over after that. The needle became slick with blood. It wasn't a professional job, but it worked to close the knife wound and stop the bleeding. He wrapped his leg with a gauze roll. With the major injury addressed, he needed to see how bad the slash across his side was. He unbuttoned his shirt and removed it one arm at a time.

Loose skin hung from his sides. Her wild swipe with the blade had caught the top of what used to be his left love handle. Now it was just skin. A small trickle of blood came from the cut. It was four inches long and an eighth of an inch deep, a minor flesh wound. He was lucky. He squinted his eyes hard, splashed alcohol over it, and searched for a gauze pad and tape. Patching the wound was a quick fix. With his knife wounds addressed, he scooted himself down from the table.

In his underwear, he grabbed the roll of painter's plastic, a scrub brush, and a set of his latex gloves. He limped back inside to the kitchen. A fly buzzed his head. He smashed it with the roll of plastic sheeting. The fly spun on its back on the kitchen floor. He hit it until it stopped moving. The fly lay dead. He tossed the roll of plastic next to its corpse. Another fly buzzed past his ear. He shooed it away.

He moved Diane's corpse to the master bath and laid her in the garden tub. The strain on his leg from moving her caused bursts of pain with each step. He hobbled back to the kitchen for the scrub brush and latex gloves. From the laundry room, he grabbed a bottle of bleach.

He stripped her naked. The smell of bleach filled the bathroom as he doused her body. The bristles of the scrub brush ripped back and forth across her skin. No evidence would be left behind. While he cleaned under her nails, he noticed a cut on her palm. It was from the knife she'd used to stab him. The cut was minor, but someone from forensics would spot it. He took a knife from the kitchen and made a few cuts across and next to it. The police would dismiss it as a form of torture. Cleaned and dried, he re-dressed her in fresh green lingerie. He wrapped her body in the painter's plastic from the kitchen.

Using just the power of his right leg for support, he pulled her plastic-wrapped body from the tub. He was weak and injured. It took him five minutes to get her out to the garage. Past his work area, parked next to the taxi, was his Range Rover. The rear quarter panel of the SUV held her body up as he opened the rear gate. He pushed her in and slammed it closed. Pain shot up his leg. He stood still until it subsided. He would dispose of her body overnight.

Chapter 13

I had a productive morning. I rolled out of bed early without the snooze button and spent a much-needed hour at the gym. I even had enough time to stop at a local coffee shop on the way to work. In addition to two large cups of coffee, I picked up a bag for the house. I sat down at my desk fifteen minutes early. A message waited on my voicemail from Terry Murphy, in our tech department. They couldn't get anything off the airport video to identify the taxi.

I put it out of my mind and plugged away at the phones for two hours. I again called every cab company on my list, that served the airport. I hoped the day shifters would remember something the night shifters hadn't. While I was still waiting to hear back from a couple places, I was starting to think she may have gotten into an unregistered cab.

Then the morning went to hell.

The captain buzzed my desk phone and told me to get to the law offices of Stanley and Wallace. We had a body.

It was a female, blond, and dressed in lingerie. Apparently, our guy had struck again. The clock read a few minutes after eleven when Hank and I left.

We drove down West Kennedy. The crime scene was under a ten-minute drive from the station. A couple of turns later, we pulled into the small parking lot for the law office. Set on a corner lot, the place wasn't much bigger than an average house. The building was a single story, beige with a terracotta roof. White pillars supported the roof overhangs over the doorways. All the windows had arched tops. The landscaping was sparse around the building aside from a row of bushes and a couple palm trees running along the back. I pulled into the first empty parking spot and killed the motor.

Two squad cars, an unmarked cruiser, and an ambulance parked near the side of the building—that was where we headed first. I spotted Detective Jones towering over the other officers and the people they were speaking with. We walked up.

"Jones, what have we got?" I asked.

"Hey, Lieutenant. It looks like we've got a case of deja vu. Woman, thirties, blond and wearing green lingerie. It's the same as the other day."

"Branded?"

Jones nodded.

"Shit. Has anyone from forensics been here yet?"

"Nah, I've only been on the scene for a few minutes. I just happened to be grabbing a quick lunch in the area when the call came in."

"Where's the body?" Hank asked.

"This way." He turned his back and headed for the side of the building. We followed a few feet behind him.

"She's right back here," he said.

I caught women's feet sticking out from the bushes as we rounded the building's corner.

"The guy that first spotted her is giving a statement to Officer Johnson out front. From what I heard, he said he parked in the last spot there and noticed her as he got out of the car." Jones pointed to a dark-silver four door.

I stopped and took in the location of the car and building. Unless you were on the complete end, in that specific parking spot, you wouldn't see the body. I pointed back to the body and resumed walking.

"Continue, Jones."

"He went to her aid and recognized the woman was deceased. He ran inside and had them call 9-1-1. That's basically it."

I nodded. We stood in front of the body. She lay sitting up with her back half into the row of shrubs. Her head rested against her chest, her arms hanging in the branches. She wore green lingerie identical to the woman we had found in the dumpster. She smelled of bleach. Noticeable ligature marks were present around her wrists and ankles. Unlike the last woman we found, this one had been beaten.

I knelt down closer to the body. My stomach turned. Her nose was crushed to one side. She had deep lacerations to both sides of her head.

"Find a purse, phone, anything nearby that could help

us ID her?" Hank asked.

Jones shook his head. "I searched around a little but didn't spot anything. I didn't want to disturb the scene before forensics came."

"Good." I stood up. "Did you talk with anyone from inside yet?"

"I haven't had a chance, no."

"Well, let's go see what we can find out."

We walked back to the front of the building.

I caught Rick from our forensics department pulling into the parking lot as we opened the front door to go inside. Three men in suits and two women dressed in business attire stood by the front counter staring at us as we walked into the building. The two women had tears in their eyes. The men had looks of worry and grief spread across their faces. Something was off.

"I'm Lieutenant Kane, with the TPD's homicide division." I motioned toward my companions. "This is Sergeant Rawlings and Detective Jones. We'll need to speak to each of you."

One of the women wiped at her eyes and spoke up. "Is it Diane?"

"Diane?" I asked.

"Diane Robins. She worked here."

"Ma'am, is there a place we can talk?" I asked.

She nodded and pointed at an office. I looked over at Hank and Jones. It appeared as though we had a possible ID. We separated the group, with Hank taking one of the men for an interview and Jones taking the other woman. I followed the woman I'd spoken with to her office. We sat.

"What is your name, miss?"

"Lisa Cotter."

I put her in her late forties. She had brown shoulder-length hair. Her red puffy eyes didn't hide the fact that she was an attractive woman.

"Your position here?"

"Attorney."

I jotted her name down in my notepad. "What can you tell me about the events that took place this morning?"

She pulled a tissue from a box on her desk and wiped at her nose. She spoke slowly. "One of Mark's clients came rushing in, yelling to call 9-1-1. He said there was a dead woman on the side of the building. I was standing at the reception desk, letting Wanda know I had someone that would be arriving and to send them back."

I stopped her. "And who's Mark and Wanda?"

"Mark Stanley. He's one of the owners. Wanda is our receptionist. Her last name is Markel. They were both up front when you came in."

I copied down the names. "Okay, continue."

She choked at her words as they came out. "I walked out to the side of the building to see what he was talking about. I didn't believe him."

"And that's when you saw the body?"

She began to cry. I gave her a moment to compose herself. "Miss Cotter, did anyone else go outside to look at the body?"

She nodded. "Mark went out after I came back. He came

back inside and wouldn't let anyone else from the office go out there." She broke into another round of crying. "It was Diane, I know it. It looked just like her."

"All right, tell me about Diane."

She used a wadded-up tissue to dab at her eyes. "Diane Robins. She's an attorney here."

"And you believe the woman outside is her?"

She nodded. "Diane missed work yesterday. She had clients scheduled all day and never called. She wouldn't do that."

I wrote down the woman's name. "When was the last time you saw Diane?"

"Monday. She went to Atlanta on business. One of her clients got picked up on a drug charge. She was supposed to be back yesterday morning."

"Did she drive or fly?"

She shook her head. "She wouldn't drive. Wanda, up front, books all of our flights."

I made a note to get the itinerary from the receptionist. "What kind of attorney is Diane?"

"Criminal defense."

The interview lasted another twenty minutes. I got as much information as I could about Diane Robins. She was single, no children, both parents deceased. She had a sister that lived out of state. I made a note to call her. Miss Cotter agreed to identify the body once it was back at the morgue. I walked out of her office to find Hank and Jones. Jones stood at the front counter, talking with the receptionist. Hank stood in the large corner office. I assumed he was speaking with one of the owners. Jones turned from the front counter and walked toward me.

"What did you come up with?" I asked.

"Just spoke with the woman from the front desk, Wanda." He looked over the notes in his hand. "Wanda Markel. She said a client came rushing in and said there was a dead body outside the building. Guess the woman you spoke with went outside to look—came back in shock. She said it was one of their coworkers. One of the other attorneys then went out to look for himself. Miss Markel made the call to 9-1-1. I got a little information on the coworker, a Diane Robins."

Detective Jones and I compared notes. We'd gotten the same story from both parties.

Jones continued. "Sergeant Rawlings spoke with one of the attorneys, a James Wallace. Now he's in with," he looked at his notes again, "Mark Stanley."

I nodded. We waited another ten minutes for Hank to conclude his interview with the attorney. I spoke with the receptionist to see if I could get a copy of the woman's itinerary. She printed me one. I was looking it over when Hank met us in the building's lobby.

"Guess they all believe the deceased is a coworker—a Diane Robins," Hank said.

"Same thing we got."

We went over everything Hank had collected from the two men. Everyone's chain of events lined up. I let the attorney I'd spoken with know where to go to give a positive identification. We informed the staff that we would be in contact if we needed to follow up. We walked back through the front doors to the parking lot. Two news vans were raising their masts, getting ready to broadcast. The coroner's van sat at the side of the building. Detective Jones went to speak with the guys from patrol. Hank and I headed toward Rick and Ed, talking at the side of the building.

Rick was holding his forensics kit when we walked up. He shook his head as I made eye contact.

"Anything?" I asked.

"Clean as a whistle. Scrubbed with bleach. No prints anywhere—no belongings."

"Damn. All right, Rick, thanks." I focused my attention on Ed, standing next to him. "What can you tell me?"

Ed coughed into his fist. "I put time of death in between three and six hours—same as the last. Ligature marks were consistent with the woman from the other day. She has some cut marks on the palm of her hand. I'd say the beating was the cause of death, but I need to check into something else first."

"What's that?" Hank asked.

"Sutures on the right side of her head above her ear. I didn't see the shaved hair around the area until we moved the body to load her. The way her hair was positioned, combined with the damage, made it hard to see."

"Sutures?" I asked.

"Yeah. Homemade. Not done by a physician, that's for sure. Kind of barbaric work."

"Another lobotomy attempt?"

"You'll be the first to know."

"How soon until you can get to her?" I asked.

"Well, we have her loaded. We're going to head back to the office with her now. I don't have anything pressing at the moment. I'll start with her right away."

"Thanks, Ed."

The media had started to swarm on the outskirts of the parking lot and seemed to multiply with each passing minute. Employees from local businesses and homeowners from the neighborhood gathered on the sidewalks to watch. I dialed the captain to let him know what we had and to ask him what he wanted me to give the press. He wanted to have a meeting back at the station and schedule a press release for three o'clock. Through the sea of reporters, I relayed the message.

Chapter 14

He'd dumped her body where she would be found and identified. His plan for her, as well as the last, hadn't been death—he would need to try again. He was halfway through a double bacon cheeseburger when chatter across the CB alerted him that they'd found her body. Between fares, the cab drivers liked to talk about the latest happenings across the city. He had found the frequency of one of the major cab companies in the area and set the station to a preset. From the way drivers were speaking on the radio, it sounded as though quite a scene was unfolding at the attorney's office. He figured he would pop in, just from a standpoint of curiosity. The thought of watching the police work entertained him. They'd interview people and cross-check everyone's stories. The forensics guys would search for any scrap of evidence left behind. He could even catch a glimpse of his new adversary, trying to solve the crime. The detectives wouldn't find anything, and neither would the forensics team. He was careful and far too smart to leave something for a stupid lab geek to find. The cops would go through a lot of trouble for nothing. They wouldn't find out who did it until he wanted them to.

It took him fifteen minutes to get to the scene. He slowed as he drove down the block in front of the attorney's office. News vans had parked at the curb, and the office's parking lot had five squad cars and three unmarked police-issue Dodges. His timing was perfect. He crawled past, doing no more than five miles an hour. Two men were loading a black body bag into the back of the coroner's van.

He continued past and made the next right. A parking spot at the end of the street came into view. He parked the cab and walked back to the scene. Pain shot up his leg with each step as he tried to hide his limp. He didn't want to draw attention to himself.

An opening appeared next to a group of people on the sidewalk. He approached and made eye contact with a man to his right. "What's going on?"

The guy shrugged. "Guess someone died or something."

"Lots of police for someone who just happened to die. The news vans, too? Nah, this seems like a bigger deal than a stiff at the office."

The guy looked over at him, appearing put off by his crass comment. "Okay, Detective."

He smirked. "Has to be a murder or something."

"Yeah, I don't know. Maybe."

He continued walking to the next group of people: three women, all dressed business casual. He put on a smile and stopped next to them. "What happened?" he asked.

The blond he addressed shook her head. "It's horrible. I heard people talking. They said they found a dead woman on the side of the building. I guess someone found her and called the police."

He nodded. "Yeah, same thing I heard. Someone back there said it was a blond woman dressed in lingerie? They found another body like that at an office building a few days ago. I caught it on the six o'clock news."

Her eyebrows raised. "Really?"

"Yeah. And now this at another office building?" He moved like he was trying to shake away the thought.

A look of concern crossed the woman's face. A reporter walked up, asking if she could interview the three women. His time to leave had come. He ducked his head and walked away. He took in the rest of the scene as he left. Detectives walked from the front of the building.

He paused when he spotted the larger bald cop in a suit. Lieutenant Kane was working the scene.

He grinned and continued walking down the block. He began limping again as he rounded the corner toward his car. The pain was intense.

Chapter 15

Everyone assembled in one of our meeting rooms. I'd just gotten off the phone with Ed. He was getting ready to start the autopsy but wanted to let me know that Lisa Cotter had positively identified the victim as Diane Robins. The captain informed me that he'd made a call to the local FBI office to see if they could lend us someone to draw up a profile. They agreed to send someone over in the morning. We asked a few of the other department heads to join us for the meeting. Rick from forensics was sitting in, as was Sergeant Timmons from patrol. Hank and Detective Jones leaned against the small table at the corner of the room. Sam James, the station's PR guy, sat at the back to listen in and determine what information from our briefing would go into the press release. He sat at a laptop, typing it up. I started the meeting.

I went over what we had found out at the scene. The same perp had killed both women. We didn't reveal to the public that the first victim had a branded hand. The killer was the only one who knew that detail.

Both women were in their thirties, blond, and found wearing green lingerie. I put Detective Jones on finding what stores sold that specific brand of lingerie. I also put him on looking to see if they belonged to any of the same groups or organizations. We needed to put the two together somewhere. If they'd stayed at the same Holiday Inn four years ago in Fresno, I wanted to know about it.

The cab was next. It was still the best lead we had. Sarah McMillian got into a cab at the airport and never arrived at her destination. I had looked into every registered cab company in the city, but that left who-knows-how-many taxis operating without licensing. I asked Sergeant Timmons to station officers from patrol at the airport. The plan was to chat up cab drivers, ask to look at their registration, and see if anything was amiss. He agreed and dispatched two cars.

Hank was going to head over to the airport and talk with Nick Waterman at the security office again. We had Diane Robins's itinerary and planned to do the same thing we'd done with Sarah McMillian. We would follow her on video through the airport to see if she spoke with anyone or got into a cab. We needed to know if the airport was his hunting ground.

Rick explained to the team that the lack of evidence told us something about our perp. He was careful disposing of the bodies. He'd left nothing at either crime scene to incriminate himself. Our team found no fingerprints or personal belongings, and the bodies were both cleaned. We were dealing with someone intelligent. However, even the most intelligent people made mistakes. He said he would take Pax back out to the scenes and have another look around. Another pass couldn't hurt.

Together, we agreed that we should disclose to the media that our perp may be driving a taxi. While we didn't know yet if Diane Robins had taken a cab, we did know that Sarah McMillian did. It wouldn't go over well with the cab companies in the city. However, there was a chance someone else got a ride from this guy and had a run in with him. We assigned extra people to man the phones. Any calls that had substance would be forwarded to me or Captain Bostok.

The captain thought we should keep the brands to ourselves for the time being. They screamed serial killer. We weren't in that territory yet.

Sam left the room to make a copy of the press release he'd put together, as well as a handout of details we felt comfortable sharing with the media. He came back a few minutes later as we mulled over our assignments.

Sam looked at his watch. "We're scheduled over in the press room in about five minutes. Take a few seconds to go over the release." He handed the press releases out.

I gave it a quick once-over.

"All right, let's get this done so we can get back to it," the captain said.

We made our way through the hall to the station's press room. It was another meeting room that the station used for budget meetings and the occasional dealings with the media. Two long tables with chairs sat in the center of the room, and more chairs lined the back wall if needed. At the front, a podium took center stage. We entered. Reporters from various news outlets and local news channels filled the room. They rustled about, finding seats. Cameramen stood to the sides to record the release.

Captain Bostok took a seat to the side of the podium. Hank and I sat next to him. Detectives Jones and Donner sat on the other side. Sam approached the podium. He gave the microphone a few taps to quiet the room.

"Ladies and gentlemen of the media, we want to thank you for coming in this morning. I'm Sam James, director of public relations for the Tampa Police Department. The basis of today's briefing is to bring you current developments and updates on two homicide cases we are investigating. To begin the brief, I turn the podium over to Captain Bostok of the homicide division and Lieutenant Carl Kane. Captain."

The captain introduced himself and gave a few highlights of our morning meeting. When he finished, he turned the podium over to me.

"I'm Lieutenant Carl Kane of the Tampa Police Department's homicide division. To my right, seated, is Sergeant Hank Rawlings. We are the lead investigators on the case. As Captain Bostok just informed you, this briefing is to cover the two homicides that are under investigation. Monday morning, we received a call that a body had been found. Our team arrived on the scene and began the investigation. The press release we had provided to the media led to a call in. That call helped us to identify the woman. She was here from out of town on business. We will not be disclosing her identity at this time as the case is still being investigated. We do have leads that we are following up on in this case."

"Today at 10:18 a.m., the TPD received a call regarding another body found under similar circumstances. We dispatched officers and detectives to the scene. From our initial investigation, we do believe these two cases to be related. The local FBI office has agreed to further help us with the investigation."

The media room burst into a commotion. Each reporter fired a different question at me at the same time.

I put my hands out to quiet the room. "Please, everyone, we will have a short question-and-answer session at the conclusion of our release. Please hold your questions until then. Let me reiterate: the Tampa Police Department is committed to bringing a resolution to this case in the shortest time possible. We have the department's full resources and staff at our disposal. That being said, we want to ask for help from the public as well. If you were in the vicinity of the Manchester office building between the hours of midnight and seven a.m. Monday or the vicinity of West Cypress Street between the hours of midnight and nine a.m. this morning and saw anything that seemed suspicious, please call the Tampa Police Department. Again, no matter how insignificant it may seem, we want you to call in and speak with one of our detectives. You can always remain anonymous."

"Where are you on the case? Do you have any suspects?" A reporter interrupted.

I nodded. "As I said, our team is still working a number of leads. From the evidence we gathered on the first case, we believe that our suspect may be a cab driver. Our first victim was last seen entering a taxi at Tampa International. What we would like to do is ask anyone who had witnessed suspicious activity involving a taxi to phone into the station. We are looking for things like verbal altercations with the drivers, especially if you are a female. We will be stationing additional officers at the airport and will be checking into the cabs and cab drivers coming and going from that area."

A reporter from the *Tampa Tribune* spoke from the back of the room. "Why are you bringing in the FBI?"

I tried to hold back my annoyance. The press in the room must have missed the part where I'd told them to hold their questions until the end.

"The TPD has a great relationship with our FBI field office. They have resources and databases that are unavailable to us at a local level. The captain called them to lend us a hand. They are sending us over a profiler to work with the team that we have assembled. Once that profile is complete, we will release it to the press."

"Lieutenant Kane, in your opinion, what kind of person are we dealing with here?"

Clearly, the press was just going to keep firing questions at me.

"Anyone who commits acts of violence on women is sick and depraved in my opinion. That's going to be it for me, guys. I'm going to turn it back over to Sam James to wrap up. Thank you."

I stepped away, and Sam took the podium.

"That is going to be it for us for today. We have to let our team get back to the investigation. I'll take a couple quick questions if you have them ready."

The media rustled around writing notes and going over what they heard in the briefing. Rich Brimley, a reporter for the *Tampa Tribune*, threw up a hand.

Sam pointed at him for his question.

"Mr. James, we heard that the women wore lingerie. Can you comment on that?"

"They were dressed in a similar fashion, yes."

"Just to confirm, lingerie?"

Sam nodded.

Chris Marks, from Channel 2, raised his hand.

"Yes, Chris, your question?"

"Are the two victims connected? And how did they die?"

"We are investigating if there is a connection now. We are not going to get into the specifics of how these two women's lives were taken. One or two more questions, and we will wrap this up here."

A voice spoke up in the back: J.R. Steele from Channel 6. "Yeah, I got a question. Are we dealing with a serial killer here?"

"Mr. Steele, I believe it's premature and reckless to jump to that conclusion. Right now, we believe the two cases are related. That is the extent of it."

"Reckless? We have two women, murdered and dumped

wearing the same outfit a few days apart? Who's to say there won't be more?"

"Mr. Steele, let's let the police do their job before foreshadowing events that haven't taken place. The TPD's homicide division has an exceptional track record of solving cases and bringing the perpetrators involved to justice. We have every confidence that will hold true here. That's all for today. Thank you."

Sam stepped from the podium. We left the media room for the hall.

Chapter 16

The phones in the police station lit up after the press release. Most of the calls were about typical arguments with cab drivers about their fare. In hindsight, I realized I should have been more specific about what we were looking for. We took all the calls regardless and weeded through them. Ed called to tell me that he'd finished the report and was faxing it over. I told him I would call him to go over the results when the report hit my desk. *Very disturbing* was his quote.

My desk phone rang again. Our secretary up front told me I had a call waiting from Lisa Cotter. I clicked over to the waiting call.

"This is Lieutenant Kane."

"Hi, it's Lisa Cotter from Stanley and Wallace."

"Hi, Lisa."

"We watched the press release from the office here, and well, I'm sure it's nothing, but we figured we should call."

"Did someone remember something?"

"Well, not really, but it might be related."

"Okay, related how?"

"Well, Diane had this client, a twenty-year-old with drug charges that he wasn't going to get out of. Diane put together a plea deal with the prosecutor. The kid wouldn't take the deal. He wanted to take his chances in court. Diane urged him again to take the deal while it was on the table. The kid refused and went before the judge and jury. They found him guilty. The judge handed down a sentence of twelve years."

"How long ago was this?"

"About a month ago. His father, Kevin O'Hare, was furious with the outcome. He blamed us. He called Diane a number of times before she stopped taking his calls. Her voicemail would be filled with the guy cussing her out and telling her she failed the family."

"So an unhappy family member of a guilty client. I'm sure that happens quite a bit. Did he make any threats?"

"He did threaten her in the last couple phone calls, and there's something else. The guy's father drives a cab."

It didn't account for the first victim. However, it was a credible threat that had to be looked into further. It was the best lead we'd gotten from the phone calls. I wrote down the guy's name and told her we would get on it. I gave Timmons in patrol a ring and asked him if he could put it out to his cars and bring him in.

I headed out of my office for the station's fax machine. Ed's autopsy report sat on top—seven pages total. I scooped it up and headed to my office. The light for my voicemail at my desk was flashing. I ticked the button to play the message, which was Hank telling me that he had her on video getting into a cab, just like Sarah McMillian. He said they had more footage of the cab than last time and he had a copy of the video in hand. He was making his way back to the station.

I called Timmons right back and told him our second victim had also gotten into a cab at the airport. He said he'd put the word out to question every cabbie that pulled through the TPA. I told him to have an officer watch for any single women that got into a cab and to get the car's plates. He agreed.

I sat down at my desk and started reading over the autopsy report. Her cause of death was comminuted skull fractures. The following page covered the other injuries she'd suffered. A word stuck out at me: *leucotomy*. I pulled up the Internet, searched it, and immediately dialed Ed.

The receptionist transferred me over to his desk. He picked up right away.

"Ed Dockett."

"Hey, Ed. Kane."

"Look at the report?" he asked.

"Leucotomy."

"I take that as a yes. It looks like we have an amateur Psycho Surgeon on our hands."

"Psycho Surgeon?" It sounded as though it came from a bad B movie.

"Well, not like that. Psychosurgery is what operating on the brain to effect a mental state is called. When you think of a lobotomy, that's psychosurgery."

I jotted down *psychosurgery* in my notes. "Got it. Is that what the stitches on the side of her head were from?"

"Yes. Underneath the flap of skin, someone used a hole saw to cut a piece of her skull away so they could access her brain."

I leaned back in my chair. "Geez."

"Well, I removed the loose piece of skull. There were slices in the brain matter of the frontal lobe, consistent with a leucotomy. This procedure was well above and beyond drilling into someone's head and pouring in boiling water."

I shook my head. "What does a leucotomy do?"

"That's the thing. It could do nothing or kill her. It could also leave her in just about any state between those extremes. Doctors tried these procedures with mental patients from the nineteen thirties to the fifties. They would slice into sections of the brain and see if they got the desired result, whatever that may be. If someone suffered from depression, they would make cuts to the prefrontal area of the brain and see what happened. If the patient suffered from schizophrenia, same thing. Doctors quit this sort of thing in the early seventies. It was pure quackery."

I grabbed a pen and wrote down the highlights of what he was saying. "Where would someone learn this?"

"They wouldn't. Our guy is experimenting."

"Great." I let out a deep breath. "Tell me about the cause of death."

"Comminuted skull fractures. She had lacerations and bruising to the right side of her head and significant skull damage to the other. The shape of the bruises is consistent with heel marks from a shoe. I think someone stomped her to death. That was after the brain procedure."

I rubbed my free hand over my head and dug my palm into my eye. "So she was alive after the leucotomy?"

Ed paused before answering. "Yes."

I shook my head. "Okay, Ed. I didn't get a chance to go over the tox screen. Anything there?" I flipped through the sheets to find the toxicology report and went down the list. There were high levels of two drugs. One was the same as the first victim, Xylazine. The other I wasn't familiar with.

"Yup, tested positive for Xylazine, the same horse tranquilizer that he used on the other woman. This time there was another, Buprenorphine. It's an opiate and an odd duck, for that matter."

"Bu-pren-or-phine." I did my best to try to pronounce the drug. "Can you spell that for me?"

He did.

"I never heard of it. Not a street drug, I'm guessing?"

"Nope. You might have your best lead there," Ed said.

"How's that?"

"It's hard to get. Real hard. Regulated like you wouldn't believe. The drug is something like thirty times stronger than morphine."

"What do they use it for?"

"It's used in treating opioid dependency, but that would be in pill form. This wasn't. There were no traces of it in her stomach, and I have a few needle marks on her arms and legs."

"So, injected?"

"Yes."

"Anything else?"

"The cut marks on her hand were interesting."

"Interesting how?"

"Well, flip to the page with the drawing of the body. It indicates where her injuries were."

I thumbed through the papers until I found the page. "Got it."

"The cuts just looked strange to me, so I put her hand under magnification and looked at the wounds. There is one with inflammation around it. The others don't show any signs of it."

"So, what do you think?"

"Well, I'm going to get Rick to come over and take a look. I want to know what he thinks before I make a definitive conclusion on it."

"Hunch?"

"Think the one was when she was alive and the others were postmortem. But like I said, I'm going to hold off on a conclusion until I get Rick's opinion."

"All right. Keep me updated."

"I will. Find this guy quick, Kane. I'm not looking forward to what comes in next if he does this again."

"Thanks, Ed."

Everything in the autopsy report got put into a file folder. I needed to give the captain an update. I walked next door to fill him in. He had his office door closed. I gave it a knock and entered.

"Cap."

He looked over at me from his computer screen and took off his glasses. He pointed to one of the guest chairs. "Have a seat. What have you got?"

"Well, we have new information."

"I'm listening."

"Good news first. I took a call from Lisa Cotter, the woman who worked with our second victim. A former client was making threats to Diane. The guy drives a cab. Timmons sent the word out to pick him up."

"Can we connect him to Sarah McMillian somehow?"

"Don't know yet. I'm going to stay here until they bring him in. I'll run the interview myself."

He nodded. "What's the bad news?"

"I talked to Ed. Our guy is experimenting with his own form of lobotomies."

A blank looked crossed the captain's face. "Experimenting with his own form of lobotomies?"

"Yeah. Well, the last one was a leucotomy. He cut a hole in Diane Robins's skull and sliced into her brain."

Captain Bostok sat quiet for a minute. "Any other good news?"

"Maybe. The toxicology screen found a drug in her system that's not easily accessible. I'm going to dig into that and see what we can come up with."

Hank knocked at the captain's door. The captain yelled for him to come in.

He took a seat next to me and surveyed the captain and me. "We get more bad news or something?"

"I'll give you the highlights in a bit," I said.

"All right. Well, we might get something from the airport's video—got a pretty good view of the cab. I just dropped it off with Murphy in tech."

The captain nodded. "This thing is going to turn into a shitstorm real quick if another body turns up. The FBI profiler will be here at ten a.m. I want you both here before nine for a morning meeting." The captain rolled his chair away from his desk. "Rawlings, we don't have enough overtime on the books. Go home. Kane, do whatever you're going to do until they bring that guy in for questioning."

We left the captain's office and closed the door. I filled Hank in on the autopsy details and told him I would see him in the morning. He asked if I would call with an update later and check in on Murphy's progress with the video. I agreed.

Chapter 17

The road split, sending him to the area for arrivals. Taxi cabs formed a single-file line. Police cruisers came into view up ahead. Police officers were patrolling the area. A cop stepped out from the curb and motioned for him to park. He pulled to the curb behind the other cabs. A cop leaned into the taxi in front of him, talking with the driver.

A knock on his window startled him. His eyes darted to the left. A fist banged against the glass again. As the man pulled his knuckles away, he spotted a badge.

He rolled down the window. "Can I help you with something, Officer?"

"We're just doing random checks. Can I see the registration for the car, your license, and proof of insurance?"

"Sure—one minute." He rummaged through the glove box and found the papers. "Here you go." He handed over the proof of insurance and registration.

The cop held them in his hand. "Driver's license too."

"Oh yeah, sorry."

From his wallet came the license. They all belonged to someone else—a former coworker. He'd lifted the wallet from the guy's desk at work. His coworker was close to the same height and build. At least he had been at the time. He hoped the cop wouldn't notice the weight difference. The hair and eye color were the same. His lack of a beard made the small driver's license photo irrelevant. The cab registration and insurance were legal, just under the former coworker's name, Dan Ellison. He'd had to check the guy's mailbox every day for three weeks to intercept the vehicle and credit-card paperwork. As soon as he did, he switched everything to paperless bills. He wouldn't need to worry about the cab registration for another year.

The cop took the information from him. "Be back with you in a minute."

"No problem." He rolled his window back up.

He sat in the car, wondering why the police were all over the airport. He wondered if it was for him.

I'll have to see what this cop knows when he gets back.

He patiently waited the five minutes before the officer returned.

The cop walked to the cab's window. "Can you remove your hat for me?"

He complied.

The cop looked at the driver's license and then him. "You dropped a few pounds, huh?" the cop asked.

"Cancer." He pointed to his stringy hair. "Treatment is eating me alive."

The cop's mouth turned to the side. "I'm sorry. Here you go, Mr. Ellison." The cop handed him back his paperwork and driver's license.

"It's just Dan. Mr. Ellison is my father." He let out a chuckle. "What's with the random check?"

"We have interest in taxis working the area."

"Well, maybe I can help. I know most of the drivers that work the airport. What are you looking for?"

"It's just part of an investigation."

The cop wasn't going to give him anything.

A fat sixty-some-year-old stood at the curb, motioning for a cab.

The cop pointed over to the man waving. "Looks like you have a fare waiting there. Have a good day, sir."

Everything told him to drive away, but it would have drawn attention. He scooped the guy up and turned up the volume on the CB. The chatter from the cab drivers on the radio told him the police had held a press conference earlier. They mentioned they were looking for a cab in connection with two murdered women. Another driver confirmed that he'd read a story about it in the *Tampa News Daily*. Halfway across town, he got rid of his passenger and headed for the nearest newspaper box. He found one carrying that paper on the corner of Fowler and North 22nd. He pulled the cab into the parking lot of the fast-food joint on the corner and hopped out. At the metal newspaper box, he fished fifty cents from his pocket and plugged it into the machine. He pulled out the evening addition and carried it back to the car.

Small text at the top corner read: *Serial killer driving the streets of Tampa? Story on page six.*

He unfolded the paper to the page and tossed the rest on the passenger seat. He browsed the article. The photo from the press conference was of Lieutenant Carl Kane, the lead investigator. The article stated the police were looking for a cab taking women from the Tampa airport. The article mentioned the lingerie but not the branding or how they died. What he'd heard across the cab's radio was all they had. While it wasn't a lot, it was enough to throw a wrench into his immediate plans. His eyes went back to the photo and then to the caption below. The caption included a quote from the lieutenant.

He flicked the photo of the cop with his finger. "Sick and depraved, huh?" He smiled and coughed. "I'll show you sick and depraved, Lieutenant."

Chapter 18

I sat glued to the monitor with Murphy in our tech department. We had played and replayed, at least ten times, the video footage Hank had brought back from the airport. We had her getting into what looked like a standard Crown Victoria taxi. Like Sarah McMillian, she walked to the taxi stand and waited, got picked up, and drove away.

We caught a glimpse of our driver in this video. Though he was no bigger than an inch on our forty-some-inch screen, he looked to be the same height as Diane Robins. He looked thin—around a hundred fifty pounds. We added it to our file. We couldn't pull any car or plate numbers from the footage. I thanked Murphy for staying late and headed back upstairs to my office.

At my desk, I sat down and grabbed the phone. I wanted to check with Timmons on Kevin O'Hare before I called it a night.

"Patrol, this is Sergeant Timmons."

"Hey, it's Kane. You get anything on Kevin O'Hare?"

"We sent a car out to his house. No one home. He works for American Taxi and Limo. We sent a car there, but he has tonight off. The dispatcher said he should be in by nine o'clock tomorrow morning."

"Okay. Thanks."

"No sweat. Want me to give you a buzz if we find him before morning?"

"Please."

"No problem." He hung up.

I called Hank to tell him what we'd gotten from the video. The phone call was short. My clock read 9:18 p.m. I couldn't do anything else at the station until morning. If they did bring in Kevin O'Hare overnight, which I doubted, I'd be fine with driving back. My keys in hand, I locked my office door and headed home.

Butch greeted me with his normal foot thrashing as he tried to escape. Corraling him and shoving him back inside the condo took a minute. I doubted he'd know what to do if he got out. Everything from my pockets was tossed on the kitchen table. A quick rummage through the refrigerator netted no results other than a beer. I decided to grab something to eat on the way in to the station in the morning. I went into the living room and flopped onto the couch. Butch came and sat on my leg. I clicked the TV on to a movie I had seen a hundred times. The television couldn't keep my concentration. I stretched out and stared at the ceiling. My mind wouldn't shut off and allow me to relax. I reviewed the evidence in my head. Ed's mention of the drug being our best lead kept coming up. I decided it would be the first thing I looked into, come morning.

The sound of my own snoring woke me a few hours later.

I pulled myself from the comfort of my couch and sauntered to my bedroom. I set my alarm for six o'clock. As soon as my head hit the pillow, my phone rang.

I rolled over, took it from the nightstand, and answered. "Kane."

"Hi, Lieutenant, it's Sergeant Mueller. Sorry to wake you. Timmons left me a note to call you if we picked up Kevin O'Hare. We just did. He's at the station now."

I pulled the phone from my ear and caught the time: 1:13 a.m. "Be there in twenty minutes."

I hung up and rolled myself out of bed. I tossed on what I had worn the previous day and splashed some water across my face. Everything from the kitchen table got jammed back in my pockets. I headed out for my car. I rolled down the windows on the drive over to the station, thinking the night air would help wake me up. It didn't.

I pulled into the station and parked. As soon as I walked in, I went straight to the lunchroom to try my luck with the coffee machine. I hit the button for a large and stuck in a cup. The machine whirred and bubbled. The word *error* flashed on the screen. I cracked my neck from side to side.

On the counter sat a coffee pot someone else must have brought in. It had just under a cup sitting in the bottom of the carafe. The red light on the side told me it was still hot. I walked over and picked up the carafe to give it a sniff. The coffee was burnt and had probably been sitting on the burner for hours. I poured it into a cup and sprinkled some powdered creamer into it. I hoped it would be better than nothing. As soon as it hit my tongue, I realized it wasn't. I grabbed a soda and a candy bar from the vending machine.

I made my way over to patrol and looked for Sergeant Mueller. He was in charge of the guys out working the graveyard shift and was sitting at his desk.

"Mueller. You have my guy somewhere?"

"Hey, Lieutenant. We have him in box number two. One of our guys scooped him up on a DUI. Someone called him in. He was using both lanes of the two-way street to get home. Be forewarned, he's not in the best of moods. Officer Quinlin is in there with him now."

"Thanks."

"Find me when you're done. We need to take him over for processing."

"Will do."

I headed to my office to grab both of the victim's files and then walked toward the interview rooms. I took a sip of the black swill in my cup. The station didn't have enough powdered creamer to put a dent in its color.

I gave the door a knock and entered.

Officer Quinlin sat on one side of the desk, Kevin O'Hare on the other. O'Hare swayed from side to side in his chair. Alcoholics all seemed to have a look about them. This guy had it. His tan was dark, his clothes dingy. He was thin and stank of cigarettes and beer. A dirty baseball cap sat on his head. Gray stubble covered his cheeks and chin.

"Kevin O'Hare?" I asked. I set the soda and candy bar

in front of him.

He swatted at them with his hand. "What are you? The good cop?" His voice slurred.

I gave Officer Quinlin a nod and took a seat.

He got up and headed for the door. "I'll be right outside, Lieutenant."

"That's fine. Thanks."

O'Hare slouched in his seat and stared at Quinlin. "Looks like your boss is here. Better run along, putz."

Quinlin smirked and closed the door.

I was always cordial with my suspects. Some officers at our station still played hard-ass during interviews. I tended to get better results from being civil and just trying to keep the conversation moving forward. That night was different. That guy was drunk and angry. O'Hare's demeanor toward Quinlin told me that my normal tactics wouldn't work. I needed to get what I could before he lawyered up or passed out.

"Okay. Kevin O'Hare. Do you drive a taxi?"

He let out a puff of air. "Doubt I do anymore. Yeah, good work tonight, guys! Great bust! Real credits to the force!" he shouted at the walls as if the guys who'd brought him in were standing there.

I checked it off as confirmed on my sheet. "Tell me about your son's attorney." I crossed my arms and waited for a response.

"My son's attorney? What the hell does that matter?"

"Stanley and Wallace. Attorney Robins. I understand there were some problems there. You weren't happy with the representation."

He jerked his head back. "Hell no! My boy got twelve years for having a handful of ecstasy. The attorneys didn't do squat."

I shook my head. "You don't get twelve years for a handful of ecstasy. I heard they offered him a plea deal."

"It might have been more than a handful but not much. He wasn't selling it. He and his stupid friends were sneaking into clubs, going to parties, shit like that and taking it. He's just a kid. He didn't have any priors. Why would he take a deal? He should have got off with a slap on the wrist. Instead, they stuck him in prison with a bunch of killers and gangbangers."

"So you threatened his attorney?"

"You know how mad I was? We hired those guys, spent thousands and thousands of dollars to keep him out of jail, and he gets locked up anyway." He slammed his hands on the table. "For twelve years!"

"What did you say to Attorney Robins?"

"I told her that she was a damn thief and someday she would get what was coming to her."

"Did that day come?"

He shook his head. "I don't follow."

I scooted my chair closer to him. "Where were you last night?"

"Work."

"Driving a cab?"

"Yeah. Why?"

"We found her body outside her office this morning. I'm

going to need more than 'you were at work.'"

He shook his head. "I didn't have anything to do with it. Check with American's dispatch. They can tell you every fare I took. When I wasn't taking a fare, I sat at the station house."

"I have to say the fact that you don't seem to care one bit is a little concerning."

"I don't care. The bitch got my son locked up. Just check my alibi. Call American Taxi."

"I'll be calling them—don't worry. Do you know someone named Sarah McMillian?"

"No. Should I?"

"I'm asking you if you know her." I pulled her photo from her file and held it up. "Ever pick this woman up?"

He sat up straight in his chair to take a look.

As soon as he sat up, I realized I was wasting my time. I didn't remember what his sheet had listed for a height and weight, but his height in the chair told me he wasn't the cab driver from the video. O'Hare had to be over six feet. He sat eye level with me, maybe a touch taller.

"Never seen her before. Look, I'm getting an attorney before I say another word to you. You guys aren't railroading me into a murder charge."

"That's fine. I would suggest you don't call Stanley and Wallace." I stood from the table and walked out.

Quinlin waited outside the door. I told him I was through and headed for Sergeant Mueller's desk.

He stared at me as I walked down the hallway toward him. "All done?" he asked.

"Lawyered up. I'm through."

"Think he's your guy?"

"Don't think so, but I'll check into his story in the morning. I know where he'll be if his alibi doesn't check out. All right, I'm heading home—going to try to catch a few hours of sleep before I'm back here in four and a half hours."

Mueller smiled. "Have a good night, Lieutenant."

Chapter 19

The cops were too thick at the Tampa airport for him to make a grab. The police patrols forced him to go elsewhere.

At 7:15 a.m., he awoke choking on his own blood. The cab sat in the cell-phone lot of the Orlando airport. He coughed and gagged. Air refused to fill his lungs. He rushed from the cab into a portable toilet. The door slammed shut at his back. He leaned over the plastic bowl and heaved. Blood ran from his mouth. A minute passed before he could draw in a breath. His illness threatened to take his life before he could complete his plan.

No. You're not finished yet. Get up.

He wiped the blood from his mouth with a piece of toilet paper and walked back to the cab.

At 7:42 a.m., a woman waved from the curb at the arrivals section. She was a little younger than the others. He put her in her late twenties. She was thin with short brown hair. The woman bounced up and down, flailing her arms in her blazer and matching skirt. He cut two cars off to get to her. He told her she had a twenty-five-minute ride from the airport to her destination.

She spent her time in the cab chatting him up. She told him she'd caught the red-eye back from Los Angeles. He learned all about the position she'd just landed as a junior executive for a pharmaceutical company in Thousand Oaks. He smiled and nodded while listening to her ramblings. She apologized for being so excited and telling him all those things he probably didn't care about. He told her to continue. She said she'd planned to pack up her things and move by the end of the week. Her hard work had paid off.

He had a solid hour-and-a-half drive back to the house in Brandon. The woman made the trip unconscious in the trunk.

Chapter 20

At nine thirty, I'd finished my fifth cup of coffee, trying to combat my lack of sleep. As long as I kept the caffeine flowing, it was holding off the drowsiness somewhat. We gathered the same team we'd had for the previous day's meeting, plus one, Major Danes. The media splashing the words "serial killer" across the papers didn't sit well with the higher-ups. He wanted to see where we stood so he could give an update to the chief. The major took up a space next to the door, his arms crossed over his red tie and barrel chest. In his dark pinstriped suit, he looked intimidating if you didn't know him. Major Danes had a thick white mustache and bald head. I imagined I would look similar in fifteen years. Anybody who knew him, however, realized he was just a cop like the rest of us. He'd worked his way through the ranks and had earned his position. I'd been out to his house for barbecues and gatherings. He was a good cop and, I would almost venture to say, a friend.

The captain had faxed everything we had on the case

over to the feds earlier. The guy they were lending us to help was going to put together a profile and come at ten. I started the meeting by going over the interview I'd had with Kevin O'Hare a few hours earlier. I'd checked out his story as soon as I got in. He had been at the taxi station between fares when the cab picked up Diane Robins, and he was across town at the time Sarah McMillian got into a cab. The guy was another dead end, someone we could cross off the list.

We went over the autopsy report of Diane Robins next. When everyone was up to speed with where we left off, I addressed Detective Jones.

"Lingerie? What did you get?" I asked.

He looked into his notes. "It's regular department store stuff. Big name brand that's sold at just about every retail outlet in the area. We're talking hundreds of stores. That's not including online sales. Needle in a haystack stuff."

I nodded. "What about connecting the two women?"

He shook his head. "Sorry, there's just nothing there."

"Okay, I have something that might be more productive for you." I printed out a couple copies of the Diane Robins toxicology report. I took one from the stack and handed one to him. "Aside from being injected with Xylazine like Sarah McMillian, Diane Robins was also injected with a drug called Buprenorphine. It's heavily regulated and normally comes in a pill form. Try to find out where someone would get the injectable stuff."

Jones nodded.

"Timmons, what have your guys got from the airport?"

"Not much, Lieutenant—a few unregistered cabs that

we cited, questioned, and then sent off. Since we talked last night, my guys have collected six tag numbers from cabs that took single females as fares. No one has called in a missing woman, though."

"Okay, keep in contact with the guys up in missing persons. If they get a call, cross-check it right away. Can we keep the cars stationed at the airport going for now?"

"Yeah, I can keep guys there as long as they are getting paid their overtime."

Timmons looked at Major Danes. Danes nodded.

"Good." I looked at Rick. "Anything from forensics? Did you meet with Ed?"

"First, we went out to both scenes again yesterday. We canvased a block in each direction. We searched dumpsters. Nothing. Pax did see two red-light cameras while we were in the area of the attorney's office. One was three blocks away, and the other was six blocks from the scene. We could try to pull those and see if we have a taxi in the area at the time. It's a shot in the dark but could be something. Someone is going to have to get it signed off on, though."

"Give me the time frame, and I'll get you guys the video," Major Danes said.

I nodded. "Thanks, Major. All right, what about the cuts on her hand, Rick? Ed mentioned he wanted your opinion."

"He gave me a call last night, and I met him there first thing this morning. He questioned the cuts she had on her right hand and wanted me to take a look. She had a wound that ran horizontally, starting in the webbing between her thumb and index finger. The shape of the laceration was consistent with the blade of a knife slipping back into her hand while she stabbed something. It's common with people who are unfamiliar with handling knives in that way. This wound had inflammation around it. Over the top of that wound and to the sides were more cuts. They were smaller in size and depth. There was also no inflammation present around them."

"So, postmortem?" I asked.

Rick nodded. "They could have been made to cover up the original cut. It's a possibility that our guy has a knife wound."

"Can you make a few calls for us, Rick? Local hospitals?" the captain asked.

"A knife wound would be reported. From him stitching up the woman's head, we know he had the materials to sew himself up if it did happen. I'll make some calls either way," Rick said.

"Thanks, Rick."

Timmons, Rick, and Detective Jones left the room. Captain Bostok, Hank, and I went over the case.

One of the girls from up front knocked on the sill of the door to let us know our profiler had arrived. The captain went, got him, and brought him back to the meeting room. We had a quick round of introductions. His name was Agent Beck. He wasn't what I was expecting. All the Feds I'd had come into contact with were interchangeable. They all seem to average six feet, all wore dark suits, and all had short hair with no mustaches or beards.

Agent Beck was five foot eight and overweight by thirty pounds. He wore a tweed suit from the late seventies or early eighties. His hair was shoulder length and graying. There was at least two weeks' worth of scruff on his face. He was either exceptional at his position or did a damn good job of avoiding whoever was in charge of FBI appearances. He took a seat and opened a folder he was carrying under his arm.

"Okay gentlemen, if you don't mind, let's get right to it." He looked up at us and waited.

We sat at the conference table.

Agent Beck cleared his throat. "Before I begin, has there been any development since last night that I should be aware of?"

"We had a glimpse of him on video. Appeared to be around five foot nine and thin," I said.

Beck wrote it down. "Caucasian?"

"Appeared so."

"Thank you." He clasped his hands together in front of him. "First, I cross-referenced everything from the case with the FBI's database. We have no one in our system that is branding victims. With nothing similar, we are indeed looking for a new suspect. Now, to be labeled as a serial killer, we would need three or more victims. You have two, but I believe—one hundred percent—the man you are looking for is a serial killer and has been for some time."

"What brings you to that conclusion?" I asked.

"His acts are planned. There is no evidence at all left with the bodies other than what he wants you to see, in these cases the lingerie, branding, and method of kill. This guy is a pro."

"So we should expect more bodies?" Hank asked.

"It's Sergeant, right? Rawlings?"

Hank nodded.

"Sergeant Rawlings, yes, I believe there will be more. Something made this guy come out of the shadows. This guy now wants to be recognized. The more victims, the more notoriety. Yet, there's more to it than that."

"More to it? Like what?" Hank asked.

"I was about to give you my thoughts on that." He flashed Hank an annoyed look for interrupting him.

Hank looked at me. His face said he wasn't sure what to make of the guy. I had a better handle on him. He was some kind of genius, and from my experience, people like that were a little strange.

I'd known a person in Milwaukee similar to that guy. Aside from being socially awkward, the guy didn't shower, dressed like a bum, and lived in a rundown little shack outside a trailer park. He'd retired at forty from designing software for the military. The guy had millions stuffed away in the bank but took a bus from city to city for chess tournaments. He competed at the master level. I bet the two knew each other.

"Sorry, go on," Hank said.

"It's the way he is killing the women. Now, if I'm a serial killer and I want to make a name for myself, what has more flair, killing my victims in a regular way or something that pops? Lobotomizing my victims sure packs more media punch than any traditional method of killing."

"So that's this guy's goal? Fame?" I asked.

"He definitely wants to stand out. All right, we ready to get into the profile?"

I nodded.

"I put our suspect in his late thirties or early forties. A self-employed taxi driver is consistent with the kind of occupation he would have. It's solitary. He'd have a hard time holding down a normal job. Normal friends and family would not be present. He is holding these women for a time, so it wouldn't allow for it. Even if he was doing it somewhere else, his frequent absences would be noted. I would say he is single, possibly divorced."

The captain spoke up, "What about them both being blond in their thirties? Does that hold any significance?"

"It could, but I'm not sure it's a deciding factor. I believe he is selecting the women out of opportunity more than anything else."

"What about the lobotomies themselves? The medical examiner told me the second procedure was far more advanced than what was done to the first victim. Do you think there is any kind of medical background?" I asked.

"No. Your suspect is experimenting. He's learning and evolving. Like you said, the second victim's procedure was far more involved. The woman's skin was removed to get at the skull. He used a different drill bit to get through the bone. He took his time, possibly following directions. As bad as it sounds, it was done pretty close to how the doctors used to do it. That is a point that is very troubling."

"Troubling how?" the captain asked.

"Well, lobotomies aren't meant to kill. I'll let that thought sink in with you guys for a while." He went quiet. "Are your heads filled with really bad images yet?"

He was right. Everything that came to mind was evil and worse.

"Where would he get the information on how to do it? Books? Internet?" the captain asked.

"I'm sure you can find enough information at either spot. I would say books though if I had to guess."

"Hank, can you get into contact with libraries in the area and see if they had any lobotomy books checked out recently?"

Agent Beck interrupted, "I wouldn't bother."

Captain Bostok looked confused by Beck's comment. "Why is that?"

"Same reason it would be a book and not the Internet. Our suspect is smart. Judging by the lack of evidence at the scenes, he wouldn't let himself be caught by something so careless. Think about it. A few women show up dead with amateur lobotomies. It would only be a matter of days before the police look into that angle, just like we have here. A couple calls to webmasters of the sites with that kind of information would give away his IP address. A book checked out would give him up just as quick. The book, if that is in fact what he's using, was either purchased at a book store, probably not in the area, or stolen. That brings up another point—I would venture to guess that he has a record."

"What kind of crimes would we be looking for?" Hank asked.

"More than likely, petty crimes. Theft, identity theft, lewd acts in public, sexual harassment. I wouldn't think there would be an arrest for anything too serious. I bet if he's local, he's already in your system for something minor."

"Now, you said something was bringing this guy out of the shadows. What would we be looking for as a trigger? Divorce, death, fired from his job, something like that?" Hank asked.

Beck rocked his head back and forth. "There is something there, I believe. Something happened that spurred the escalation. What it is may not register to you and me, though."

"Explain," I said.

"Well, something like a cheating spouse or getting fired can set a person on a rampage. You know—a guy gets fired from his job and goes and shoots the place up, or a man finds his wife in bed with another man and kills the two. Yet, that's a reaction for someone who has a mental breakdown. Serial killers are different. They already kill. These people don't live within the boundaries of normal society, so a normal trigger may not fit."

I nodded.

"You have to remember—the feelings we have of sadness, guilt, right and wrong, morality—none of these things apply to our suspect. Take, for instance, Ted Bundy. Everyone tried to find the answer to why he killed, the reason he took people's lives. Do you know what his reason was?" He looked around the room for an answer but didn't get one. "He said he liked doing it. That was it. He liked killing people."

I was going through my notes, looking to see if he had covered everything I wanted to ask him.

"What about the brand? Did you find anything on it?"

Beck shook his head. "From everything I saw, it's something original. It looked like a set of two triangles on top of each other facing left, a quartered circle in the center and two more triangles in the same orientation facing right. Sorry, I don't have anything for you on it, but I have a feeling you'll get the meaning to it when you find the perpetrator. I have copies of the profile I put together printed up for you guys." Beck looked at each of us. "Anything else?"

I found the word *drugs* circled in my notepad. "One more thing, Agent. What is your take on the drugs being used, and how does that tie into the profile?"

He grinned. "Good question. Opportunity is the answer."

"Can you explain that?" I asked.

"From my research, these aren't the kind of drugs that are purchased on the street. When I say opportunity, I'm referring to these drugs being available to him in some area of his life. Obviously, a taxi driver wouldn't have access to these sorts of things, but perhaps he stole them when the opportunity presented itself in the past."

"Thank you, Agent Beck. If we gather more information, you will add it to the profile?" the captain asked.

"Absolutely."

Beck handed his copies of the profile to the captain and saw himself out.

Chapter 21

He started on her as soon as he got home. Unhappy with the results of his last procedure, he read up on something new. When he finished branding her, he began. The book he was working from referred to it as a *transorbital* lobotomy. It was much easier than his previous method and didn't leave him covered in blood when he was through. He used a small spoon wedged between her upper eyelid and eyeball to give him the space needed. An ice pick with depth-gradation marks at two inches and two and three quarters was inserted at the top corner of her eye above her tear duct. With a medium-sized rubber mallet, he pounded the pick into the thin bone behind her eye. His ears caught an audible *snap* as the pick broke through. He continued tapping it into her brain until the depth was to the first etched mark. The book told him to sweep the pick horizontally through her brain toward her other eye. He did. At the pick's original position, he tapped it in another three quarters of an inch to the next gradation mark. He repeated the procedure on the other side. Once he completed his procedure, he transferred the woman to his makeshift recovery room.

He'd been checking on her between naps. Ten hours passed since he'd completed the surgery. Three hours passed since he last checked on her. He rolled from the couch to go see how his girl was doing.

He walked through the house to the master bedroom. The woman lay strapped to the bed. Her driver's license showed that her name was Anna Smith. She was twenty-seven and weighed a hundred twenty-four pounds. She was smiling ear to ear in her license photo. He hadn't dosed her with any of the tranquilizer since the operation. He abandoned using the opiate. When the last woman had pulled out the IV, the solution emptied onto the carpet. The only thing she had received was a small dose of Alprazolam that he had just given her. She would wake up soon, and he wasn't looking for a repeat of the last occurrence. The drug would keep her in a nice, docile fog.

He headed out to the living room and plopped down onto the couch. The room was dark, with the blinds shut and curtains closed. He tossed his feet up on the coffee table. A jolt of pain ran through his left leg. He swatted at a pesky fly that buzzed his ear as he powered on the TV and brought up the guide. Searching through, he found channel six and selected it from the menu.

"Let see what's on the news."

He tuned in just in time to catch the end of the replay of J.R. Steele's report from the press release the police had given the day before. The daytime anchors, Joyce Meekins and Dan Rutton, came back on.

Meekins said, "And that was J.R. Steele reporting from the Tampa police station. It's just tragic, Dan. A spokesman for the TPD has ensured us they are using everything at their disposal to pursue and apprehend the person or persons responsible for these attacks."

Dan Rutton responded, "Here's hoping they have someone in custody soon. Again, the TPD has asked for any support they can get from the public. If you or someone you know has any information about this case, we urge you to please call the Tampa police department. They have a tip hotline where you can remain anonymous, if desired."

The news anchor rattled off the number.

"I wouldn't get my hopes up too high about having someone soon." He flipped the TV back to the guide. A fly landed on the end of the remote control. He shooed it away. He scrolled up and down, looking over his choices.

"Looks like talk shows or soaps. What do you think, babe?" he asked.

There was no response.

He flipped on one of the talk shows and took in a deep breath. The foul smell of decay filled his nose. He shook it off and lay back on the couch. Within a few minutes, he dozed off.

Chapter 22

"So what did you think of our profiler?" Hank asked.

We sat in Captain Bostok's office, going over the suspect profile Agent Beck had handed out.

I browsed the sheet again. "He was a little different, but everything he said had merit. At the same time, we can't take everything he said as gospel."

"I agree." Captain Bostok reached into the mini refrigerator under his desk and brought out a soda. "I'm going to put someone on checking into the libraries and website hits on lobotomies anyway."

"Are we planning on sending this profile out to the press?" Hank asked.

The captain cracked open his soda and took a sip. "I think we should."

"Still want to keep the branding thing under wraps?" I asked.

He nodded. "I don't want to help give this story legs."

Someone knocked on his office door.

"Yup," the captain shouted.

Detective Jones took up most of the doorway as he walked in. "Got a little issue here."

"I'm listening," Bostok said.

"Well, tracking down these drugs might be a little much for one person to handle. Not that I don't like a challenge, but this is beyond that. We have pharmaceutical companies, pharmacies, clinics, hospitals, rehab centers, and more with the opiate. The tranquilizer is another story. They use the drug on deer farms, cattle ranches, horse ranches, you name it. The list just goes on and on."

"Are they found together anywhere?" I asked.

"I didn't find anything."

"All right, let's split it up. Jones, you take the tranquilizer by itself. Find every place that has Xylazine within a hundred-mile radius and see if they have any missing stock. Hank, I want you to stay on the opiate with the clinics and hospitals. I'll see what I can do to place the two drugs together."

"Okay," Jones said.

"Yeah, that's fine," Hank said.

"You guys get to it," the captain said.

I walked back to my office and got on the Internet. I searched the drugs and every brand name they came in. After twenty minutes of different combinations of the names, I got a hit for the veterinary field. For the better part of the next four hours, I dialed one number after the other. My search results showed over sixty vets in the greater Tampa area. When you added the suburbs, the number ballooned. Most of the places carried the tranquilizer, yet all of it was accounted for in each circumstance. Only two places out of the group I had already called dealt with the opiate. The FDA hadn't approved the drug for animal use, but vets could still legally prescribe it. They used it to treat severe pain in felines. Neither clinic had noticed any gone missing. My stomach growled. I took a break and headed for the lunch room with plans to raid the vending machines.

The food machine offered a selection of two sandwiches or a bruised apple. I plugged three fifty into the machine, and it kicked out a sandwich. I peeled open the cellophane bag and gave it a sniff. The label said ham and cheese. It looked like it could pass as such. I stuck another dollar fifty into the soda machine and punched a button. With a little banging, a twenty-ounce bottle of soda hit the bottom of the machine, shaken to perfection. I let it sit for a minute while I ate the sandwich at one of the lunch tables. It wasn't half bad, but I was still hungry. A single sandwich remained in the entire machine. Unless I wanted a beat-up, two-dollar apple for dinner, I had to buy it. I dug through my wallet and found enough money.

On a whim, I hit the button on the coffee machine for a large Columbian roast, just to see what it would do. It started whirring and making noise, then I heard the water. I grabbed a cup from the rack and stuck it into place. Coffee flowed from the machine into my cup. *Ding!* The machine finished. I took the cup from the spot under the machine's spout and raised it to my lips. The coffee was steaming. I took a sip through my teeth in case it was filled with grounds. Nothing—the coffee was perfect. I dumped in some creamer. With the bottle of soda and sandwich in one hand and coffee in the other, I walked back out into the station. Hank sat at his desk.

I walked over and sat across from him. "Anything?" I set my coffee and soda down on his desk.

"That's not from the lunch room, is it?"

I unwrapped the plastic covering the sandwich and started in. "The coffee? Yeah, the machine cooperated today."

"I know the coffee machine works. They had a repair guy in here this morning. Where do you think the coffee people kept bringing you earlier came from?"

I shrugged and took another bite.

Hank pointed at my food. "I'm talking about the sandwich."

"Yeah, bought it from the vending machine. Why?" I spoke through a mouthful of bread, meat, and processed cheese.

"There have been two sandwiches sitting in that machine for a week plus. The guy from the vending company must have been on vacation or something last week. He never came. I think someone had it unplugged for a day or two as well."

I looked at the label on the sandwich's plastic. It had expired six days prior. A closer inspection of the bread probably would have shown some green specks, but I wasn't going to go down that road. I tossed the last bite in my mouth and chewed. The mayo did taste a little tangier than it should have.

"You're going to get food poisoning."

"Maybe I can sue the station," I paused to swallow the blob of chewed old meat and cheese, "and retire early."

"Good luck with that."

"So, what did you come up with?" I asked.

"I got the main hospitals and bigger clinics checked off the list, for the most part. It's not looking like we're going to get anything there."

"Why is that?"

"Injectable. None of the hospitals or clinics carry it in that form. Either way, nothing has come up missing at any of the places I talked with. I'm about to move on to the smaller places and see what we get. How about you?"

"It's not very common, but it looks like they can be found together in the veterinary field. I've been calling every vet in town. Nothing so far."

"Should we focus our efforts there?"

"I got it. Just keep doing what you're doing."

Hank slouched back in his chair. "Man, I hate working the phones. The last guy I talked to kept me on the phone for twenty minutes telling me about how Buprenorphine and other drugs are distributed across the country. Would you like to hear how it gets from point A to point B?"

I took a sip of coffee and smiled. "Enlighten me."

He read from his notes as though he was giving a presentation. "There are two pharmaceutical companies that produce Buprenorphine in the United States, neither of which is in Florida. From the manufacturers, it travels to one of a few main distributors. The main distributors, again not in Florida, sell the drugs to the big hospitals and clinics. Then there is the secondary wholesalers, also called the gray market. They buy the drugs in bulk from the distributors. The secondary places supply the smaller clinics that don't have enough purchasing power to get medications from the big distributors. The gray market, while still legal, seems to do a lot of shady things with the drugs. They price gouge small hospitals. They repackage it and trade it back and forth between themselves. All that happens before it ever lands in a patient's hands. Legal drug trade 101."

"Sounds similar to the illegal drug trade."

Hank nodded.

I stood and grabbed my coffee and soda from his desk. "All right, keep dialing. Couple hours left."

He picked up his phone.

I headed back to my office to continue making calls. I thought back to what the profiler had said about this guy being an opportunist. Getting the drugs from the veterinary field made the most sense. The two drugs weren't found together in any other profession. Plus, the vets used the injectable version. I had fifteen vets still left on my list. The red light on my phone was flashing—I'd missed two calls while out. I hit the button for the messages. The first was Rick telling me that none of the local hospitals had reported a knife wound. I hit the button to erase the message. The second message started. My sister's voice came through the speaker giving me the third degree because I hadn't called her the day before, as I'd promised. I hit Erase in the middle of her rant. I didn't remember promising her that I'd call. Her message did remind me that I wanted to call my father.

I rubbed my eyes and found some resolve to power through the last few calls to the vets. I hammered five out quickly—no leads. The next name on the list was familiar. It was the vet that I took Butch to. I dialed them up.

"Tampa Paws. How can I help you?"

"Hi, this is Lieutenant Kane. Is Doctor Reynolds in?"

"Is there a problem with Butch?"

"No. Butch is good. This is police related."

"Oh. Okay, I'll transfer you to the back and let him know you're on the line."

"Thanks."

"Tell Butch we miss him. Hold on."

I sat on hold, waiting for Doctor Reynolds, wondering if the receptionist was being sarcastic. We hadn't had a good experience the last time I brought Butch in for his checkup. I put him on his leash and walked him toward the front door. He pranced across the parking lot just as a dog would. I scooped him up when I walked through the door and let them know we were there for his appointment. We were going to have to wait a couple minutes, so I sat down with Butch on my lap. He was being good. He was looking around but just sitting there on my lap. I let his leash drop to the floor and patted him on the head. I had never seen him so civilized, that was, until someone opened the front door. He leapt from my lap before I could get his leash and made a run for daylight. A woman walked through the door with a German shepherd in tow. She stopped in the

143

doorway to try to catch the escaping cat. She should have just let him through. The German shepherd clogged the other side. Butch went for the dog. A flurry of cheetah-spotted fur circled the dog's face. Butch hissed and gave the dog an onslaught of right and left swats as he stood on his back legs. When he finished his boxing, he started with the biting. Anything that was soft, he sank into. The German shepherd let out a high-pitched yelp when Butch pierced his left ear with his teeth. The dog tried to backpedal out the door while its owner fought to pull him back inside.

It all happened in a matter of seconds. I ran over and pried my hissing, swatting, devil cat from her dog's face and apologized. She gave me the speech about having him in a crate. I offered to cover her vet bill for the day, but she refused. She was fine with just shaking her head at me every time I made eye contact with her.

Doctor Reynolds came to the phone. "Lieutenant Kane. How are we doing today?"

"Fine. I just wanted to ask you a few things."

"Sure. Debbie told me this is police related?"

"Yes."

"Well, anything I can do to help. What do you need?"

"Do you use Xylazine or Buprenorphine there?"

"We use a generic form of Xylazine as an anesthetic on horses. Don't have the Buprenorphine though."

"Is all the tranquilizer accounted for?"

"I don't know why it wouldn't be. It's just me and Doctor Ferrin back here, plus Debbie up front. Sometimes my son comes in and helps out after school. He's here today.

We didn't have any break-ins or anything like that."

"Is it possible for you to just check for me while I have you on the line?"

"Yeah, I guess. Give me one minute."

I waited on the line for him to come back. I heard the honk of a truck horn through the earpiece, followed by Doctor Reynolds yelling for someone to get the delivery from the driver. It reminded me of something Hank had said earlier. Doctor Reynolds came back to the phone a minute or two later.

"All accounted for."

"Okay, good. I have another couple questions for you if that's all right."

"No problem."

"How do vets get their medications for the animals?"

"We order through a wholesaler or distributer on some of the more common items. The wholesaler makes it easier for something we just need a small supply of. I'd say that's pretty typical of most veterinary clinics."

"Are the places local?"

"Big one no, small one yes. The distributer we go through is called D&Z, out of Atlanta. They are the main place for most of the vets on the east coast. The place we go to for everything else is right here in Tampa. That place is called Pet Med Plus."

I wrote down the names. "Are there other smaller wholesalers for pet supplies in the area?"

"There is one more, but their prices are a little higher, and they don't deliver. They are about a half hour south of the city."

"Can I get the name of that one too?"

"Wholesale Pharm and Supply."

It got copied into my notepad.

"Thanks for the help."

"Sure."

I hung up and looked up the numbers for the wholesalers.

Chapter 23

He awoke from his nap ready for a long night. He went into the bedroom where he was holding Anna Smith. She was awake. He went to her side, his hand on a kitchen knife tucked into the back of his waistline. There wouldn't be a repeat of the incident with the last woman.

"How do you feel?"

She stared at the ceiling. He shook her head and stuck his finger in her mouth. If she was with it, she would try to bite him. She didn't.

He untied her one strap at a time. She didn't try to move. He sat her up and waited. She did nothing. He got her to her feet.

She walked herself out to the living room as he limped along, keeping her steady. He helped her sit down on the couch and took a seat across from her in the recliner. He watched her. She didn't react. Her mouth hung open, her eyes rolled toward the top of her head. Every few seconds, her eyes would move around the room and float back up.

She didn't speak, yet she didn't do much of anything. She just sat there with a blank look on her face. He had her dressed in the familiar green lingerie, the same his ex-wife had worn. They were twins.

He'd give her another few hours before he made his decision for the evening. He had just the thing to kill some time—a little bit of reconnaissance on the lieutenant. If his time spent in the military had taught him anything, it was to know your adversaries. He locked Anna back up in the bedroom and left the house.

Chapter 24

It was a little after five thirty when I called the wholesalers. I got voicemail for both, which included their hours. Both places closed at five, but one opened at eight, the other at nine. I'd have to wait until morning to get in touch with them.

I heard a tap at my door, and Hank walked into my office. "Hear the news?"

I glanced up from my desk. "What news?"

"Just got the red-light camera footage brought by. The guys down in tech are going over it."

"Good. Let's hope they get something. How about you?"

He shook his head. "Everyone I talked to said everything is accounted for. I'm not a hundred percent sure that I'm buying it, though."

I stretched my back in my chair. "Why is that?"

Hank sat on my couch at the back of the room and crossed his leg over his knee. "Think about it. What clinic or hospital wants to be associated with having missing drugs? It makes them look bad. My guess is there were quite a few that were missing things. I'm sure they just fired whatever employee took something and called it a day."

I took in a deep breath and tried stretching again. My body ached, probably from sitting all day and talking on the phone—if that was possible. "You could be right. We have to weed through them either way."

"Yeah, I know. What about you? Leads?"

"Could be something, could be nothing, but I can't follow up on it until morning. I'm going to look into the wholesalers of the pet meds in the area. So far, all the vets I called told me the same thing—nothing missing. Looks like most of the places are starting to close up. I'm going to see if they got anything from the red-light cams and then head home. Maybe grab a beer at Lefty's."

"You're starting to be a regular over there, huh?"

"They have decent food, and the place is close enough to my house. I wouldn't call myself a regular, though."

"And here I thought you went over there to see your little girlfriend." He smiled, pleased with his jab.

"She's not my girlfriend. You have anything going on? Want to head over there with me and grab a beer?"

Hank shrugged. "Sure. Tonight is Karen's poker night with her friends, anyway."

"Poker night? Don't women go to book clubs or scrapbook? I've never heard of a women's poker night."

"She plays with a bunch of DEA people from work."

"So she dresses you, packs your lunch, and then tells you

she's staying out late to play poker with a bunch of the DEA guys?"

He leaned back and crossed his arms over his chest. "Do you have to bust my balls now? I'm not in the mood, Kane."

A smile crept across my face. "I wouldn't be, either." With a wave of my hand, I motioned for him to get out of my office. "I'm going to lock up and go check on the tech guys. We can take off when I get back. Go finish up whatever you're working on."

"Sounds good."

I took the elevator two floors down and walked the length of the hall to the tech department. I walked in and found Keller sitting at a desk, staring at a video screen. "You looking at the red-light camera video?"

He nodded his head.

"Just you here?"

"Yeah, Murphy already checked out for the night. They gave us everything from nine o'clock at night until six in the morning. I have it going at three-times speed, and I'm pausing it at each car. This is going to take a while. When I'm done, I have another camera view from up the street. I'm planning on staying late." He glanced at the clock on the wall. "Technically, I'm here late now. I'll put in another couple hours and have to resume tomorrow. I've been here since eight a.m."

"That's fine. I'd look over the hours of midnight until four a.m. It would be the smallest number of people on the streets that could have witnessed the guy. I think we'll have our best shot there." I turned toward the door. "Give me a buzz on my cell phone if you spot anything of interest."

"Will do, Lieutenant."

Hank had cleared his desk by the time I got back upstairs. We left the station around six. He followed me to my condo. I dropped off my car and rode over to the bar with him. I planned to take a cab home since Hank never stayed out very long.

When Hank and I walked in, we made a beeline for the bar. A middle-aged couple had control of the pool table. The man was eyeing his next shot while the woman fed singles into the jukebox. From her clothing, I guessed we'd be listening to country music. Aside from them and an old man sitting at the far end of the bar, the place was empty. Callie served the old man a beer and looked over at us with a smile.

Hank nudged me with his elbow. "Hey, what do you know? Your girlfriend is working."

She walked over to where we sat. "Hey, Kane. Can't get enough of me, huh?"

I smiled at her. "Never."

"Rough day, hon? You look spent."

"You could say that," I said.

"Yeah, I saw you on the news yesterday. Catch the guy yet?"

I shook my head. "Nah, still looking."

"You get any sleep last night?"

"A little."

"You need to start taking better care of yourself." She motioned to Hank, sitting next to me, and leaned in. She spoke in a whisper. "It's Hank, right?"

I nodded.

"What's with all the whispering?" Hank asked.

"I'm telling him a secret." She looked at Hank.

Hank offered his hand. "Hank Rawlings. We've met once or twice."

She shook it. "Sergeant, right?"

Hank nodded.

"Callie Green. Nice to meet you again. What can I get you?"

"Gin and tonic."

"Sure, coming right up. What about you Kane? The usual?"

"Yup."

She leaned across the bar. Her feet came off the ground. "You want anything else?"

I put on my innocent face. "Like?"

She shook her head and smiled. "Are you guys eating too?"

"Yeah."

"All right. Need a menu?"

"Please," Hank said.

Callie bounced back down from leaning on the bar, reached beneath it, and brought out a menu, which she handed to Hank. "I have to run into the back to grab another bottle. Be right back."

As soon as she disappeared, Hank mimicked, "Can't get enough of me? Nah, never, babe."

"Yeah, yeah," I said.

"You need to take better care of yourself, hon. You want anything else?" He smiled as he flipped open the menu to browse through it. "What's good to eat?"

"I get the steak sandwich. It's pretty good. I've had the burger a handful of times, too."

Callie walked over with a glass and set it on a coaster in front of Hank. "Need a lime, Sarge?"

"Please."

She grabbed a slice of lime from her tray and propped it on the edge of Hank's glass. He flicked it in and took a sip.

She grabbed a mug from the freezer, topped it off with beer, and placed it in front of me. "Shot?"

I shrugged. "Might as well."

Callie grabbed two shot glasses from below the bar. "You want one too, Hank?"

"What are you drinking?"

She smiled. "Jägermeister."

Hank waved his hand. "No way. Thanks, but no thanks."

Callie poured two shots, picked one up, and slid the other one to me. We touched glasses before knocking them back.

Callie wiped her mouth with the back of her hand. She looked at Hank. "Decide on something to eat?"

"I hear the steak sandwich is good. I'll try it."

"No problem. Same for you, Kane?"

I nodded.

"I'll go put it in. Should be fifteen minutes or so." She winked and walked into the back.

Hank shook his head. "I don't know how you drink that stuff."

"I usually only have one," I said.

Hank took a sip of his drink from its tiny red straw. "Well, I think one shot of that is too much. The smell makes me gag."

The couple playing pool replaced the cues on the wall and left. The front door clanged as it closed behind them. Though they'd left, the country music continued. From the amount of money I'd seen her stuff into the jukebox, I was guessing we'd be listening to country for some time.

"Pool?" I asked.

Hank took another sip from his drink. "Sure, why not."

I walked over to the change machine and pulled out my wallet. A ten was the smallest I had. "Hank, you got a couple of singles or a five?"

He popped open his wallet. "Nope. Eighty bucks in twenties."

I pulled the ten from my wallet and stuck it into the change machine. The machine rumbled then spat quarters at me as if I'd hit the jackpot. I jammed my hand into the slot to catch the change before it spilled onto the floor.

"What the hell did you stick in that thing?" Hank asked.

"A ten. I know exactly where most of these quarters are going, though. I have to play something else in this jukebox if I want to keep my sanity."

"Not a country fan?" Hank asked.

"I know every word to every country song ever written. The ex-wife was a fan. Thus, I am not." I handed Hank a handful of change and plugged eight quarters into the jukebox.

Hank pushed the change into the table and racked the balls. "What are we playing for?"

"Bar tab?"

"Two out of three or three out of five?"

I took into account the weight of change still in my pocket and answered, "Three out of five is good."

I'd grown up playing pool in bars with my father every weekend. He would take money matches with the various bikers and patrons.

"Five bucks a head, and I'll play with my kid," he would say.

We seldom lost, and by the age of twelve, I was playing in adult pool leagues. My father and I still had heated matches at the local bar when I visited him in Wisconsin. I needed to visit him or at least call.

Hank flipped a coin, and I got the break. I gave him the first game so he could save a little face, then I took the second and third in just a few minutes.

Callie brought out our food before the start of the fourth and put it down next to our drinks. "Who's winning?"

"Pretty close right now," I said.

"Don't let your food get cold. Good luck, hon." She gently swiped my side with her nails on her way back to the bar.

Hank snorted. "Your break, hon."

I smiled and walked to the table. I didn't have a comeback at the ready, but I didn't need one. The eight ball sank on the break. "Looks like you get the tab, buddy. Thanks for dinner. I think I'll get another beer, too."

We sat and dug into our meal.

Callie walked back over. "How is it?"

"Perfect," I said.

"Real good," Hank said midchew.

"Another beer, Kane?"

I nodded.

"What about you? Another gin and tonic, Sergeant?" Callie asked.

He wiped his mouth and crumpled up his napkin. "Nope. I'm good. Just the tab."

Callie looked to me. "Are you leaving me already?"

"Nah, I'm going to stick around for a bit, yet."

She smiled. "Good, I'll be right back." She walked back behind the bar.

"You had enough, Hank?" I asked.

"Yeah, I want to get home before Karen does."

"You didn't get a hold of her earlier, did you?"

Hank shook his head. "She turns off her phone when she's playing poker."

"That doesn't bother you?" I finished the last of the beer in my glass.

"No, not at all. The only thing that bothers me is when she comes home smelling like an ashtray from smoking cigars."

"Karen smokes cigars?"

"Just when she's playing poker."

"Seriously? Your wife smokes cigars while she's out

playing poker with the guys? Yeah, you better get home. Make sure you do the dishes. You don't want to get the belt. You know, from her pants."

Hank laughed. "Whatever. We make it work. You need a ride or what?"

"Nah, I'll grab a cab in a little bit here."

Callie returned with the tab and my beer, smiled, and then headed for a group of four that was grabbing stools at the bar.

Hank tossed down the money to cover the tab and stood. "Okay, don't stay too late."

"Yup. Think this is my last beer. I want to get a little of… damn, what's that called?"

"Sleep?" he asked.

"Nailed it," I said.

"See you in the morning."

Hank walked toward the door.

I grabbed my beer and found a spot at the end of the bar.

Callie came over. "How long are you sticking around?"

"I'm going to head out after this one. I didn't get much sleep last night. Need to play catch up."

"Stay and have one more. It's on me."

"I'll think about it."

She smiled and walked to the guy at the end of the bar waving a five-dollar bill. I watched her do her rounds through the bar while I sipped my beer. Ten minutes later, Callie was back, and my beer was empty.

"Decide?" she asked.

"Sure, what the hell. Last one."

She poured me a mug and set it down on the bar. "Kane, let me go close that group of people out. I'll be right back. I want to run something past you."

"All right." She walked off toward the other end of the bar.

I dialed up the cab company to send a taxi. They said it would be fifteen minutes or so. I hung up and focused my attention on the bar's TV. A fishing show played on the little screen. I squinted and tried to make out what was going on. The guys on the flats boat appeared to be fishing for snook. Either my eyesight was getting bad, or the bar needed a bigger TV. I chalked it up as a combination of the two.

Callie walked around the bar and sprang up onto the stool next to me. "When was the last time you had a real meal?"

"What do you mean? I just had the best steak sandwich in town."

"No, I mean something that someone cooked that didn't involve a microwave or a bill when you finished."

I kicked the question around in my head for a few seconds, replaying what I'd eaten from the last few days, then weeks. I came up with TV dinners, expired vending-machine food, and takeout from various greasy spoons around work.

"It's been a while."

"You like Italian?"

"Food?"

She smiled big. "Yeah food, dummy."

"Of course. Who doesn't?"

"Let me cook you dinner."

I looked at her, sitting next to me. My mouth moved faster than my brain. "Okay."

"How about Sunday night? I don't have to work. Around eight o'clock?"

"Well, I'd have to check my social calendar."

"Whatever. Let me give you my address." She pulled a pen from the waistline of her low-riding, tight-fitting jeans. She jotted it down on a napkin from the bar and handed it to me.

I gave it a quick glance. "No phone number?"

"Nope. You can't cancel, that way."

I stuffed the napkin into my wallet. "I'll see you Sunday." I tried to be nonchalant.

"The food will be ready by eight thirty. Don't be late."

"You mean delivered?"

"I can cook, you jerk."

"Guess we'll find out." I smiled. Through the front doors, I could see a cab waiting at the curb. "Looks like my ride is out front. Here, hold on." I motioned for her pen, and she handed it over. I wrote my cell number on a napkin. "In case something comes up, you can get a hold of me."

She took it, smiled, and sprang a hug on me that I wasn't expecting. She wrapped her arms around my neck and pulled me close.

"Can't wait." She whispered it into my ear, followed by a kiss on the cheek. She let go and turned to get back to work. I waited there for a second, still a little shocked, before I headed for the door.

Things were looking up, at least in the personal-life department. Work was another story altogether.

Chapter 25

He returned from his trip across town and cleaned Anna's body before they left the house. She wasn't playing possum like Diane Robins, he was certain. If she had anything left upstairs, she would have protested being scrubbed with bleach.

The black tint of his Range Rover's windows wouldn't allow anyone to see the woman or him inside. With the police searching for taxis, taking his own vehicle would limit the risk. He belted her into the passenger seat beside him and buttoned her blazer around her. Underneath the jacket, she was wearing the familiar green lingerie. On her back was a message written in magic marker.

He had found the perfect high-traffic area to set her loose. The location had no cameras, which would allow him to leave unseen, he hoped.

A block and a half down from Seventh Avenue in Ybor City, he saw people walking in the lights of the street ahead. The particular part of town was a bustling area for nightlife.

He looked at the parking lot approaching on his left—it sat behind the buildings of the strip. The lot was three quarters full with cars but dark. He had scouted the place out in the daylight the week before. He didn't spot a single camera. The lot had no guard shack or security, just a small machine nestled next to a group of shrubs where you paid and got a parking pass. He pulled in and curled the SUV around to the back. A parking spot came into view at the rear corner of the lot. He backed in and killed the motor.

He sat in the darkness and watched a car pull in and park. A group of college kids piled out and walked toward the street. After they left, the area went quiet. No cars were coming in, and no one was walking the lot. He looked over at Anna. Her eyes were open, staring forward. Her head lay against the headrest. He reached over with his gloved hand and unbuckled her seat belt. He unbuttoned her blazer. Taking it off of her took him longer than he liked. She wasn't doing anything to help the matter.

He looked around at his surroundings. The lot was still empty of people coming or going. He opened his door and went around the back of the SUV to the other side. She stared out her window at him. He pulled the handle but stopped before the door swung open. Two women walked across the lot in his direction. He left the door and crouched down in the darkness between the cars.

He listened to their conversation. The women laughed and joked about some jerk that had hit on them in the bar. They came closer. His lungs constricted. A cough tried to escape. He placed one hand over his mouth and fought to keep it down. The women were one car away. His body jerked. He squeezed his nose to keep the air from escaping. The women passed. When he heard the second car door close, he took his hands from his face. He placed his shirt over his face and coughed. Blood spattered the inside of his shirt. It was better to be on him than the ground, where a forensics team could find it if they searched the area.

The women pulled out of the lot in a newer Toyota Camry. He waited until they turned onto the street. The lot was clear.

He went back to the Range Rover's door and opened it. He paused and examined his rubber gloves in the light from inside the truck. They were blood free. He took Anna by the arms and pulled her out. She rocked on her feet. He moved her around the car door and closed it.

He pointed out in front of her. "Walk toward the lights."

From behind, he shoved her. She stumbled and took a step—then another. She walked mindlessly.

He got back in the car and started it. The latex gloves stretched and snapped as he pulled them from his hands. Through the windshield, he watched her. She swayed left and right but continued forward toward the next row of cars. A mirror from a pickup truck caught her on the shoulder and spun her. She fell into the car next to her.

He pulled from the lot and made a right onto Seventh Avenue. He waited at the red light. A sea of people made their way across the street at the crosswalk. The strip was busy—people sat outside the bars and clubs laughing, drinking, and enjoying themselves.

She'll be found within five minutes.

He turned on the police scanner he'd bought earlier in the day.

Chapter 26

The sound of my phone buzzing on the coffee table woke me up. I jammed my fingers into my eyes for a quick rub. I'd fallen asleep on the couch, watching television. The clock on the cable box showed a few minutes after midnight. I'd been asleep for an hour. I shooed Butch off my lap so I could sit up and grab the phone. He found his pillow at the other end of the couch and stared at me. He looked annoyed that I'd disturbed him.

I figured Keller had stayed extra late and had something on our cab. The caller ID said it was the captain. That late at night, the news wouldn't be good. I hit Talk.

"Hey, Cap."

"Get up. Get dressed. I'll be out front, waiting. We need to go over to Tampa General."

"Why? What happened?"

"We have another victim from our guy. This one is alive."

"What?"

"Just get down here. I'm pulling up now." He hung up.

Tampa General was a two-minute drive from my condo. I could see the hospital from my patio. The complex was lit up just across the edge of the Hillsborough Bay. I pulled myself from the couch and went to the kitchen. I grabbed everything from my pockets off the table and walked out. Butch didn't try to escape. He was in sleep mode, which is where I should have been. The captain sat out front, idling at the curb in his dark-blue sedan, a newer Ford. I got in.

"Figured this is easier," he said.

I pulled the seat belt over my shoulder. "Now, what's going on?"

"Got a call from Sergeant Mueller about forty-five minutes ago. One of his guys in patrol picked up a woman stumbling around a parking lot in Ybor City. Green lingerie. The woman had no ID and didn't respond to the officer's questions. Something was wrong with her. He took her to the hospital. I guess they admitted her right away."

"Stitches on her head?"

"It wasn't mentioned."

"Did she get away?"

"I don't know."

The captain pulled to the side in the hospital's drop-off area behind a police cruiser. We headed toward the sliding glass doors. An officer was standing near the front desk. The doors opened for us, and we walked into the lobby. I recognized the patrolman when we got inside. His name was Tate. I'd seen him around the station when I stayed into the night shift.

"Where is she?" I asked.

"They took her up to the second level. The attending is a Doctor Winters."

"Did she say what happened to her?" I asked.

Tate shook his head. "Something is wrong with her. I picked her up—she didn't say a word. Asked her name—she didn't respond. I asked if someone hit her—silence. She just sat in the car, staring forward. She smelled of bleach. Like she'd bathed in it."

"Were there stitches on her head?" I asked.

"I didn't see anything like that. Looks like she may have been roughed up, though."

"How did you find her?" I asked.

"A call came over the radio about a woman in distress behind Seventh in Ybor. I was just down the block. I arrived on the scene and saw a couple standing next to a woman in a state of undress. As I got out of the car and approached, I noticed she wore the same green lingerie as the two murder victims. I called it in to Sergeant Mueller right away. The couple told me they'd found her roaming the lot. They asked her if she was okay, but the girl wouldn't respond. They saw she had black eyes, so they called it in. When I realized the state she was in, I brought her here."

"Thanks, Tate. Second floor, you said?"

He nodded.

The captain and I headed up and found the nurse's station. A woman sat behind the counter, dressed in scrubs. She looked up at us as we walked up.

"There was a woman brought in by an officer a little

while ago that you had admitted."

The girl nodded. "We have her in room two twelve. Doctor Winters is in there with her now. You guys can follow me. I'm heading back that way."

She came around the counter, and we followed her down the hall and around the corner. At the room, she poked her head into the door. A doctor emerged.

"You Doctor Winters?" the captain asked.

"Yes."

"The woman that was brought in, how is she? Can we speak with her?" Bostok asked.

"She's awake but unresponsive. I haven't gotten a single word out of her."

"Are there stitches on her head anywhere?" I asked.

"Stitches? No, I didn't see anything. Why?"

The captain shook his head at me to drop the subject.

"Can we see her?" I asked.

"Follow me."

I followed Doctor Winters into the room. The captain came in behind us. A woman in a hospital gown lay in the bed, staring at us. She didn't blink or move. She had two black eyes.

"Miss, I'm Captain Bostok, and this is Lieutenant Kane with the TPD's homicide division. Can you tell us what happened?"

She didn't respond. She just sat there.

The doctor pointed at me. "You're Lieutenant Kane?"

"Yes. I'm Lieutenant Kane. Why?"

"You need to see something." He went to the woman's

side and pulled her gown up to expose her back.

In black marker on the small of her back, it read, "Sick and depraved? I've got my eye on you, Lieutenant Kane."

"What the hell is this?" I asked.

"That's how she came in." The doctor pulled her gown back over the writing.

I took a step back. "Miss, can you tell us your name?"

She didn't look at me or respond.

I looked to the doctor. "What can you tell us?"

"We have just started to run our tests. We drew blood and had it sent to the lab for a tox screen. We are still waiting on the results. From every test I've run, she's unresponsive to any form of stimulation."

"Do you have an idea of what is going on with her?" the captain asked.

"Too soon for me to give you an answer. We'll need to run more tests."

"Physical injuries?"

"Well, it's kind of odd. You can see she has black eyes, but the bruising that is visible isn't consistent with being struck. She also has a brand on the back of her hand."

"A quartered circle? Triangles on the sides?" the captain asked.

"Here." The doctor rolled her hand over to show us the brand.

It was the same as the others.

I spotted ligature marks on her wrists.

The captain let out a puff of air through his nose. "Are there ligature marks on her ankles as well?"

"Yes."

"But no stitches anywhere on her head?" I asked.

"Stitches, no. That's the second time you have asked. Why would she have stitches?"

The captain took the question. "There have been two homicide victims dressed like this woman. Both victims had holes drilled into their skulls and damage to the brain," Bostok said.

"Lobotomy?"

He nodded.

"There is a waiting area down the hall, please wait there. I need to look at something." He herded us out the door. "They used to perform lobotomies through the eye sockets." He closed the door to her room.

We waited where he'd instructed. An hour passed before the doctor came back out and met us. His face showed that we didn't have good news.

"Let's go to my office," he said.

We followed him to the end of the hallway and sat across from him in his office.

"We took her for a CT scan. She has lesions to both frontal lobes of the brain. Someone performed a transorbital lobotomy on her. They broke through the bone behind her eye sockets and cut into the brain."

The captain dug his palm into his eye. "What the hell. Can she recover?"

"I believe that this is permanent. She has extensive brain damage."

We sat quiet. No words could describe how I felt. Someone

had destroyed this woman, had taken her very identity—her mind. That might have been worse than killing her.

"We received the results from the toxicology screen. She has trace levels of a tranquilizer in her system."

I nodded. "The tox screens on our other victims showed a tranquilizer as well, Xylazine. What about Buprenorphine?"

"Buprenorphine? No. The only other drug in her system was Alprazolam."

"What is that?" I asked.

"Xanax."

"Enough to put her in the state she's in?" I grasped at a hope that her condition was drug induced.

A bite at his lip and a quick shake of the doctor's head told me the answer was *no*. I wrote the name of the drug down in my notes.

"We're going to run some more tests and a rape kit. If we find out anything further, I'll have someone contact the police department."

"Can we get as much information on the woman as we can before we go? Height, weight, hair color, eye color, identifying marks? I'd like to be able to give the guys in missing persons a profile of her in case we get a call."

"Sure, Lieutenant."

He gave me all the information he could put together from the woman. After the captain asked him if he and his staff could keep a lid on the woman until we found her identity, we left his office. Officer Tate's car was gone when we reached the captain's Ford. We hopped in and pulled away from the hospital. The captain was quiet for the short drive. He pulled up to the curb in front of my condo. I reached at the door handle to get out.

The captain threw the car into park. "What do you think was with the message written on her?"

"Who the hell knows? Guess the guy saw the press release we held. If this sick son of a bitch thinks he can play a game with me, he won't like the outcome."

"We should give this one to the feds, Kane."

I pursed my lips and let the car's door handle snap back. "Why?"

"This is getting out of control. We won't be able to keep all the details out of the press much longer. It's all that will be on the news. It will be splashed across every television, radio, and newspaper."

"Give me more time. I'll get something."

"A day. No more."

I got out and headed inside.

Chapter 27

I was up before the sun. My lack of sleep would eventually catch up with me, but if that was my last day on the case, I planned to make the most of it. I made a cup of coffee for the road and sprinkled food in Butch's dish. He dove from the couch and ran for the kitchen as soon as the first kibble hit the bowl. I gave him a pat on the head. His breakfast would distract him from the door as I walked out. I called my father on the way to the station. He was fine, as I'd predicted. As I expected, he made me feel guilty for not visiting. I let him know that I'd put in for time off and would come visit in the next few months.

I made it to the station by seven and to my office a few minutes later. The voicemail light on my phone was flashing. I hit Play.

The message was from Keller in tech. He let me know that he had watched both videos in their entirety. He spotted eight cabs on the footage. He got all the tag numbers and ran them. They all checked out as legitimate fares. He went on to tell me that he'd stayed until one in the morning.

I hit Erase. The red-light cameras were a bust.

I put it out of my mind. At the top of my list was calling the pet-medication wholesalers. The more I thought about it, the more I felt that was our best lead on the drugs. I woke up my computer and plugged Alprazolam into a search engine along with the other two drugs. Every result had something to do with the veterinary field. I was on the right track. We just had to find where it had come from and who'd taken it.

What Hank had said about the hospitals and clinics not wanting to own up to missing medications rang in my head. The same could be said about the vets I had called and the wholesalers I was about to contact.

I powered up my computer and got the addresses for both places. If I didn't find a lead with the wholesalers, I was prepared to make face-to-face visits with the vets I had already spoken with. I dialed up Hank. He picked up within two rings.

"Hey, Kane. What's up?"

"How long until you can be in?"

"I can come now. Karen just left for work. I'm just finishing up breakfast. What's going on?"

"I want to stop in by the veterinary wholesalers and talk with some people face to face. I was thinking about what you said about these places not wanting to own up to missing drugs. People will have a harder time lying to two cops face to face."

"Sure, I can leave in five minutes, be at the station in twenty. It's only a couple minutes past seven. What are you doing at the station already?"

"This is our last day on the case. One way or another."

"What do you mean?"

"We had another victim last night. This one was alive. They found her wandering in Ybor, wearing lingerie. The captain and I went to the hospital and spoke with the doctor—another lobotomy. I'll go over the rest when you get here."

A long silence came from his end of the phone. Hank cleared his throat. "I'm on my way."

He walked into my office a little after seven thirty. We grabbed an unmarked cruiser from the lot and headed out.

"Where are we going to first?" he asked.

"The place is called Wholesale Pharm and Supply. They open at eight." I looked at the clock on the dash. "We should be there a couple minutes after."

I filled Hank in on everything the doctor had told the captain and me on the ride over, as well as the message in magic marker.

The wholesaler was in an industrial park out in Ruskin. It was a thirty-minute drive south from downtown—well out of our jurisdiction. The navigation on my cell phone told me that the address was coming up on our right. I saw it in the distance. It was a long, multiunit beige building. On the outside of the corner unit was the name of the business we were looking for. The remaining four units in the building were empty. Two cars were parked on the side and one in the front. I pulled up and shut off the car.

We walked in. A jingle of bells strapped to the top of the door sounded our presence. A man dressed in a black polo shirt emerged from the back hallway. He was in his fifties, tan and a hundred pounds overweight. A gold necklace wrapped his neck, and a gold bracelet sat on one wrist, a gold watch on the other.

"Morning," he said. "What can I do for you gentlemen?"

"Good morning. I'm Lieutenant Carl Kane. This is Sergeant Hank Rawlings. We're with the Tampa Police Department's homicide division."

He jerked his head back, causing the fat under his chin to wiggle. "Homicide division?"

"Yes, sir. We would like to speak with whoever is in charge here."

"I guess that would be me, though sometimes I don't feel that way. I'm Paul DiMarini, I'm the owner. What can I do for you?"

"We would like to talk about the products you carry and if any have come up missing."

"We have a ton of stuff missing."

"Excuse me?" I asked.

"We just did inventory last week. First time this year. A ton of stuff might be an exaggeration, but as the owner, I don't want a thing missing. What are you looking for?"

"Xylazine, Buprenorphine, and Alprazolam."

"Xylazine we have. Buprenorphine and Alprazolam we don't carry—never have. You want to see the count?"

"Sure," I said.

He opened a drawer under the front counter and pulled an inch stack of papers from it. "Here's our inventory." He thumbed through the pages, mumbling the word *Xylazine.* "Ah, here we go—Xylazine. Says here we should have forty-eight bottles. Let's go check the shelf." He motioned over his shoulder to follow him back into the warehouse, so we did.

He stopped at a rack and found the stock. I watched him count the bottles of Xylazine in front of him one by one.

I multiplied the bottles in the rows. "You have forty-two there."

His mouth curled to the side. "Hold on." He walked into an office in the warehouse and came back with another stack of papers. He flipped through them. "Pick sheets from the week." He pulled one out and turned it toward me.

It was an order from a vet for Xylazine—quantity, six bottles.

We thanked him for his time and showed ourselves to the door. The next stop was Pet Med Plus in Brandon. The business was twenty minutes away as we headed back toward the city.

We pulled into the parking lot just before nine. A large gray warehouse with tinted glass front doors stood before us. A couple cars were parked on the side. We walked up to the front door. The business's name was plastered across the front in stickers. I gave the door a yank—locked. I peered through the glass and didn't spot any employees. We'd have to wait.

I leaned against the side of the car. Hank rested his arms

on the roof on the other side. I checked my watch—8:58 a.m. My phone buzzed in my pocket. I pulled it out. The caller ID said it was the station. I hit Talk.

"Lieutenant Kane."

"Where are you? You see Rawlings?" the captain asked.

"He's with me. We're looking into some pet-med wholesalers. On our second one."

"So you're not here?"

"No. Why?"

"The lights in your office were on, so I knew you were already in this morning. I've been walking around the station for the last fifteen minutes looking for you so we could start our morning briefing about last night."

"This place should be open in a few minutes. I'm guessing we'll be back within the hour."

"Did you already fill Rawlings in?"

"Yeah, earlier."

"Then don't worry about it. I'll go over everything with the guys here. You guys keep working on what you're doing."

"Sounds good."

"Come to my office when you get back."

"Yup." I hung up.

"Captain?" Hank asked.

I nodded.

"This might be our guy here." Hank pointed to a newer black two-door pulling into the parking lot.

The car pulled past us and continued around the back of the building. We saw the lights inside flicker on a few minutes later. A man came to the front door, unlocked it, and pushed it open. He stood in the doorway. He was shorter than me by a few inches but made up for it in width. His shaved arms stretched the sleeve holes of his T-shirt. His chest pulled the fabric around it tight. He held a water bottle filled with a bright-pink liquid—creatine or an after-workout drink was my best guess.

"Morning, officers." He smiled, exposing bright-white veneers.

Hank and I walked up. "I'm Lieutenant Kane." I nodded at Hank. "This is Sergeant Rawlings. Wanted to see if we could talk with who's in charge."

"That's me today. The name's Don. I'm the office manager. What can I do for you?"

"We're looking into a case that involves drugs used in the veterinary field. Wanted to see if you had anything come up missing."

"Not that I know of."

"Mind taking a look for us?" Hank asked.

"Sure, I guess. Come on inside." He held the door, and we walked in.

He walked past us and went behind the front counter. We stood across from him.

"So, missing drugs, huh? Do you know what medications you're looking for?"

"Xylazine, Buprenorphine, Alprazolam," I said.

"Let's check the stock." He clicked a few keys at the computer sitting in front of him. The printer at the side of the counter started making noise and shot out two sheets.

He pulled them from the printer's tray. "Buprenorphine, quantity seventeen. Xylazine, seventy-six. Alprazolam, fourteen. I'll head back and check the inventory."

"Mind if we look over your shoulder?" Hank asked.

He slapped the inventory paper against his hand. "Not at all. Come on." He stood from his chair and motioned for us to head into the warehouse.

We followed him through the door to the back. Three delivery vans sat parked inside. Rows of shelving rose to the ceiling. A couple of warehouse workers entered through the service door at the back and punched in at the time clock on the wall.

"The Xylazine is right over here." He pointed to a shelf an aisle over. "Have to get the stock picker to check on the Buprenorphine and Alprazolam, though. The stuff we don't move a lot of sits higher on the shelves."

We walked over to where he had pointed out the Xylazine. He pulled a bin from the second row of the shelf and set it on the ground. I saw two boxes and a handful of loose vials inside.

"Boxes have thirty a piece in them." he said. He stacked the two boxes on top of each other.

I cocked my head and looked at them. Each vial had plastic shrink wrap around it.

He counted them. "Missing five. There might still be stock in the vans."

I nodded.

He slid the bin back onto the shelf and headed for the parked cargo vans. He went through them one at a time.

Each van was empty.

He stood and looked at his inventory sheet when he closed the back of the last van. "Hmm," he said.

"Missing?" I asked.

"Our inventory is computerized. It's dead on. It updates with each order."

"When was the last time you took a physical inventory?" Hank asked.

His face said he was thinking. "Five months ago. We do it twice a year—next audit is next month."

"Let's check on the other ones," I said.

He waved his hand over his head at the guy walking toward the back of the warehouse. "Jerry! Can you bring the picker over?" he shouted.

The guy gave him a nod.

He rubbed at his eye and then pointed. "Buprenorphine is in the row over there."

We walked over. The warehouse worker he'd called drove around the corner with the picker a few seconds later. "Bin six, fourth row—Buprenorphine," he said to the guy.

The warehouse worker raised the platform on the stock picker up to the shelf. He pulled the bin and made his way back down.

"There you go," he said. The guy handed the bin to the office manager.

He set it on the ground to go through it like the last one. The vials sat in the bottom of the bin, four by four. He didn't need to count. "One missing," he said.

"I would venture to guess that you are missing some

Alprazolam as well," I said.

"Let me check."

He rattled off its location to his guy on the stock picker. He brought the bin down, and it was two vials short.

"I don't know who would steal from here. You would think someone would jump out at me, but I just can't see anyone here doing it."

"How many employees do you have here?" I asked.

"Sixteen, not counting myself and the owner."

"Has anyone been fired, quit, anything like that?" Hank asked.

"We have some turnover with drivers and warehouse workers. Maybe ten that have been let go or quit this year."

"Think we could get a copy of your past and present employees?" I asked.

"I don't have the authority to give that out. You would have to talk with Todd, the owner."

"Can you call him?" I asked.

"Um, yeah, one minute."

We followed him back to the front of the building. He ducked into an office toward the back of the room and grabbed a phone. Hank and I walked back around the counter. We sat and waited at the front desk. Minutes passed as the guy spoke on the phone.

"Think he'll give us a copy?" Hank asked.

I saw the guy hang up. "Guess we'll see. Here he comes."

The office manager returned to the front counter. In his hand were a few sheets of paper. "The owner said okay. Here are copies of all of our staff from the last year." He set the papers on the counter and slid them over to me.

I glanced over the sheets. Addresses and phone numbers sat next to the names. I counted roughly twenty-five employees.

We thanked him and made our way back to the station to dive in.

Chapter 28

He'd been flipping the local news channels back and forth through the night and all morning. He was looking for anything on the girl he'd released. None of the local stations were reporting anything. He didn't understand why it wasn't getting any coverage. The call of a woman in distress had come through the police band around half past midnight. He heard the officer radio back to dispatch to tell them he was taking her to Tampa General Hospital. After that, the police radio went quiet about her. There wasn't so much as a peep about her on the police band all morning.

He pulled the lever on his recliner and kicked his feet up. He slid his phone out of his pocket and called information, and they put him through to the hospital.

A receptionist picked up. "Tampa General Hospital. How can I direct your call?"

"Hello. This is Sergeant…" He looked around the room for a name and coughed to buy himself time. "Excuse me.

Sergeant Watkins with the Tampa Police. I wanted to speak with someone about the Jane Doe one of our officers brought in last night."

"Hold one second for me."

Hold music played in his ear as he waited on the line.

"This is Doctor Wallace. I handle the day-shift patients for Doctor Winters."

"Sergeant Watkins with the TPD. I wanted to send an officer by to pick up the lingerie the Jane Doe wore when she arrived last night. We wanted to have our guys in forensics take a look at it."

The doctor's response would tell him everything.

"We have it in a bag in her room. Just have the officer ask for me, Doctor Wallace."

"Thank you." He hung up.

"Hmm." He curled his mouth to one side in thought.

The cops must have told the staff at the hospital to keep quiet. If anyone from the media knew about the woman, the news would have been everywhere already.

He'd take it upon himself. The police weren't telling the media enough about the women. So far, they had been keeping the branding and the lobotomies under wraps. He'd fix that. He dialed information and had them put him through to every television station and newspaper in the area.

While coughing and hacking, he informed each news outlet about the lingerie, the branding, the lobotomies, and the woman at the hospital. He stayed on the phone for over an hour. The press would run with the story. He clicked the volume up on his police scanner and went back to flipping the channels. He started to doze off to the daytime talk show that was on.

Chapter 29

Television crews and reporters engulfed the front of the police station—never a good sign. We parked the car in the structure and got out. A couple of back-entrance-savvy reporters rushed out at us as we walked toward the door.

A reporter jammed a microphone in my face. Not far behind the microphone was a television camera. "What can you tell us about the lobotomies?"

"No comment."

"What about the woman who was found alive?"

I didn't respond.

A Channel 6 microphone held by J.R. Steele blocked my path. "Lieutenant! Lieutenant! The media is calling this guy the Psycho Surgeon. Care to comment?"

Hank turned to me. "Psycho Surgeon?"

I shook my head and held out my palm toward the camera. "No comment." I continued walking.

Steele followed me with the microphone. "Why has this killer singled you out?"

I stopped. "Singled me out?"

"We have a source that said that the lobotomized woman found last night had a message written on her to you."

I shook my head and walked inside.

The ringing of telephones was filling the station. We made our way to the captain's office. He was sitting at his desk, talking on the phone. He hung up when we walked in.

"Looks like we have a leak. Where did it come from?" I asked.

"Either the hospital or someone here at the station. It could be a combination of the two. Nothing we can do about it now except lay it all out for them. I have a press release scheduled in an hour."

"One of the reporters called him the Psycho Surgeon," Hank said.

Bostok pushed his chair back. "Great. So they gave him a name?"

"Not a very clever one," I said. "Anyway, we found the place the drugs came from. We have a list of all employees from the last year. About to go through it now."

Captain Bostok nodded. "Do it."

Hank and I split the list of employees. He took his half to his desk, and I did likewise. I clicked away at the computer. One by one, I checked backgrounds and called each employee, past and present. Nobody I managed to speak with could think of anyone who might have committed a workplace theft. Most of my stack was gone when Hank burst into my office.

"Third guy I called is on his way in. Says he may have something."

"What's the something? When is he coming?"

"He mentioned a video. On his way now."

"What's the name?"

"Bob Cross."

"Past or present employee?" I asked.

"Past. Looks like he quit a few months back."

I nodded. "Let Cap know we got someone on the way in. See if he wants to sit in."

Hank nodded and walked next door.

I plugged the guy's name into the system. He was clean. His address was listed out in Carrollwood. I printed his sheet off.

Hank walked back in. "Cap says he has his hands full with the press but wants an update if we turn over anything during the interview."

I finished looking into the rest of the employees in my stack. They all looked clean. Within an hour, we got the call that our potential witness was waiting. I popped into the lunch room to get my standard offerings and headed to the interview boxes. An officer from the front sat him down in box one. Hank waited for me outside the door, and we entered together. A thin man sat at the table. He was wearing an old T-shirt and khaki shorts. The front of his hairline receded. The rest of his hair was chin length. A beard covered his face. I looked at the weight on the sheet again. That guy was fifty pounds lighter than what was listed. I set the soda and candy in front of him.

"Mr. Cross, I'm Lieutenant Kane. This is Sergeant Rawlings. You have some information to tell us?"

We took seats across from him.

"Yeah, I have to say I was surprised to get a call." He scooped the candy bar off the table and began unwrapping it.

"Surprised how?" I asked.

"Well, I'm pretty sure I have your smoking gun here."

"We're listening," I said.

"I think I have the guy you are looking for on video." He took a bite from the candy bar and chewed with his mouth open. He popped the soda and took a big gulp.

"On video doing what?" I asked.

"Stealing the drugs in question. Like I said—smoking gun."

"Do you have the video here? Can we see it?"

"Yeah, sure."

He removed his cell phone from his pocket and clicked a few buttons. He turned the phone so Hank and I could see the screen and then pressed Play. A video began. I recognized the inside of the Pet Med Plus warehouse.

The video looked to be filmed from behind a product rack. The man in frame stood in front of the bin where the Xylazine was kept. The man put some items from inside the bin into a bag and walked out the warehouse doors. The video stopped.

"His name is Chad Packard. He's one of the delivery drivers." He took another sip of soda.

I wrote down the name, which wasn't one from my stack of employees. "How do you know that those were the drugs in question?" I asked.

"After he walked out, I went to see what he took. It was a couple vials of Xylazine. I'm not sure about the other two the sergeant here mentioned, but I'm positive about that one."

"And you're sure it is this Packard guy?" I asked.

"A hundred percent."

"We'll need that video," I said.

"Sure, whatever." He slid the back off his cell phone and popped out the small memory card. He let out a couple coughs into his shoulder and set the card on the table in front of him.

"How did you acquire this video?" Hank asked.

He raised his eyebrows. "I recorded it."

"Why?"

"Well, here's the thing." He squinted. "My medical bills were starting to pile up." He paused.

We sat in silence.

"Short version, I'm dying of cancer and don't want to leave my wife with a pile of debt."

"So this was going to help that how?" I asked.

"I don't know, I thought maybe I could... I don't know."

"Extort him for stealing?" Hank asked.

Cross shrugged. "I'm in a tight spot. I can't work anymore because of my illness. Our money is running low. I guess I just figured if I could get a few hundred bucks or so out of the guy, it may help at home. Not really one of my finer moments or brightest ideas, I guess."

"Did you get any money out of this guy?" I asked.

"No. Here's the kicker in your case, though. Before I could even attempt to get any money out of the guy, he quit at Pet Med Plus to start a taxi business."

I had a question bubbling. It was bothering me. "So, why didn't you come forward earlier?"

"I would have if I would have known what was going on. I don't watch the news or read the papers. What do I care about what's going on in the world? I just want to spend some time with my wife before I go. We have one rule: nothing depressing. That means no news, basically. The world's problems will still be there after I'm gone, or so my wife says."

Cross rattled his fingers across the top of the desk.

I glanced at his left hand—no ring. No tan line from a ring. No indentation from a wedding ring. It normally wouldn't be a big deal. Wearing a wedding band could be hazardous on countless jobs. The problem was he was unemployed and just gave us a yarn about his wife.

"Your wife doesn't mind that you don't wear a wedding ring?"

He rubbed at his finger. "Technically, we're still divorced. We're actually getting remarried next Tuesday. When she found out about the illness a few months back, we reconciled, and I moved back in. It's funny how death can bring two people back together. We have known each other since we were kids."

I nodded.

"Can you give us a minute, Mr. Cross?" Hank asked.

"Yeah, sure."

Hank stood and motioned for me to follow him out. I grabbed the memory card with the video on it and followed Hank. I closed the door behind me.

"What do you think?" Hank asked.

"It's too good. Was this Packard guy on your list?" I asked.

"Yeah. Didn't see anything of concern, though."

"Come on." I walked toward my office. Hank followed.

I sat at my desk and plugged Chad Packard into the computer. He showed up right away. He was local. I rattled off his information to Hank, "White male, forty-two, hair brown, eyes brown. Height, five foot ten, weight one seventy-five."

Hank leaned against my doorway. "Do you think it's the guy on the video?" he asked.

"Hard to tell."

"I don't remember seeing any priors," Hank said.

I shook my head, "None." I scrolled down the screen to double-check. I ran through his DMV record. He only had a minivan registered.

I clicked the button to print off the sheet with his information.

I let out a breath. "This just seems fishy."

"What seems fishy?"

"The guy in the box. He brought the case to us on a silver platter. It's too perfect. When was the last time someone walked in with a case gift wrapped?"

Hank shrugged. "Never."

I nodded. "Exactly. I'm not sold on the dying-husband love story, either. Let's go run it by the captain and see what he thinks."

"Works for me," Hank said.

We went next door to Bostok's office. I gave the captain's door a knock and walked in.

He gave us his attention. "Well?"

I gave it to him in short bursts. "The guy has a video and a story. Video is from the warehouse of Pet Med Plus. It shows a guy named Chad Packard putting drugs from a bin in question into a bag and then leaving. Claims that Packard quit to start a taxi business."

"Do we know that for sure?"

"I checked DMV records—just a minivan under his name. The cab could be registered through a business, though," I said.

I handed the captain the memory card with the video. "This is the video here."

"Why does he have the theft on video? Did he work security there or something?"

"His plan was to blackmail the guy," Hank said.

The captain shook his head. "Because that's always a good idea. What do you think, Kane?"

"Too perfect, and I don't get a good feeling from the guy."

"Explain."

"I think he might be full of shit, but in case he isn't, we

need to get the warrants for this Packard set and get out there. The place is just a couple minutes away."

"I'll get tech to make us some copies of this and get on the phone for the warrants. What do you want to do about the star witness?" Captain Bostok asked.

I thought for a second. Something about Cross was really rubbing me the wrong way. The more I thought about him, the more other things started bothering me. He hadn't come forward with the information on his own. The case was everywhere. You couldn't miss it, no matter how hard you tried. The fact that he planned on blackmailing a coworker spoke about his character. He worked at the place the drugs came from. This guy could have just been trying to steer us in the wrong direction. However, we wouldn't be able to hold him just because I had a feeling.

"I'd like to put Donner on him if that's okay. Just a gut feeling."

The captain nodded. Hank and I left his office.

I called Donner.

Chapter 30

We got word on the warrants within twenty minutes. The video had persuaded the powers that be to sign off on an arrest and a search warrant. We put the wheels in motion. Timmons sent out a page to the members of our SWAT team out on patrol. The address was just outside the city but still within the TPD's jurisdiction. It was a ten-minute drive from the station. We wouldn't need to contact any local departments.

We assembled in the station's parking structure. The SWAT guys dressed in their gear. We had six SWAT members plus Jones, Hank, and me. We put on our lapel mics and ear radios. Each of us put on body armor and snugged the straps tight. We didn't know who we were dealing with, and our protocol was to be prepared for the worst possible situation.

SWAT would take three cars, and Hank and I would take an unmarked cruiser. Jones would drive himself in another.

Sergeant Collison was our SWAT-team lead. He was in his forties and just a touch smaller than me. Short gray hair covered his head. He sported a goatee manicured to perfection. It looked fake. He spread a map out on the trunk of our unmarked cruiser and laid out the plan. We'd park at the east corner and approach the residence. The neighboring house would give us cover until we were right upon the property in question. His team would take the lead and get the door. Hank, Jones, and I were to follow when they had cleared the room—simple but effective. We left the station.

The lights flashed, and sirens wailed as we drove through the city. Four blocks away, we went silent and killed the red-and-blues. The neighborhood was middle class. Single-story bungalows built in the forties lined the sides of the street. Big oaks and palm trees filled the yards. We pulled up where Collison had instructed and killed the motor.

Collison went around and performed a mic check. His men took their weapons from their cars. He instructed one of his men to bring the door ram. I drew the Glock 22 from my shoulder holster. Hank and Jones did the same. We took up the rear and stayed low as we followed SWAT around the tree line toward the house.

Collison stopped and looked back. "We got a taxi—Crown Vic," he said.

I saw the yellow of the cab parked in the driveway. It was the same make and model from the airport videos. Our witness might have been telling the truth after all. The tension rose. We stayed single file as we approached the house, a brown single story with a white fence around its small front porch. Outside the porch was a four-foot pygmy palm and flower garden. The yellow taxi cab and a minivan sat parked in the driveway. A neighbor across the street and one house up stopped watering her flowers in the front yard to watch us. Collison and three members of the SWAT team climbed the steps up to the porch. They took the sides of the front door. The other two went to the back of the house. Hank, Jones, and I stayed at ground level.

Collison looked at us. "Ready?"

I gave him a nod.

Collison banged his fist on the door. "Search warrant, Tampa Police!" He looked at his men ready at the door with the ram. The front door opened before they could break it in. I saw a kid standing at the doorway. Collison grabbed the boy and pulled him outside. The other three officers went in, one after the other. The sound of a dog barking echoed from inside the house. We heard Collison's men yelling for someone to get on the floor. In just a matter of seconds, the *all clear* call came through our earpieces. We climbed the front steps and entered the house. Collison sat the boy down on the living-room couch.

We proceeded through the living room and found everyone in the kitchen. A man and woman were facedown on the tile floor. Black zip-tie handcuffs held their arms behind their backs. The man demanded an explanation. The woman cried out for her son in the next room.

I walked over and knelt next to the man's head. "Are you Chad Packard?"

"Yeah, what the hell is this?"

I pulled the warrants from my pocket of my shirt and showed it to him. "We have a warrant to search the property and a warrant for your arrest."

"For what? I didn't do anything."

"The theft of narcotics."

"I didn't steal any narcotics."

I read him his rights and lifted him to his feet.

As I pulled him up, he grunted then looked at his wife, still on the ground. "Deb, I didn't do anything."

Hank and I escorted him out of the house and over to the back of my unmarked cruiser. I pushed down on the top of his head and sat him down inside.

I looked at Hank. "Can you sit on him for a second? I have to go talk to Jones."

"Yeah, I got him."

I walked back to the house. Jones stood on the front porch.

"You want to run the search on the house? Try to hunt down the drugs, but keep an eye out for anything that looks suspicious. Find me something on lobotomies. Search every tool in that garage. If you spot anything, stop and wait for forensics."

He nodded. "I got it."

"We're going to take him back to the station and get started."

"I'll give you a call as soon as I'm through. What should I tell the wife?"

"Let her know where we're taking him."

"No problem."

I thanked Collison and the team and made my way back to the car.

Mr. Packard demanded an explanation from the backseat on the ride back to the station. He pleaded his innocence.

I tried to tune him out. We'd find out soon enough.

We brought him into the station and parked him in the first interrogation box. Hank headed into the observation room to watch him, and I went to tell the captain we had him in the building. I saw the major sitting across from Captain Bostok in his office through the window. I gave the door a knock and stuck my head in.

"No incidents. I have him in the box. Jones is searching the house."

The captain waved me in. "Come in."

I did and closed the door.

"What did you see at the house? Were there any signs that this could be the guy?"

"I was only inside for a minute. Jones is running the search."

"Tell me how it went."

I ran through it for the captain and Major Danes.

"They will toss the drug charges if we don't come up with something at the house," the major said.

"The hell with the drugs—I'm looking for a confession to multiple murders."

"Get the drugs first and then move into it." The captain pointed at a DVD on his desk. "Keller in tech burned the video footage to something we could play up here. Question the theft, and when he denies it, play the footage. See what we get out of him."

We walked toward the interrogation rooms. I hit the lunch room for the standard can of soda and candy bar. We discussed how we wanted to proceed with the questioning before I went inside the box. Captain Bostok and Major Danes entered the observation room with Hank. Prepared to question the suspect solo, at first, I walked into the interrogation room.

Chapter 31

I took a seat and placed the candy bar and soda in front of him. Worry covered his face. He stared at the food, at me and then the floor. He sat upright, with his elbows on the table.

"Mr. Packard, can I call you Chad?"

He nodded and let out a breath in anger.

"Chad, I'm Lieutenant Carl Kane. I'd like to ask you a few questions and get your side of the story about this theft. I would like you to be able to speak with me freely, and if you request legal counsel, you might not be able to do that. Now, I have already read you your legal warning at your house. Would you like an attorney?"

He looked up and shook his head. "I don't need a lawyer. I didn't steal any drugs. None of this makes sense."

"I also need to inform you that this interview is being recorded. Now, I'm going to give you a chance to be honest with me. If you have anything to tell me, now is the time."

He put both hands on his head and let them fall to his

sides. "I have no idea what the hell is going on here."

"Okay Chad, first, does the taxi at your house belong to you?"

"The cab? Yeah, I started a taxi service a few months back. Why?"

"Prior to that, you worked at Pet Med Plus as a driver?"

"Yeah? Why?"

"Tell me about your time there."

He rolled his eyes. "What is this? Why do you want to know about this?"

"I'll connect the dots in a second for you. Now, Pet Med Plus, tell me about it."

"I'm not sure what you want me to tell you. It was a job. I worked there for a couple years until I had enough money saved up to open my cab service."

"Okay Chad, now about your taxi service, do you work the airport area?"

"I work all over the city. You said this was about drugs. Why the hell do you care what I do for a living? The SWAT team busts into my house on a bogus drug warrant while my family is eating dinner, and now you want to talk about my taxi business? This is bullshit."

I held my hand up in an attempt to calm him down. "We're going to need some information, Chad. Now, you said you work the airport area, did you happen to pick up any women there this week?"

"I'm sure I did. Monday through Thursday, I work ten-hour shifts—eleven a.m. to nine p.m. I've had over a hundred fares this week."

"And you never work late or on Fridays?"

He shook his head. "Not if I can help it. I stop taking fares at eight thirty p.m. on the weekdays so I can get home in time to put my boy to sleep. I don't work Fridays so we can have a family dinner together. That was what we were doing when you busted in."

I wasn't quite ready to buy his Father of the Year story. "Mr. Packard, did you work with a Bob Cross?"

"Bob Cross? Yeah, I worked with him."

"What was your relationship with him?"

"He was another driver. I wasn't friends with him. He seemed sketchy."

"Sketchy how?"

"He was weird. I wasn't a fan—put it that way."

"Chad, he was here earlier and had some interesting things to say about you."

He jerked his head back. "Like what?"

"Well, we'll get to that. First, what can you tell me about Xylazine, Buprenorphine, and Alprazolam?"

He shook his head. "They were things I delivered when I worked at the warehouse. Why? Are they important or something?"

"Is that your extent of knowledge about the drugs?"

"Yeah." He put his hands in the air and let them fall to the table. "Come on, man. What is this? Why am I here?"

His level of anger was increasing. I decided to give him a couple minutes to cool off.

I pretended to check something on my cell phone. "Excuse me for a second. I'll be right back."

I walked out and over to the observation room. Hank, Captain Bostok, and Major Danes sat inside. I stood before them and leaned my back against the wall. "Any word back from Jones yet?"

"Haven't got word," the captain said.

"How does he look from in here?" I asked.

"Pissed," Hank said.

"Run the DVD footage and see what he says," the major said.

I nodded. "Where's the DVD?"

"It's loaded in the player." Hank pointed to the rolling cart that held the television and DVD player.

I rolled it from the observation room back over to the box. Hank held the door open, and I wheeled it in. Packard looked at me. A confused expression covered his face.

I plugged everything in, grabbed the remote, and took a seat. "Chad, I'm going to play something here, and afterward, we'll talk about it."

I clicked Play. The video began to roll. I didn't watch the screen. I stared at him, looking for a sign, anything that would tell me he knew what he was looking at. It took a few seconds, but then his facial expression changed. It was recognition. I had him.

I paused the video. "Here comes the part where you walk out with the stolen drugs." I hit Play again.

He stumbled for words before the video even played through. "Those aren't stolen drugs."

"What are they?"

"I bought heartworm pills for my dog. Why would you

have video of that?"

"Excuse me?"

"Heartworm pills. They are still at my house in the bag with the receipt. They are under the kitchen sink. That was like a week before I quit. I stocked up so I wouldn't have to pay retail."

"Chad, another officer and I stopped by the warehouse. The bin where you are doing this is where the Xylazine is kept."

"Yeah, it's also the same bin the X-tra Guard heartworm pills are sometimes kept. The stock in the warehouse is alphabetized. Some items share bins."

"I didn't see any heartworm pills in that bin when we were there," I said.

"Call the place and ask."

I hit the power button on the system. "Give me a minute." I walked out.

Captain Bostok and Major Danes stood outside the door.

"Tell Jones to look under the kitchen sink for a bag filled with heartworm pills," I said.

Hank walked out from the observation room with his phone to his ear. "Already called him. He's checking now."

"Think he's telling the truth?" Major Danes asked.

I shrugged.

Hank gave a nod and cupped the mouthpiece. "Jones said he found a brown paper bag filled with X-tra Guard heartworm pills under the sink. There's a receipt. The boxes even have stamps from Pet Med Plus."

"Give me that." I took the phone from Hank. "Jones, you see anything that looks remotely suspicious out there?"

"Nothing. A few of the guys stuck around to help me look. We're coming up empty."

"No signs of any of those drugs? Did you check everywhere?"

"Nothing out of the ordinary. Normal-looking medicine cabinet. Nothing prescription. Searched high and low."

"Tools? Did you go through them?"

"This guy owns about as many tools as my grandmother. There's just nothing here, Kane."

"Did you get a look in that cab?"

"A once-over. Nothing of interest, unless you want to get forensics out here to go through it."

"Let me see what our plan is here. I'll get back with you in a few minutes."

"Sounds good."

"Okay, thanks." I hung up.

"He says there is nothing there. We have no stolen drugs and nothing of interest."

"Son of a bitch," the captain said.

"Hold on." I pulled up the Internet on my phone and searched for the Pet Med Plus phone number. I hit the button to dial.

"Pet Med Plus, this is Don."

"Lieutenant Carl Kane, I was in there earlier."

"Sure what can I do for you?"

"Do you store X-tra Guard heartworm pills in the same

bin as Xylazine?"

"When it just comes in, we do. We run low on shelf space, so sometimes we combine things after a big shipment."

"Thanks." I hung up.

I looked to the captain. "This Packard guy might be telling the truth."

The captain let out a long breath. "Call Donner. Find out where Cross is. Get his ass back in here."

"What are we doing with Packard?" I asked.

"We're sitting on him. No one of interest is leaving this station."

I nodded.

Hank and I headed to my office to make the call.

"Think Cross might be our guy?" Hank asked.

"He just moved up the list."

While Bob Cross might have gotten himself out of the station, he hadn't done so without a tail. I enlisted Detective Donner to follow Cross from the police station. I dialed up Donner, and he picked up right away.

"Donner."

"Hey, it's Kane. You still on Cross?"

"Yup. I'm looking at him now."

"Where is he?"

"At the mall."

I could hear the sounds of faint music and people talking. "The mall?"

"Yeah, the mall in Brandon. I followed him here, parked, and found him inside. I've been following him around from store to store since. He's sitting in the food court now, eating."

"He hasn't spotted you, has he?"

"Nah, no way. I've been keeping my distance."

"Well, it doesn't matter now either way. Bring him back here."

"You want me to ask him to come back in, or you want him brought back in?"

"Brought."

"Ten four. I'll go get him."

"Let the mall security know what you're doing."

"You want mall security to back me up with this guy? That's a joke, right? I'll just go grab him and be on my way back."

"Let them know. He might be our guy. We don't need an incident. Call me when he's in custody." I hung up.

"Hank, find me something on Bob Cross. I mean anything."

"Will do." Hank left my office.

Chapter 32

When he got the call from the sergeant, he got the perfect opportunity to get a little face time with Lieutenant Kane. Bob wanted to see what kind of person he was—to see how much of an adversary Kane could be.

Bob had always been planning to use Packard as a patsy if needed. While he'd gotten the time he sought with the lieutenant, and gotten out of the station, he hadn't done so without a tail. Bob might have underestimated the lieutenant's level of intelligence. The cat-and-mouse game had begun.

He first spotted the tail as he left the station. A gray late-model Dodge Charger pulled from the parking structure after him. He kept tabs on the car following in the side mirror. He made a few extra turns. With each one, the car reappeared in the Range Rover's mirror—never more than a few car lengths back. Bob headed back toward Brandon. He figured the cop would stop where his jurisdiction ended. He didn't—he kept following. He couldn't take the cop to the house. Bob opted for the mall. It should have been an easy place to ditch the tail.

The cop wore a suit. He was alone. He followed Bob from store to store. Bob looked at clothing. He stopped, checked prices, and even tried a few things on in the store's dressing rooms. The cop stayed close. Bob looked for an opportunity to elude the detective's surveillance, but he was never more than a hundred feet away.

Bob wondered if they'd found Packard yet. The cab idea had come from him. Chad talked about it every day. He had a countdown. Each day, Packard would announce he was one day closer to starting his cab business. One day, it clicked. It would be the perfect way to get the women. When he overheard Chad asking about getting heartworm pills for his dog, Bob decided to record him grabbing them from the bin. Bob had taken the Xylazine the next day.

He smiled, thinking of his intelligence. A burst of pain shot up his leg and interrupted his smile. He'd been trying to disguise his limp and walk normally for hours. After just a few more feet, he could rest.

He walked his tray of food over to an empty table at the food court and sat. He unwrapped his cheeseburger and dug in. From the corner of his eye, he spotted the detective walking to a table. He picked away at his french fries and washed them down with a mouthful of soda.

The cop sat at the other end of the food court, staring at him. He talked on the phone. He was probably giving whoever was on the other end an update on his whereabouts—maybe Lieutenant Kane.

Bob finished his meal, wiped his hands with a napkin, and got up. He walked his tray over to the trash and then headed for the bathrooms at the edge of the food court. He stopped in front of a hat store to watch the scene behind him in the glass. To anyone looking, he appeared to be checking out the merchandise inside. He caught the detective getting up in the reflection. Bob made for the hallway. A hundred feet, at most, separated the two. He'd have to use the distance to his advantage. Bob made his way down the length of the hall and past the men's room. He waited at the back door marked Emergency Exit until he saw the detective coming down the hallway. They made eye contact. Bob pushed the door open with his back and went through. He had entered a back hallway of the mall. An exit door led outside a hundred feet farther down the hall.

As the door was closing, the cop shouted, "Mr. Cross! Bob Cross! Stop right there!"

Bob stood on the other side of the door. In his hand was a syringe filled with ten milliliters of Xylazine, which he'd been carrying in his pocket. With his back against the wall, he waited with it ready to strike—his thumb on the plunger. The door burst open, and the detective rushed through. They made eye contact as Bob plunged the needle into the back of the detective's neck. The cop grabbed Bob by the shoulders, and they struggled. Bob thumbed the plunger down, pushing in the fluid. The detective let go and reached for his neck. He stumbled backward and crashed to the floor of the hallway. He tried to reach for his gun, but Bob pounced on him and held his arms above his head until the drug took full effect. Within ten seconds, the cop was out. A violent coughing attack overtook Bob, and he spewed blood into the unconscious cop's face.

Bob went through the cop's pockets. He took his car keys, wallet, phone, and badge. He reached into the cop's sport coat and took his service pistol from the holster under his arm. Something else was there, something useful. He took off the cop's shirt and took the item he wanted. The detective would be out for a couple hours.

He walked down the hall and pushed each door open until he found a storage closet. He pulled the cop over and closed him inside. He left the mall out the back and walked around front.

Bob stopped in his tracks. Another problem presented itself—the Range Rover. They would be looking for the vehicle if his tail had reported what he'd been following. It was registered to his wife. They would find the house. Bob needed to get his equipment and taxi out of the garage as soon as possible. He'd leave the Range Rover at the mall.

From his pocket, he pulled the keys he'd lifted off the cop. A remote control dangled from the ring. He walked through the front of the mall's parking lot, holding down the button until he spotted the cop's unmarked cruiser honking its horn. He walked down the aisle and got in.

The drive back to the house was short, the stop inside even shorter. He removed the rest of the green lingerie from the house. Back in the garage, he gathered his operating tools and backed the taxi out. He pulled the detective's car into the stall where the taxi had sat and closed the garage door. In total, it was under a five-minute stop. He thumbed on his police scanner, adjusted the volume, and drove back toward the city.

Chapter 33

I called Detective Donner three times. He didn't answer. I left another message and hung up. I decided to give him a few minutes to call back before calling mall security to ask if someone could try to find him. Hank tapped my door and walked into my office. "What did you get?" I asked.

"There isn't a ton there other than the basics. No criminal history. He spent time in the Army. Honorable discharge." He tossed a sheet of paper with the info on my desk. I picked it up and gave it a look.

"Family?" I asked.

"Records show both parents deceased. No children. He was married in 2009. Divorce finalized a couple months ago. His address is listed in Carrollwood. I found an address for a Tina Watkins, his ex-wife, out in Brandon. It's on the sheet there."

"Finalized a couple months ago? That doesn't sound like reconciliation to me. Didn't he say he moved back in there?" I found her name on the sheet. "No phone number?"

"Unlisted."

"Wait. Where did you get the number for Cross?"

"His sheet from Pet Med Plus."

"Was it a mobile or home?"

Hank shook his head and shrugged.

"Where is his employee sheet from Pet Med Plus?"

"Hold on. I'll get it."

Hank left my office to retrieve the sheet. He walked back in a few seconds later and passed it to me.

I looked it over. It was a Brandon phone number. I grabbed my desk phone and dialed it. No one answered after multiple rings. A voicemail told me I'd reached Tina Watkins. I hung up. "He answered at the home number for his ex-wife."

"So he has been staying there," Hank said.

"Donner tailed him out to Brandon. If he was going back to Carrollwood, he wouldn't have driven all the way out there to go to a mall."

I looked over at the clock—7:06 p.m. "What the hell is Donner's deal? It's not like him to not report back. Is the captain still in his office?"

Hank looked out my door. "Yeah, he's still in there."

"Go tell the Cap what we just talked about. Tell him I can't get a hold of Donner. See what he wants to do."

Hank nodded and walked out.

The files from the two dead women lay scattered across my desk. We still didn't even have an identity on the woman found alive. I took the paper Hank had given me and tossed it on top of the rap sheet I had on Bob Cross. I leaned back in my chair and bounced a pencil on my desk. I rubbed my eyes until my vision blurred. I reached for the phone to call the mall's security office. Something on my desk caught my eye. It was a photo of Sarah McMillian's brand. I grabbed it and spun it toward me. I hung up the phone.

"Son of a bitch!"

I traced the outline with the pencil.

"Son of a bitch!"

I grabbed the photo and went to the captain's office. I burst in and stuck the photo of the brand under the captain's and Hank's noses. "What's that say?" I asked.

"It's a photo of the brand with pencil scribbling around it," Hank said.

"Read it."

"The pencil makes it look like it says Bob."

"With a cross inside the *O*. The damn brand says Bob Cross."

The captain squinted and looked at the photo. He shook his head. "Shit. You can't get a hold of Donner?"

"No. He tailed Cross to the mall in Brandon. I told him to grab him and bring him back to the station. It's been a half hour. He hasn't answered the phone or reported back," I said.

"Did you call mall security?"

"I was about to when the photo of the brand caught my eye."

"You and Rawlings get out there. Find Donner and Cross."

"Cross said he was staying in Brandon. He answered the phone at his ex-wife's place out there. You want us to call the Hillsborough County Sheriff's Department to check it out?" I asked.

The captain stood from his desk. "You two go to the ex-wife's address. Get HCSD to assist. I'll take Jones and go to the mall. Call the HCSD on your way. Go."

"Sounds good, Cap."

We grabbed the address and left. The place was a twenty-minute drive from the station—all freeway. I called the Hillsborough County Sheriff's Department while we were en route. A couple of deputies would meet us at the house.

I made a right off the main road into the subdivision. The street was two lanes in each direction. Palm trees and flower gardens lined the median, and white picket fences sat just beyond the sidewalks. Landscape workers bustled about, blowing away debris and pruning trees, their day almost complete. I saw the sheriff's cruiser up ahead. I flashed my lights as I passed. The sheriff's car pulled from the curb behind me. We turned right onto Munson Court. The house was the first on the corner. I pulled to the curb across the street and parked.

Hank and I got out. Two deputies exited their cruiser, and we got together. The driver's nameplate read Ortiz. He looked to be in his forties with short black hair. His partner's nameplate read Saunders. He was a big mid-twenties-looking kid with a blond buzz cut. We introduced ourselves. I explained the situation to them.

We walked up into the driveway, guns drawn. The house was a newer beige ranch with a two-and-a-half-car garage at the front. The grass and flower gardens didn't show one weed. Three big palm trees stood at the front. A fence wrapped the backyard. I wouldn't have imagined a psychopath living in that house. I nodded at the deputies.

"You guys want to try and get a visual around the back?"

Ortiz nodded and pointed the younger deputy around the corner. I reached out, rang the doorbell, and took a step back to the side. We waited and listened. No one came. A window sat to the right of the home's front door. The blinds were turned shut but not pulled all the way down. I crouched to look in and saw a formal dining room with the lights out. Chairs lined the wall but no table. Something caught my eye. Dead flies covered the window's ledge. I looked at them more closely—blowflies, hundreds of them.

I looked over my shoulder at Hank and Ortiz. "We may have a D.B. Either of you two smell decomp?"

Hank got by the base of the window and took in a deep sniff. "I can't smell anything."

"We need to get a look inside this house."

"Around back? Patio doors maybe?" Ortiz asked.

I agreed.

"Ortiz, stay on this front door."

He nodded.

Hank and I walked to the gate in the fence.

Saunders walked back toward us. "The whole back here is fenced in. No entrance other than this one. No one ran."

I yanked the fence gate. It was locked from the other

side. I pulled myself up and over. I unlocked it for Hank and the deputy. We walked around the side of the house to the lanai out back. Bushes, landscaping, and various palm trees surrounded the screened-in area. Hank walked to the other side in search of the entry. "Got a door over here," he shouted back.

We headed over to Hank and followed him into the lanai. A custom pool had a small rock waterfall bubbling away at the back near a hot tub. Tropical plants in planters lined the perimeter. A wicker table, chairs, and footrests sat next to a small outdoor fireplace. We went to the sliding backdoor.

Hank reached out and gave the door a tug. "Open. Do we go in?"

"Hold on." I looked at the base of the door—more blowflies.

"Just open the door a crack."

Hank slid the door open.

Saunders yanked his head back away from the door. "Someone's dead. We have to call this in."

"Do it," I said.

He made the call. I pointed into the house and gave the command to enter. I motioned at Hank and the deputy. They fell in behind me.

"Tampa Police Department!" I shouted.

No response.

"Tampa Police!" I yelled.

Again, no response.

We stepped into the house. It was an open floor plan.

From where we stood, in the dining room, the entire house was visible, except down the hallway to the left. The kitchen was to our right. We cleared it and walked to the living room. The television was on, playing an infomercial for a juicer.

A woman was sitting on the couch with her back toward us. Just the top of her head was visible over the couch back.

"Tampa Police. Put your hands up."

I advanced on her and rounded the side of the couch.

She didn't move. As soon as I got in front of her, I realized she was the source of our blowflies and odor. The woman was dead and had been that way for some time. A cycle of flies and maggots had already been through her body. She wore green lingerie—at least some places of it were still green. Blood mixed with her decay had stained the rest of it.

We cleared the living room and then headed toward the hall. Another door stood next to the hall entrance. I gave Hank the sign to wait and opened the door. It was the garage. Plastic hung from the ceiling and covered the floor. A few workbenches and toolboxes lined the back wall. Tools scattered the area. The dark silhouette of a car parked at the back showed through the plastic. A dining-room table, also covered in plastic, sat in the first garage bay. That was apparently where he had operated. I looked left and right— no people. I closed the door, and we continued into the hallway.

The deputy cleared the first room in the hall, a home office. Hank and I walked toward the master bedroom. The light was on, the door open. I stopped when I noticed something odd. I got Hank's attention and pointed to the deadbolt mounted to the bedroom door. It could only be engaged from the outside.

He nodded.

With Deputy Saunders at our back, we continued into the room. I spanned left and right. An unmade queen-size bed took up most of the floor space. A pair of ratcheting straps were balled up on the floor. An IV bag hung from the headboard. A dresser and a large television were on the wall to my left. We made our way through the room to a hallway leading left, to the master bath. A closet door was open with the light on inside. I spun around the door. The small room had nothing but clothes inside. I poked my head into the master bath.

I holstered my weapon. "Damn. He ain't here."

We walked back outside to get away from the smell of decomp and wait for the other officers to arrive.

Chapter 34

Hank and I watched them wheel the woman's body from the living room, down the front step, and out to the driveway where they'd parked the coroner's van. The captain's Ford pulled to the corner of the street. He and Jones got out and walked over.

"Cap, Jones," I said.

"They give you any problems?" the captain asked.

"No, they called it in, but as soon as they got word from their superiors, they backed off and gave us the scene. We've been waiting on the okay from forensics to go back in the house. What did you get from the mall?"

"Nothing. No signs of Donner or Cross. Donner's car wasn't in the mall's parking lot. He never talked with anyone from security about taking someone out of the mall. I gave them descriptions of Donner and Cross. They're going to look on their surveillance videos and call me back."

"What about Packard?" I asked.

"I had the guys at the station cut him loose. It's pretty

obvious now he's not our guy," the captain said.

Ed was standing at the front door of the house, so we walked over.

"Don't suppose she died of natural causes?" I asked.

"Not unless it's natural to have over a dozen holes drilled in the side of your head."

"A dozen holes?"

Ed nodded. "A dozen might be on the low side."

"How long has she been sitting there?" I asked.

"My guess is ten to twelve days. He did this one before the others."

"Damn. Can we ID her? Is it the ex-wife?" Captain Bostok asked.

"Height, hair color, and weight are pretty close to the information we have on her. We'll have to get her dental records to confirm, though."

"Okay, Ed. Thanks. Give me a call when you have her report ready," I said.

"Won't be until tomorrow, but I will."

I saw Rick in a clean suit inside.

He noticed us standing at the door and walked over, pulling the mask from his mouth. "This place is something else."

"What have you got so far?" I asked.

"I'm just working in the living room and kitchen right now. Pax is looking over the rest of the house and the garage. So far, I have blood from a number of different sources. There is cast off all over the kitchen. The kid and I are going to be here a while. Cap, I'd like to get an entomologist in here. He should be able to get us a better time of death from all these flies."

"That's fine, Rick. Whatever you need," Bostok said.

Rick flipped the mask over his nose and mouth and walked toward the kitchen. We walked back outside to get away from the smell.

"Well? Now what?" Hank asked.

"We need to find Donner. Something is wrong." I pulled my cell phone from my pocket and dialed his number. It rang and went to his voicemail.

Pax burst from the front door of the house. "You guys, come on. Come here."

The tone of his voice said he'd found something bad. We followed him into the house and out to the garage. Pax had pulled down the plastic separating the parking stalls. I saw the reason for his emotion. One of our unmarked Chargers sat parked in the last garage bay. We rushed over to the car. I didn't see blood. I put my hand on the hood. It was still warm. I looked at Hank. "Call the tag into the station."

Someone from patrol confirmed it as ours. The car number had been checked out to Donner. I dialed his phone again to see if I could hear it ring in the garage.

On the seventh or eighth ring, someone answered.

"Hello?" I asked.

I could hear breathing from the other end of the phone. He cleared his throat. "Did you think I wouldn't spot your tail, Lieutenant Kane?"

It took me a second to recognize the voice and realize

what we were dealing with. I squeezed the phone in my hand until my knuckles were white. "Where's my detective?"

I pointed at my phone and mouthed the word *Cross* to the captain and Hank.

"Oh, I wouldn't worry about him. He'll turn up sooner or later."

"Where the hell is he?"

"How is my wife? Was she still watching the television? That's all that bitch ever did."

He knew we were at the house. I covered the mouthpiece on the phone. "Hank, get some officers to search the area. He knows we're here."

I uncovered the phone. "So, you are confirming that you killed your ex-wife?"

"We were as happy as ever for the first couple days after her procedure. Then she kind of started to go downhill. I kept drilling more holes, pouring in boiling water, but she just wouldn't respond. Tell me, Lieutenant, how does it feel to know you had me sitting right in front of you and you guys were too stupid to see it?"

"I'm going to find you."

Cross made a sound like a yawn. "Did you like the girl found in Ybor the other night? I think her name was Anna or something."

The girl was probably staring at the wall in her hospital room. The thought made my blood boil. I didn't know what else to say to him. He didn't just need to be caught. He needed to be taken out of the population permanently.

"What do you want? Why are you doing this? Where is my detective?"

He laughed. "I want notoriety—just a few moments in the spotlight, so to speak. Now that we're acquainted, I may have found a better way to get it." He paused.

I figured he was waiting for me to comment on his statement. I didn't.

"The fun is just starting. Your detective is stuffed in a supply closet at the mall. I'd hurry. I gave him a pretty good-sized dose of Xylazine. It might have been enough to kill him. I'm not a hundred percent sure. See you soon." He hung up.

"Come on." I slid my phone back into my pocket and headed for the car.

The captain and Hank followed. "What did he say?" Bostok asked.

"Said Donner is stuffed in a supply closet in the mall. He drugged him. Call 9-1-1 and have paramedics meet us there. I'm going to get a hold of the mall's security office and get them searching. Is there a way we can get a GPS location on Donner's phone?"

"I'll call tech," Bostok said.

I hopped into our cruiser, and Hank jumped in the passenger side. The captain and Jones got in the captain's car and followed us over to the mall. I made the call to security on the way over. The man I spoke with told me one of their guys would meet us up front when we arrived. We parked our cars at the front curb of the mall, and I led us in. An older man in a security uniform met us at the doors.

He had a white mustache and a large beard. He might have been the mall's Santa during winter.

"You the officer I spoke with?" he asked.

I nodded. His nametag read Jerry Ott.

"We just found your detective. He's in the back hall by the food court. This way."

We followed him in and past the food court. The mall was set to close, and it was mostly empty aside from employees and a couple last-minute shoppers. He led us to the emergency exit at the end of the hall containing the restrooms. He pushed the door open and walked through. Twenty feet down the hall, another man in a security uniform knelt next to Donner in the middle of the hallway. We went to his side. The security guard's name badge read Caffe. I looked down at Donner. His face was covered in spattered blood. He was breathing but unconscious.

"This how you found him?" I asked.

He jerked his head toward the door a few feet away. "Found him in the janitor's closet over there. He's breathing but not responding."

I felt for Donner's pulse. It seemed strong. His jacket hung open, his service weapon missing.

"Jones, can you go and wait for the ambulance? Show the first responders where we are."

He nodded.

The security guard we'd met at the front doors, Ott, accompanied Detective Jones back into the mall.

"What happened here?" Caffe asked.

"A man we are after attacked him. Show me the closet

you found him in."

The captain waited with Donner while Caffe showed me into the janitor's closet. It was five feet by five. A mop bucket sat on the floor. Miscellaneous cleaning supplies filled a shelf at the back. None of Donner's belongings were on the floor. His service weapon was nowhere in sight. We went back to Donner and the captain. I felt Donner's jacket and pants pockets. The captain flashed me a questioning look.

"Service weapon is gone." I checked the final pocket inside his sport coat. "No keys, badge, wallet, anything."

Jones led the EMTs back to us. They loaded Donner onto a gurney and started administering a hand ventilator. One of the attending technicians came over to us.

"How does he look?" I asked.

"We are just trying to get some extra oxygen into him right now. His breathing is a little shallow."

"The blood on his face?" I asked.

"Not his. It looks like it was expelled on him."

"Is he going to be all right?" Hank asked.

"Well, we are going to take him over to Brandon Regional Hospital. You should be able to speak with a physician there later."

I rubbed my head. "Thanks."

The EMTs wheeled Donner out the exit at the end of the hallway, and the door slammed shut.

Captain Bostok paced back and forth in the hall.

"Did tech get anything on his phone?" I asked.

"No signal." Bostok shook his head. "We're done, guys.

I'm going to make the call to the feds in the morning."

"You can't," I said.

"It's done, Kane."

I had no intentions of turning the case over. "You know how much backlash you'll get from the other officers if you give up a case where one of our own was attacked."

He fired back, "That's why I'm turning it over to the FBI. I won't risk my men."

I protested more, but the captain held his stance. The feds were going to come in either way.

We argued back and forth for another ten minutes. The captain closed the conversation with the threat of time off if needed.

I left the mall angry. I stewed in the car as Hank and I made our way back to the station.

He was the first to break the silence. "You have to see the captain's dilemma. He does have a point."

I nodded. "He has a point all right—covering his ass. The coverage from the media is going to get out of hand. If Cross is not brought in soon, it will threaten our jobs and positions within the department. Bostok is trying to cover his ass to keep his job."

Hank decided he was going to try to be the voice of reason. "What we found at his ex-wife's house isn't normally what we deal with. This guy is on another level. This is the kind of case that the feds have the ability and resources to investigate."

I'd had enough of Hank's talking and didn't respond. Cross was a psychopath and not one who I was looking to deal with any longer, but I wanted to be the one to remove him from society.

The day had been one of my longest and worst on the job. I just wanted to get back to the station, drop off Hank, get in my car, and go home. A beer on the couch and then bed—I was interested in nothing else until morning, when I'd resume my argument with the captain about keeping the case in house.

We parked the Charger in the station's lot and walked in. Still steaming, I walked fast and hard to my office to grab my car keys and lock it up. On my way out of the station, my cell phone rang. I didn't recognize the number, but it was local. I let out a deep breath to relax and clicked Talk.

"Carl Kane."

"Hello Carl, this is Candice, a couple doors down from you."

I wondered how she'd gotten my phone number. "Hey, Candice. What's up?"

"Well, I found Butch here roaming around the hallway. He walked right in my door when I opened it. Looks like he got out somehow—just wanted to give you a heads-up."

That explained how she'd called. My number was on Butch's tag. "All right. I'm heading home now. I should be there in around ten minutes if that's okay."

"Sure, that would be fine."

"Thanks for grabbing him. I'm on my way."

"No problem." She hung up.

I wasn't sure how Butch could have gotten out into the hall. The front door and patio were the only ways in or out.

He didn't go five stories off the patio and walk back up. He didn't get past me out the front door that morning. *Did he?*

I got into my Mustang and drove the short distance back to my condo. I parked in the underground structure and took the elevator up to the fifth floor.

Candice lived in unit 500A. I stopped at her door and knocked. It opened. She stood, holding my cat in her arms. Butch purred and licked at her hand. I'd never seen him that loving before. I was tempted to leave him with her. She passed him over, and I carried him back to my door. He squirmed, trying to get away.

Chapter 35

He tossed the phone in a pond after making the call, sure the cops would try to get a location on it, and Bob didn't want Kane to know where he was just yet. Finding out where the lieutenant lived had been easy. Bob kept it simple. He just followed Kane after he left work Thursday night. Bob even found out what bar he liked to go to—all very valuable information. He decided to pop in and learn more about the good lieutenant.

He let himself into Kane's condo. A troubled youth had taught him the finer points of lock picking. As he opened the door, a big cat rushed past him and disappeared down the hall.

He closed the door at his back and walked inside. Bob took in his surroundings.

He let out a catcall whistle. "Nice pad, Lieutenant Kane."

Bob walked across the dining room to the kitchen. He dug through the lieutenant's kitchen drawers. Aside from silverware, foam beer holders, and junk, he found nothing of any significance. He walked over to the refrigerator and opened the door. He took out a beer.

"Don't mind if I do."

He cracked the can's top, took a drink, and set it on the counter. He walked to the living room. A rack of DVDs stood in the corner. Bob thumbed through them, inspecting the titles. He smiled—they had similar tastes in movies. He walked through the rest of the condo and rummaged the drawers and cabinets. In the back of the master bedroom closet, he found a standing safe. He pulled at the handle. The four-inch-thick metal door swung open.

He laughed. "Nice security."

Firearms, ammo, and related items filled the safe. He already had the detective's gun from the mall stuffed in his waistline, so he didn't need another. He preferred a more personal approach, anyway. On the top shelf sat a file of paperwork. He dug through it. They were divorce papers, dated almost two years prior. He looked at the names—Carl and Samantha Kane. He dug through the rest of the file and found paperwork from Carl Kane and Samantha Merray.

Must be her maiden name.

An address caught his eye under her name. Bob noticed the time on Kane's alarm clock next to his bed. The lieutenant could return at any moment. He started toward the door. Out of the corner of his eye, he spotted a dry-erase board on the refrigerator. A list of groceries was written there. He grabbed the beer he'd set down on the counter earlier and took another swig. A smile crossed his face when he thought of a message to write. He wiped the grocery list off and took the marker from the bottom of the board.

Chapter 36

I put my key in the door to unlock the deadbolt, and the door pushed open. Someone had broken into my condo. I always locked my door. I set Butch down on his feet in the hallway and pulled my gun from my shoulder holster. With the barrel of my gun, I pushed the door the rest of the way open. Things were out of place and drawers opened. Butch ran past me and jumped onto the couch—stupid cat. *The one time I set him in the hall to run the other way, he runs inside.* He didn't seem concerned that someone might be in the condo. I went through the entire place, clearing the rooms one by one. The place was empty. I contemplated not calling it in or waiting until morning to report it. I noticed the beer on the counter and walked over. The beer was sweating. Whoever had been in my condo had just left. Then I saw the note.

The dry-erase board, which I seldom used to write my grocery list, had a message written across it. It read, "My next will be the best yet. At least for you." It was signed with a sketch of the brand Cross had been placing on women.

I didn't care to try to interpret the message. All it told me was that Cross had been there and was planning to hurt more women. I called the station and reported the break-in to Sergeant Mueller, working patrol. When I hung up, I dialed the captain to let him know what had happened. Then I sat and waited. I expected the place to be filled with feds within minutes. Instead, a half hour later, I had a condo full of cops from my precinct.

The captain walked into my condo and approached. "Cross?"

I nodded. "Where's the feds?"

He ignored my jab. "Show me the note."

I took him to the dry-erase board in the kitchen. Pax dusted it for prints. He looked up as we stood in front of him. "Pulled a few prints from it. I'm going to take the beer can back to the lab too." Pax set the dry-erase board, now sealed in a large see-through bag, on the breakfast bar so the captain could read it.

"What do you make of the message?" the captain asked.

I shrugged. "Another taunt of some kind from Cross."

Bostok let out a deep breath. "Anything missing?"

"Not at first glance, no."

The captain took a seat at the breakfast bar. "What's his deal with you?"

"Who knows, Cap."

"He's got something for you. You've never run across this guy before?"

"Never." I shrugged. "Your guess is as good as mine."

He nodded. "I thought about our conversation earlier."

"Yeah, I wanted to apologize."

"No, I understand a hundred percent. You want to catch this guy yourself. I'm going to make a call to the local Bureau and ask them for assistance. I'm not going to let them take over. You are still going to be the lead. This is going to remain our case. You'll just have the feds at your disposal."

"Are they going to go for that?"

"No state lines were crossed so they can't just take the case from us if we don't hand it over to them. Plus, when we find Cross, they can look good because they helped."

"What about jurisdiction issues?"

"We're owed enough favors to make it work."

"Thanks, Cap."

He stood. "Find Cross, Kane. We can't afford to have another body or lobotomized woman."

"I will."

"I'll see you at the station in the morning." Bostok left.

Butch wailed from behind the bathroom door. I'd locked him in there when the guys from the station arrived and informed everyone in the house to not open the door. There would be hell to pay when he got out. He didn't like being confined.

The officers looked at everything, touched everything, and dusted everything. I tried to take a mental inventory of everything in my condo. My recent lack of sleep was making it difficult. After I went from room to room three times with the night-shift detectives, nothing appeared to be missing.

As much as the thought of Bob Cross wandering around my condo was disturbing, I just wanted everyone to get out so I could go to sleep. He wasn't there, and if he came back while I was home, he would have problems. The last of the police left a little after one in the morning.

I let Butch out, and he repaid me with a violent thrashing of my leg, which I'd expected. Cross, the prick, had drunk my last beer. I headed straight to bed. Sleep came in short bursts. Every sound jarred me awake. Every creak sounded like a footstep. My service weapon spent the night stuffed under my pillow.

Chapter 37

The door lock clicked and allowed him entry. He relocked the door behind his back. The house was dark except for a small amount of light coming from the laundry room. Bob searched the wall for a security system but didn't see anything. He'd gotten the address straight from the divorce papers.

The address was double-checked online on his way over. A number of results all showed the same owner's information, Samantha and Martin Bridgeman. Bob took the gun from his waistband with his left hand. He held it just as a precaution. In his right hand, he held a needle filled with Xylazine. His pocket contained another. He crept through the lower level of the house, room by room. They were all clear. He walked to the laundry room, where a door sat beyond the stainless-steel washer and dryer. He opened it and peeked through into a garage with two cars inside—they were home. Children's bikes sat along the garage's back wall. He went back into the house and found his way to the staircase up to the second level.

Bob wondered if the kids were home. He continued up the steps until he hit the landing of the second floor. A night-light lit the back area of the hall. Some construction paper, spelling out the word *Belle*, covered the door. Bob turned around. The master bedroom had to be the other way. He pushed open the doors on his way to the end of the hall. He passed two closets with folding doors, a bathroom, and what, through the crack of the door, looked like a boy's bedroom. He stopped at the cracked-open door at the end of the hall. It had to be the master bedroom.

He listened for any noises coming from inside the room and heard what seemed like the faint sound of a man snoring—he wasn't sure. He rested his thumb on the syringe's plunger and pushed the door open. Bob lurked into the room. A streetlight out front provided a small amount of light through the drawn blinds. He saw the couple in bed, asleep. The woman lay closer to Bob. The carpet masked the sound of his footsteps. Bob crouched at the foot of the bed and remained quiet, his breathing echoing in his head. He tried to calm himself. He needed to deal with the larger threat first.

Bob crept to the man's side of the bed, where he lay facing outward, snoring. Bob moved right in front of the man's face and caught the smell of whiskey hanging on the guy's breath. Bob switched his grip on the syringe and held it like a knife ready to strike. He raised his arm and stabbed the needle into the man's neck, thumbing down the plunger as soon as it hit skin.

The man awoke in an instant and spun over. His movement ripped the needle from Bob's hand, and it disappeared into the bed sheets. The man sat up and kicked himself back across the bed. Bob ducked to the floor. The man's frantic movements woke his wife.

"Honey, what's wrong? Spider again?" she asked, still half asleep and unaware of what had taken place.

"What the… There's a… Sam, call…" The man fell back to the bed, unconscious before he could warn his wife.

"It was just a dream. Go back to sleep." The woman pushed the man back toward his side of the bed.

Bob reached into his pocket and pulled out the other pre-filled syringe.

The woman lay on her stomach. Her right leg and half of her buttocks stuck out from the sheets of the bed. It might as well have had a bull's-eye on it. He jammed the needle into the side of her buttocks and thumbed the plunger down. She swatted at it in her sleep and made contact with Bob's hand holding the needle. She flipped over and pulled the covers to her chin. Bob didn't try to hide.

"Oh my god! Marty!" she screamed.

Bob lunged at her. He grabbed her in a bear hug and whispered in her ear. "It's time for us to have some fun, Samantha."

They'd be the last words she'd hear before going limp in his arms. He dropped her to the floor and went in search of the children. When he finished, he went back to the master bedroom and dragged Samantha down the stairs and out to the garage. Bob took the keys to one of the cars from the key hook on the wall. He popped the trunk to a newer black Lexus. He dumped Samantha inside and closed it.

The man was next. Bob dragged him down the stairs and out to the garage. On the workbench, he found a spool of wire and used it to hog-tie the man. He dumped him in the trunk of the other car and slammed the lid.

He backed the Lexus containing Samantha out of the garage and parked his taxi inside. His cargo from the taxi was transferred over to the Lexus. He hit the button on the visor to close the garage door and left.

He needed to find a cheap motel with ground-level entry—a place where he could get her indoors and perform a procedure without a bunch of people nosing around—something seedy and out of town. He knew just the place. It was a half hour away.

Bob made a right off of Highway 41 into the trashy little motel in Gibsonton. Most of the town was populated by carnival folk, drug addicts, cheap hookers, and drunks. The neighborhood didn't look any better during the daylight. The sign in front of the Weary Traveler Motel would have said Vacancy if all the letters were lit. It was a run-down single-story building shaped like a U. Bob's options were seven dollars an hour or thirty-two for the whole night. He dug through his wallet. He had only twenty bucks. The wallet he'd taken from the cop was empty aside from a couple credit cards, which were sure to be canceled or tracked by then. He thumbed back through his wallet and pulled out a new Visa. He peeled off the activation sticker.

The name on it was Dan Ellison. He gave the hollow-eyed front-desk woman the card. She didn't ask for ID. She handed him a couple metal keys—they had plastic tags with room numbers on them. He moved the car to room 118. Darkness lay over the motel's parking lot. The only light came from a halogen motion light mounted to the outside of the office. When it clicked off, he popped the trunk of the Lexus and pulled Samantha into the room.

Chapter 38

My alarm woke me just after six in the morning. After a quick shower, I went through the usual routine of getting dressed and throwing on my shoulder holster. I walked out to the kitchen to deal with Butch. I opened the cupboard and grabbed his food. As soon as it hit his dish, he came running from the living room. I started some coffee and went to the fridge to get the creamer. An empty one-foot-by-one-foot square—where the dry erase board had been—stared me in the face. I tried to put the thought of Bob Cross standing in my kitchen out of my head.

I sat down at the breakfast bar to drink my coffee and watch the morning news. Every local news outlet was airing coverage of the case. They had footage of his ex-wife's house. Bob Cross played on every channel. Every photo had the name Psycho Surgeon below it. They were doing their best to make him famous. He wouldn't be able to hide for long with the kind of exposure he was getting.

I took a sip from my coffee and set it on the counter. I

grabbed the report from the break-in and looked it over. The rustling of the paper must have sounded like food to Butch. He jumped up on the breakfast bar and sent my coffee splashing toward me in a brown tidal wave. I did my best to dodge the flying coffee but still caught a good portion of the liquid with my suit jacket and pants. I let out a deep breath. That was probably an accident, but it also might have been payback for locking him in the bathroom.

I walked to my bedroom to change. When I pulled open the closet door to grab a new suit, something in my safe caught my eye. My safe door stood open, and I stared inside. The other officers and I had gone through my safe to make sure all of my firearms were accounted for. They were, but I hadn't noticed that the manila envelope containing my divorce papers looked as though it had been gone through. I pulled it from the shelf in my safe and opened it.

I had looked over the documents a thousand times. Our divorce hadn't been quite as clean as I would've liked, and my father had always stressed that I should never sign anything I didn't understand. I went over the entire bundle of documents so many times that I had memorized them. Samantha wasn't going to get anything more than she deserved, especially after cheating on me. I couldn't imagine why the detectives would have gone through it. I dug through the sheets of paper. Everything was there.

A thought of what Cross had meant by his note on the fridge bubbled up in my head. *"My next will be the best yet. At least for you."*

The "at least for you" part bothered me. He might have

246

had Samantha's name and address. As much as I hated it, I needed to call and check on her. I found the last number I had for her and dialed. It went to voicemail. I needed to find a phone number for Samantha's house. If I could get her on the phone, it would at least put my mind at ease. I didn't have a phone book, and didn't feel like turning on my computer and running a search. The quickest way to get her number was to call my sister. She picked up right away.

"Hey, Carl. We're just getting up. What's going on?"

"Hey, I need a number for Samantha. It's work related."

"Work related, huh? Don't give me that. What do you want to talk to her for? You remember that she's remarried, right?"

"I don't have time for this. Just give me her damn number."

"Geez. Whatever. Bite my head off."

"Mel, what's her number?"

"Hold on."

She got it and rattled it off in a snotty tone. It was the same number I already had.

"What's the phone number for her house?"

"You can't call their house. What are you, crazy?"

I'd had enough arguing with my sister. If I told her the real reason why I wanted to get a hold of Samantha, she would freak out.

"Forget it. I'm sure he's in the phone book. Don't worry about it."

I hung up.

Whether Sam was in any kind of danger or not, I didn't

know. However, if I told my sister my reason for wanting to contact her, she would be planning a funeral within a day. I fired up my computer and searched for their house phone number. Martin Bridgeman's home phone number came up right away. I tried the number twice but got no answer.

I looked at my watch. I had enough time to get out to their house and be back to the station before my shift started. Though I'd remembered the general area of Samantha's new house, I wrote the address down in my notepad to be sure. I finished getting dressed, grabbed my keys, and headed downstairs.

Around seven thirty, I pulled into their neighborhood, a twenty-year-old subdivision filled with upper-class homes. At the top of the market, the homes in the neighborhood were worth a million dollars each.

I squinted at the numbers on the mailboxes and houses. I caught a house number over a garage and continued up the street. I stuffed my notepad back into my pocket. "Four more."

I'd been to Doctor Bridgeman's house once in the past. Samantha insisted we go and eat dinner with the dentist and his wife. Little did I—or his wife—realize they were already sleeping together. Another half a block up, I found the address. I slowed as I passed, hunching down to get a better view of the house through the passenger side window. The driveway was empty. Everything looked normal.

The home was smaller than I remembered. It was a tan two story with a terracotta tile roof and expansive landscaping. A pair of king palms took center stage along the sidewalk leading up to the front door. A two-car garage stood to the right, as well as another for one car—three cars total.

I pulled to the curb and walked up to the house. I stopped outside their front door. A carved wooden sign sat in the landscaping to the side. It read, "The Bridgemans".

I shook my head in disgust and knocked on the front door. I prepared myself for the most awkward greeting imaginable. No one came. I tried the doorbell. No response. I continued waiting for another minute or two and checked my watch—just after seven thirty. They could still be sleeping.

I walked to the edge of the house and turned at the garage. Two first floor windows sat on the side. The location of the one closest to me told me it belonged to the garage, and the other sat toward the back of the house. I walked to the first window and tried to peek inside. The thick blinds did a great job of preventing me from making anything out in the garage. I tried the next window at the back. Again, blinds blocked my view inside.

I walked back to my car to head out. Nothing looked out of the ordinary. They weren't home, were asleep, or had seen me and didn't want to answer. I decided to keep trying to call her throughout the day—maybe even to call Marty's dental office to see if it was open later. That was all I could do.

I pulled up to the station a few minutes after eight o'clock. Just as the day before, the media had taken up permanent residence in front of the building. As I pulled around the station, I spotted the television crews recording from the sidewalk. I pulled in and parked. As I walked toward the door of the station, Officer Johnson greeted me.

"Morning, Lieutenant." He opened the door to let me in.

"Johnson." I nodded. "You take a job as the doorman here?"

He smiled. "Looks like it. We had reporters sneaking into the employee parking and trying to get interviews. Sergeant Timmons put me out here to shoo them off."

"For how long?"

He shrugged. "Whole shift, I guess. Until I'm told otherwise."

"Well, have fun."

"Tons."

I walked inside and made my way to my office. I could see the captain and Major Danes talking in the captain's office next door. The captain saw me walking past and waved me in.

"Major. Cap."

"Morning, Lieutenant. I hear you had a break-in. Cross?" Major Danes asked.

"Appears so."

"You didn't find anything missing, though?"

"No, nothing missing, but…"

"But?" Bostok asked.

"I didn't notice it until this morning. My divorce documents had been gone through."

"Do you think it was Cross?" the major asked.

I shrugged. "I guess there's no way of actually knowing if it was Cross or not. It could have been one of the detectives."

The captain appeared to be kicking something around in his head. "Call your ex-wife," he said.

"Tried. No answer. I even tried stopping there, but they could've been asleep or out of town for all I know. I haven't talked to my ex-wife in almost a year."

"Did anything look off when you went to the house?" the captain asked.

"Not that I saw."

"How hard did you look?" Major Danes asked.

"Not that hard, I guess. I rang the doorbell, knocked, and took a quick look into a couple windows. I left within a few minutes."

"Any signs of a forced entry?"

"If there had been on the front door, I think I would have noticed it. I never went around back."

The major set his jaw. "Go back over there and have a better look around. Take an extra officer from patrol with you."

His words came across more like an order than a suggestion. I nodded.

"Okay. Kane, before you head out," the captain cleared his throat, "I called and enlisted the help of the Bureau this morning. They are going to send us over two agents later this afternoon. In the meantime, they have put alerts out on Bob Cross's credit cards and bank account. If he accesses either, we'll have his location. I want you to have a meeting with the agents when they arrive."

"That's fine. Anything else?" I asked.

"That's it."

"Any word on how Donner is doing?" I asked.

"They kept him overnight and sent him home this morning. He's fine."

"Good."

Chapter 39

Roaches scattered across the worn carpet when he flipped on the lamp. A coughing attack had woken him from his sleep. His hand was covered in blood from his lungs. He wiped it on the edge of the chair he sat on. Samantha lay bound to the bed. She wore the familiar green lingerie. Bob looked back at the digital clock that sat on the nightstand—8:16 a.m. He'd woken up a few times in the last hour from Samantha making noise. She was coming around. He needed to give her another dose of the tranquilizer. In the middle of the night, a couple in a drugged stupor had rented the next room. He didn't want Samantha coming to enough to realize the situation she was in and scream. He went to her side.

Her eyes rolled around in her head before coming straight and focusing. She fumbled her words. "Where am I?"

"You're in a motel room."

"Why?"

"Because this is where we'll have to work."

"Wha… Who are you?"

"I'm Bob Cross. The press has been calling me the Psycho Surgeon, though."

She squinted and shook her head. "What?"

"Psycho Surgeon."

"Where am I?"

"I just told you. You're in a motel room."

"For what?" She started to fade back into unconsciousness.

"I'm going to cut into your brain." Bob got up and walked to the small desk. He grabbed a vial of the Xylazine and loaded up a syringe. "I've had enough small talk." He walked back over to her and stuck the needle into the side of her neck. He pushed the tranquilizer in—silence.

"It's time to brand you," he said.

She didn't respond.

Chapter 40

Johnson got relieved from his door duty to make the trip with me over to my ex-wife's house. I tried calling her phone a few more times on the way, but the calls still went straight to voicemail. I pulled up to the house and parked at the curb. Johnson pulled his marked cruiser in behind me and got out.

"This is us here." I pointed to the house.

We walked up the driveway and went to the front door. I reached out to the bell and pressed it in hard. It dinged inside the house. I heard no one rummaging around inside, no footsteps, and no voices.

We waited another minute. No one came to the door.

"Johnson, you're in uniform. Why don't you check around back?"

"No problem."

I stood at the front door and rang the bell again. I waited. Johnson came around the other side of the house.

He shook his head as he approached. "Everything looks normal."

I knelt down and inspected the front door opening, searching for any kind of pry marks or anything of the sort. The door and sill looked normal. I twisted the knob—locked.

"You check the garage?" he asked.

"I tried earlier. You can't see inside."

"Let me have a look."

Officer Johnson walked to the side of the garage, and I followed. We got to the window. Johnson started contorting himself, trying to see in. He cocked his head one way, crouched, and then stood on his tiptoes. His final method was to look through the tiny slits that the string that operated the blinds passed through.

"Are you seeing anything?" I asked.

"Not really."

A thud came from inside the garage. Then another. Then more.

"You hear that?" I asked.

Johnson nodded his head, "Yeah. It's coming from inside."

I turned my head and stuck my ear against the garage window. The thuds grew louder, and then I caught something else. Someone shouted, "Help!"

"Call it in." I motioned for Johnson to stand back and put my elbow through the window. I cleared away the glass and pulled myself through. The thuds came from the trunk of a black Acura—parked next to it was a yellow taxi. I pulled my weapon.

The shouting for help continued from the trunk of the

car, followed by repeated thumping. Someone was kicking from inside.

I rapped on the top of the trunk lid. "Be quiet. We'll get you out of there in a second."

I motioned for Johnson to come in. He climbed through the window and drew his service weapon. I spoke just above a whisper. "We need to see if anyone is in the house."

He nodded.

I went to the door leading inside and slowly twisted the knob. Johnson and I entered the house. It was quiet—no footsteps of anyone running, no cries for help. We moved room to room and cleared the lower level. No one was there. We moved upstairs—no children, no Samantha, and no Bob Cross. We headed back for the garage.

I gave the lid a rap with my knuckles. "Who's in there?"

"Martin Bridgeman. I live here. Get me out."

I opened the car and searched for a trunk-release button. The button was recessed at the left bottom of the dash. I thumbed it down—nothing. I went back to the trunk. "Where are the keys?"

"They are in here with me. I'm tied up. Find something to break in. There are tools up on the work benches."

"You don't have a spare set of keys?"

"I don't know where they are. Just break in."

I pulled a crowbar from the bench and jammed it down into the gap between the trunk and rear bumper. I pressed down with all my strength, but the trunk didn't budge.

"Johnson, give me a hand with this."

He came over, and we both put all our weight into it.

The metal of the car's trunk lid bent, popped free, and flew up. Inside was my ex-wife's husband, hogtied in his boxer shorts. I looked at him lying there in his urine-soaked underwear. He was pathetic. He was out of shape and balding and had some stupid-looking mustache sitting on his lip. *This is what Samantha left me for? This is the guy she cheated on me with?* I made a scissors sign with my fingers toward Johnson, and he brought over a set of snips from one of the workbenches. I cut the wire that bound Marty. We got him to his feet.

Marty sat on the rear bumper of his car. "Carl, what the hell are you doing here?"

"Trying to find Samantha. Where is she?"

"I don't know. Who the hell tied me up and locked me in my trunk? Why is there a taxi in my garage?"

"Tell me what happened. Do it quick," I said.

He pointed to his boxer shorts. "I wet my damn underwear. Can I go change first?"

I stuck my finger in his face again. "Tell me where she is. Tell me what happened."

"I don't know. I don't know what happened. We went to sleep like normal. When I woke up, I was hogtied in a trunk."

"Were your kids here?" I asked.

"No, this is their mother's weekend."

"You don't know who did this to you?"

"No. The last thing I remember was going to sleep last night." He looked around the garage. "Samantha isn't here?"

"No."

"Are you going to tell me what the hell is going on here and why there's a damn taxi cab in my wife's parking spot?"

"What does Samantha drive?"

"A black Lexus IS."

"What's the tag number?"

He gave it to me and I called it in as stolen. I pointed at the door leading into the house and gave Bridgeman a shove. "Inside."

He stumbled forward. "Fine."

We went back into the house. The smell of the place brought back bad memories. Samantha had often come home with that exact odor stuck on her. It wasn't a bad smell, but at the moment, it made me want to hog-tie Bridgeman again and stuff him back into the trunk. My feelings for him needed to be pushed aside. The only thing that mattered was finding her.

I sent Johnson with Marty to his bedroom. I instructed him to give it a quick search while Bridgeman cleaned himself up. Johnson came back out a few minutes later, holding a syringe on a piece of paper.

"Cab, syringe—had to be the Psycho Surgeon, right?" he asked.

I looked at him out of the corner of my eye. "It's Bob Cross. Leave the Psycho Surgeon crap for the media."

"Yeah, that's what I meant, Bob Cross. Why would he leave evidence? He never did before."

"Because he doesn't care. We know who he is. And now he has my ex-wife. He left the cab here so he can move around without being spotted." I rubbed my eyes.

I had to tell Bridgeman what was going on. A serial killer had taken Samantha because of me. Bridgeman shouted profanities and put on a show. He flailed his hands in the air and called me every name in the book. He stormed halfway across the kitchen at me but stopped dead in his tracks when I cocked a fist. I still owed him for sleeping with her when she had still been my wife. He retreated and took a seat at the kitchen table.

We needed to go through the house room by room and look for anything Cross could have left behind—any little scrap or clue that could tell us where he'd taken her. We needed to dig through the taxi and see if we could find anything there. I dialed the captain. He said he'd send Rick, Jones, and Hank out. Johnson and I were to sit tight until everyone arrived.

I sat down at the kitchen table. After a few minutes of waiting, my phone buzzed in my pocket. The caller ID said it was an unknown caller. I clicked Talk.

"This is Lieutenant Kane."

"Hey, Carl."

"Who the hell is… Cross? Where is Samantha?"

"I may have overestimated you. I gave you fair warning that I was going to take her."

"If you touch one hair on…"

Cross interrupted with a laugh. "Please. Cliché threats, Lieutenant? You can do better than that. Tell me, what's it like sitting in the house with your replacement? Does it stir bad feelings? Are you sitting with your rival now? Oh, you did find him in the trunk, didn't you?"

"How do you know where I am?"

"Don't bother scouring the neighborhood. I'm not watching you. Your report of her car being stolen came across my trusty police scanner."

"What the hell do you want? Where is Samantha?"

"Why so much concern for an ex-wife? Do you still love her, Lieutenant?"

I didn't respond. He wanted to play some kind of sick mind game with me, and I had no interest in giving him the satisfaction.

"You better answer, or I'll start tinkering with her right now. Listen."

I heard the sound of a drill in the background. "Yes."

"Yes what?"

"Yes, I still love her."

Marty stared at me from the corner of the kitchen.

"Isn't that nice? We have a lot in common. My wife left me too. It's too late for Tina and me, but I'm sure you can still get Samantha back if you try. You've got to just keep drilling down to get to the root of the problem."

His words disgusted me.

He chuckled into the phone, finishing with a snort. "Did you get the joke there?"

"Yeah, it wasn't funny. Tell me what you want, Cross."

"Well, I'm kind of getting a late start this morning. Samantha and I had a long night."

"What did you do to her?"

"I just got done branding the little cow. That's it. Like I

said, I'm getting a late start today. I figure I'll probably go grab a bite to eat and run a couple errands before I come back and start on her. So you'll have a little time to find us. It wouldn't be any fun if you didn't have a chance. I'll make sure you get some clues to where we are."

"I'll find you."

"Maybe. Here's the reason for my call though, Carl. I want you to tell me which way I should do it. Transorbital or leucotomy? I figured I'd let you choose."

"I'm not choosing."

"Choose, or I do it now."

His end of the line went quiet.

I said nothing.

"I'm going to count to three. One… Two… Thr—"

I interrupted him. "Don't."

"I'm waiting for an answer."

I was silent, again.

He laughed into the phone. "All right, fine. I won't make you pick. I'll surprise you."

"I'll kill you if you do anything to her."

"Maybe. I'm thinking that I'll do the procedure while she's alert and awake. What do you think? Think she'll like that?"

"I'll find you, you sick piece of shit."

He yawned. "I'm just so weary from all this traveling." The sound of a drill filled the phone. "See you later, Carl." He hung up.

I slammed the phone down on the table.

Chapter 41

His claim that I had time didn't hold any weight with me. I didn't want to think about her being held against her will or what he might be doing to her. I was going to find him in the shortest time possible.

I went to the cab first. It belonged to Cross, so any clues would most likely be found there. I wasn't going to wait for forensics or anyone else. I looked for any trash on the floor. Maybe he had left something behind, indicating where he had been. I was digging around the floor of the cab when my eyes caught the taxi registration card on the dash. The name was Dan Ellison. The photo looked like Cross might look without the beard. I opened the glove box and searched for the vehicle's registration, which I found in an envelope with the insurance. They were both in Dan Ellison's name. *Who the hell is Dan Ellison? Why does that name sound familiar?*

I called the plates in to dispatch. They came back legal and up to date—issued to Dan Ellison. We got his address from the vehicle's registration. We confirmed it as current with the station. I hung up. Ellison and Cross were either connected or the same person. If Samantha was being held there, I didn't want to give him a forewarning.

Hank, Jones, and Captain Bostok walked into the kitchen. I talked to them about the conversation I'd had with Cross and what I had found. I also told them about Dan Ellison.

"Take two squad cars from patrol as backup. You, Jones, and Hank lead. Use your head," the captain said.

"Address is out of our jurisdiction," I said.

"Where is it?"

"Apollo Beach."

"I'll call ahead to the Hillsborough County Sheriff's Department. You'll be fine—just go."

"What about a warrant?"

The captain thought about it for a second. "If it's Cross or you see any sign of him, we already have the warrant. If it's not Cross, get this Ellison back to the station. His name is all over a vehicle involved. It's enough to bring him in."

The plan was loose, but it was all we had. I got Marty's home and mobile phone numbers. I told him I'd update him with anything I found. Jones and Hank got in my car for the ride over to Ellison's house. The address was twenty-five minutes south. Johnson followed us in his patrol car. Officer Henry met us en route. An HCSD car sat a few blocks from the address. He filed in behind us after we passed. We pulled into the subdivision and parked at the curb a block away from the house. We got out, and I went to the trunk of the car and put on a vest.

Hank flashed me a confused look.

"Someone has to go to the door," I said.

The deputy approached us. "Who's heading this up?" he asked.

I cinched the Velcro straps tight on the vest with my left hand and reached out for a handshake with my right. "Lieutenant Carl Kane, TPD Homicide."

He shook my hand. "Deputy Scott Tanner."

I introduced the rest of the team.

"What can I help with?" he asked.

"We have a person of interest at the address. Not sure if he's home and not sure the level of what we are walking into. He might be innocent and unaware of why we are there, or we could be walking up on a serial killer with a hostage, the hostage being my ex-wife."

His eyes grew. "Geez."

"I'm going to go to the door and try to make contact." I pointed to Hank and Jones. "The two detectives here will have my back. I want you backing us up, if you're all right with that."

"That's fine."

"I'm going to send my guys from patrol around the back of the house to make sure we don't get a runner."

We made our way up the street toward the house. It looked to have been built in the early 2000s. The outside was light-tan stucco. A ten-year-old oak tree sat in front of the house's front bay window. Low shrubs surrounded the front. The officers from patrol headed around toward the back—one in each direction. I walked to the front entryway while Hank and Jones went to the blind side of the doorway against the house. The deputy was behind them to the right.

"Ready?" I asked.

They nodded.

I knocked on the door. A flash of darkness and then light flickered in the peephole. Someone was looking out. I moved to the side of the door. It opened.

"Can I help you?"

I looked at the man standing there. He was clean shaven, short, and a little overweight. His hair was a few inches long and dark brown. He wore a red polo shirt and black slacks. He wasn't Bob Cross, but he wasn't that far off in appearance, minus the weight difference. Behind him, some kids sat in the living room playing video games on a big-screen TV. A woman sat in the kitchen, talking on the telephone. The man who'd answered the door looked me up and down, trying to figure out who I was and why I was there. From his position, he couldn't see my backup with their guns drawn.

"Are you Dan Ellison?"

"Yes."

"Mr. Ellison, I'm Lieutenant Carl Kane with the Tampa Police Department." I showed him my badge. "I need you to answer some questions for me."

His reaction would tell me about his involvement. I waited for him to run, to slam the door in my face, something. He just stood in the doorway.

"Questions? About what?"

"Bob Cross."

"Bob Cross? What do you want to talk to me about him for?"

"So you know him?"

"I used to work with him, yeah."

"Where?"

"Pet Med Plus."

It dawned on me why his name sounded familiar. He was on my sheet of employees for the place.

"We need to know why he is driving a taxi that belongs to you."

"What?" He stepped from the front door of the house and closed it behind him. He spotted Hank, Jones, and the deputy with their weapons drawn. "Whoa, what's going on here?" He held his hands up at shoulder level. "I didn't do anything."

"Step out here," I said. I brought him ten feet from the front of his house. "Do you have any weapons on you?"

"Weapons? No."

"Mind if I check?"

"Go ahead. I don't have anything on me."

I gave him a quick pat down. I nodded for the men to holster their weapons.

"Mr. Ellison, why is Bob Cross driving a taxi registered to you?"

"Taxi? I don't own a taxi. Never did."

"There is one titled to you, registered to you, insured by you."

"It must be a different Dan Ellison because it isn't me."

"Your address is on all the forms."

"Look, I'm telling you I don't own a taxi. I've never even

ridden in one."

I stared at him. He looked as if he was thinking about something.

"Wait a minute. That little prick."

"What?" I asked.

"He had to be the asshole who stole my wallet from my desk at work. So he registered a cab in my name? Is that what this is about? What did he do? Hit and run?"

"You haven't been watching the news?"

"No."

"He killed two people and incapacitated one. Right now, he is on the run with another."

He shook his head in disbelief. "What?"

My cell phone buzzed in my pocket. The caller ID on the screen said it was the captain.

"Sit tight for a second for me, Mr. Ellison." I motioned for Hank to follow me and for Jones to keep an eye on Ellison. I walked to the sidewalk and hit Talk. "Cap?"

"What's the scene?"

"This guy was a coworker. Said Cross may have stolen his wallet."

"Have Jones bring him back to the station either way. I just got word from Timmons. HCSD just called us. They located Samantha's car."

"Where is it?"

"Out in Gibsonton."

"Gibsonton? Where?"

The captain rattled off the location.

"Okay. I'm leaving now."

Chapter 42

He ditched the car a couple blocks away and walked back. A shiny new Lexus sitting in front of the ratty motel would've screamed that something was off. He left Kane a clue inside the car. It wouldn't matter either way.

Samantha Bridgeman lay strapped to the bed. Her hands and feet remained zip tied together. The blinds were drawn shut, so the room was dark. An old television in the corner provided the only source of light—it was playing a Saturday-afternoon movie from the seventies. Bob paced the room and focused on the small alarm clock on the night stand. It showed a couple minutes after two o'clock. He called in the location of Samantha's Lexus to the sheriff's department. He walked over and gave her another dose of the tranquilizer.

He left the drill, scalpel, and suture needles, but he stuffed the branding iron, ice pick, hammer, drugs, and lingerie into a pillowcase from the bed. He decided to hang onto the cop's gun just in case.

Bob headed out. He'd watch the show from a distance before continuing with the rest of the night's activities.

Chapter 43

Jones took Ellison back to the station and dismissed the other officers. Hank and I were nearing where her car had been spotted. I saw the Lexus from half a block away. Aside from the fact that there was a sheriff's cruiser behind it, in that neighborhood, it stuck out like a sore thumb. Hank and I pulled into the parking lot that the car was sitting in. We stepped out, and the deputy walked over to us.

"You my detectives from TPD?" he asked.

"Lieutenant Kane." I nodded toward Hank. "This is Sergeant Rawlings."

"Deputy Richard Williams. I guess someone called our station and reported a stolen vehicle and its location. I shot over and ran the plates. It came back as stolen. The alert said to contact the TPD."

"Thanks. Do you know if it's open?" I asked.

"Open with the keys in the ignition. That's why I'm still sitting here. It was stolen once—doesn't need to be stolen again."

I reached out and opened the door.

"Don't you want to have someone print this thing?"

I shook my head. "We already know who stole it."

He gave me a confused look.

We hopped in and searched for any sign of a clue that could point us to where Cross was holding Samantha. Hank put his face down to the carpet and searched under the passenger seat.

"Anything?" I asked.

"It's clean."

I grabbed the keys to look in the trunk. When the lid flipped open, I noticed hair on the trunk's carpet. It was the same color and length as Samantha's. At least it was the last time I saw her. I didn't see any blood, so I closed the trunk lid. We'd have to get the car towed back to our station so forensics could go over it. I hit the button on Samantha's key fob to lock the Lexus. I looked at the keys. One was old and worn. It was on the same ring as a number tag—118. I flipped the tag over. It came from a motel in Gibsonton. Underneath the name, it read, "hourly rates". My ex-wife wouldn't be caught dead in a rent-by-the-hour motel.

I looked at Deputy Williams. "Where is the Weary Traveler Motel?"

"Up the street here a mile or so."

"We need to get there now." I started for our car. "Can you lead the way?"

"Sure." The deputy went to his cruiser.

"Call back to your station for support on your mobile phone. The guy we're after has a scanner."

He nodded.

"Come on, Hank. Let's go."

We hopped into our car and followed the deputy from the lot. He flipped on his lights and sirens.

I called it into our dispatch from my cell phone. I didn't want Cross to know anyone was en route if he was monitoring the police bands. We headed south a little over a mile, weaving in and out of traffic. Deputy Williams cut the lights and siren a few blocks from our turn. He made a right into the motel's lot and pulled up to the side of the building. We followed in behind him. We were the only police there.

We piled out, and I asked the deputy to get our backs. He followed us to the room. The curtains were closed, so we couldn't get a visual inside. I pulled my service weapon and took the far side of the doorway. Hank tucked in behind me. The deputy covered us from behind. I pulled Samantha's keys from my pocket and slipped the hotel key into the door. With my gun in my right hand at my hip, I twisted the knob with my left and pushed the door open. I could see a good part of the room before I stepped to the side. No one ran out, and no shots were fired. I peered around the corner of the doorway. The room was dark. I spotted a lump in the bed, a person. We stayed low and entered—all guns pointed into the room.

Hank flipped on the lights. The room was empty except for the woman strapped to the bed. It was her.

"Sam!" I went to the bedside. Hank cleared the rest of the motel room. The deputy stepped inside.

"What the hell is this?" he asked.

Plastic covered the bed. The nightstand held a drill covered in blood and a scalpel. A few bottles of alcohol and needles for stitching lay across the nightstand. She lay in a pool of half-dried blood. Both sides of her head had been shaved. Above each ear, at her temple, were stitches. I checked her for a pulse and found it faint. I unhooked the straps holding her.

"One of you have something to cut these zip ties?" I asked.

Hank pulled a pocket knife from his pants, flipped it open, and passed it over. I cut away the ties on her hands and feet. Her hand was branded. Hank grabbed his phone and requested an ambulance.

I picked her up and laid her on the second bed. I leaned over her and opened her eyes with my fingers. "Samantha? Samantha?"

She didn't respond or wake up.

I sat there until EMS arrived. They couldn't tell me anything about her condition. They loaded her on a gurney and wheeled her out. I followed. The parking lot was filled with HCSD cars. I walked with the EMTs over to the back of the ambulance, where they loaded her inside. They told me they were going to take her to Tampa General Hospital and closed the doors. They hit the lights and sirens and pulled out. I walked back to the Charger and called Bridgeman.

"This is Marty."

"It's Carl. I found her."

"Well, let me talk to her."

"She's being taken to Tampa General."

"What the hell happened to her? Is she going to be okay?"

"I'm not sure. She was unresponsive when we found her."

"Unresponsive. What the hell is unresponsive?"

"Just go to Tampa General. I'll meet you there." I hung up.

Hank walked around the corner toward me as I leaned against the car.

"Any signs of Cross?" I asked.

He shook his head. "HCSD has a description of him. They are looking around the area. Nothing yet. The woman inside the motel office said the occupant of room 118 came in late last night. She gave me a copy of the invoice." Hank handed me the piece of paper. "The room was billed to a Visa belonging to Dan Ellison."

"How is that going to help us now?" I asked.

"Get the feds to watch Ellison's accounts. See if we get a hit somewhere else."

I nodded. "I'm going to the hospital. Are you staying here, or do you want me to drop you back at the station?"

"We have our forensics guys and people from the station coming out here. I'm going to stick around. I'll hitch a ride back."

"Okay, I'll talk to you later." I ducked into the car, closed the door, and pulled out.

Chapter 44

He opted not to stick around the scene any longer than needed. Bob sat at the bus stop two blocks away, waiting on a ride out of town. He'd watched a sheriff's car and an unmarked Charger fly past ten minutes prior and turn into the motel. Since then, more squad cars and an ambulance had pulled in. The bus pulled up, and Bob climbed the stairs. He took a seat and smiled.

Chapter 45

I parked in the visitor's section of the parking structure and walked across the parking lot to the emergency wing. I'd called on the way over. No one could tell me anything. I walked through the front doors and stopped at the reception area, where the woman at the counter stopped typing at her computer and looked up.

"What can I help you with?"

"I'm looking for Samantha Bridgeman. An ambulance brought her a few minutes ago."

"Are you a relation?"

I pulled out my badge. "Lieutenant Carl Kane, Tampa Police Department."

"She's being seen right now. If you'd like to have a seat in our waiting area, a doctor will let you know as soon as there's any information."

"Thank you." I walked over to the chairs and took a seat.

I sat there for ten minutes before Marty burst through the hospital's sliding doors. He bypassed the front desk and came straight toward me.

"What the hell happened to my wife?" He shoved me.

I let it go and took a step back. "The doctors are looking at her now. They will let us know as soon as they have any information."

He stuck his finger in my face. "I swear you'll pay for this. This is your fault. You're responsible."

I tried to ignore him.

"You and your stupid job. You're the one who put her in danger."

I looked at the floor.

He stepped closer. "If you were capable of doing your job, my wife would be at home safe right now."

Bridgeman was starting to test my resolve.

"Big dumb cop. All brawn and no brains. You'll pay for jeopardizing my family, Kane. You'll pay for jeopardizing the safety of my wife. Believe it." He shoved me again.

That was enough. Before I could weigh the consequences, I punched him as hard as I could in the stomach. My fist sank into his flabby midsection, and he folded. I grabbed him before he fell to the ground and pulled him in close. "If you weren't a worthless piece of shit that went after married women, she'd still be my wife in the first place." The words left my mouth through clenched teeth. I pushed him down into one of the empty chairs. "Now, sit down and shut up before I lose my temper."

He glanced up at me, his face red with pain. He looked as if he was about to say something but stopped before the words came out. I took a seat a few chairs away from him.

We sat quietly for over an hour, waiting for someone to give us news, any news. No one came.

Bridgeman broke the silence. "You want a coffee? I'm going to the cafeteria."

I nodded, and he walked off. I assumed the coffee to be a peace offering. Hank walked through the front doors of the emergency wing's entrance a few minutes later.

He spotted me waiting and came over. "Any news?"

I shook my head. "Still waiting. What about the scene? What did you guys come up with?"

"Forensics bagged and tagged everything. We haven't found Cross. He wasn't in the area. His face is all over every news channel, and every cop in a hundred-mile radius is on the lookout. It's just a matter of time."

Bridgeman walked back up, carrying two cups of coffee. He handed one to me and gave Hank a nod. Then he went and sat down out of earshot.

"How's Bridgeman dealing with all this?"

"He's just concerned about Samantha. We had a talk right when he got here. I think we're on the same page now."

Hank nodded.

A doctor approached from down the hall. I stood to greet him.

"I'm Doctor Anderson. You the officer inquiring about Samantha Bridgeman?" he asked.

"Lieutenant Carl Kane." Bridgeman walked over from the waiting area. "This is her husband, here. What can you tell us?"

"Well, she appears to be sedated with something. When they brought her in, the sutures on the sides of her head were still seeping blood."

"Sutures?" Bridgeman interrupted. He stared at me.

The doctor nodded and continued. "The sutures were fresh. We cut them away. I inspected the area and, well, I don't even know how to say this. Someone performed an operation on her brain."

"A what!" Bridgeman shouted.

Cross had lobotomized my ex-wife. Bridgeman went into a rage. He hurled questions at the doctor, spewed threats at me. I tuned him out and got the doctor's attention.

"How bad was the damage to her brain?" I asked.

"It's hard to tell. She's still under the influence of whatever she was sedated with. She's on an IV right now to flush her system. We'll have a better idea of her condition in the next few hours."

As soon as the doctor finished telling me about Samantha, I felt an impact and pain on the left side of my face. Bridgeman, the little weasel, had blindsided me with a punch when I wasn't looking. I turned to face him. Hank took him to the ground before I could react. The doctor took a few steps back to remove himself from the flying bodies. Hank pulled Bridgeman's right arm way up behind his back and put a cuff on him.

Bridgeman yelped in pain when Hank pulled up his other arm.

"Hank," I said.

Hank clicked the second cuff around his wrist and got off Bridgeman's back.

"Assaulting an officer. Real smart," Hank said.

Bridgeman grunted and groaned, lying on the cold hospital floor.

"Hank, take the cuffs off him."

"He just sucker punched you."

"Just take them off."

Hank put a knee in the small of Bridgeman's back and unhooked him. He put his face down next to Bridgeman's head. "One more swing, asshole, and I'm arresting your dumb ass. I don't care what he says." Hank stood and walked into the waiting area.

Bridgeman pulled himself to his feet. He turned to the doctor. "Can I see my wife?"

"Not yet. I'll let you know when you can. Are you guys going to be all right here?"

I nodded.

I stood at the windows overlooking the hospital's parking lot. Hank sat a few feet away, thumbing through a magazine.

Half an hour passed before the doctor came back.

I walked up. "How is she?"

"The effects of the sedative are starting to wear off. She spoke her name when asked. She stumbled with some of the other questions and tests. It's too soon to tell if her mental state is impaired from being drugged or the damage to the brain itself. We have a neurosurgeon on his way. As soon as he gets here, we'll have to get her into surgery to fix the damage to her skull. I can let you see her now if it's quick." Doctor Anderson motioned for us to follow and headed down the hall.

Marty looked back at me when I didn't start walking. "Are you coming?"

I shook my head. I didn't want to see her again in that state. They walked off.

Hank came to my side. "Hey, that's good news. She spoke."

I let out a deep breath. "It's my fault she's here in the first place."

"No, it's not. Why is it your fault? Because you used to be married to her?"

"I should have recognized that he was going after her sooner."

"Okay, by that logic, we should have caught him after the first woman or when he sat right in front of us at the station. Don't start thinking like that. We'll get him. He'll pay for this."

"You're right. He will pay."

Chapter 46

Hank left when Marty came back from seeing Samantha. Marty told me she'd recognized him and asked what happened. The neurosurgeon arrived around seven o'clock, and they took her into surgery. A few minutes after ten o'clock, Doctor Anderson met Marty and me in the waiting room.

"Well?" Marty asked.

"The surgery went well. We just moved her into the ICU for recovery."

"What did the surgeon say about the damage to her brain?" I asked.

"He spotted lacerations in the white matter of her prefrontal lobes."

"What does that mean? She's going to live, right?" Marty asked.

"She will. Now, with this kind of brain damage, I have to inform you that she may suffer some long-term effects."

"Long-term effects?" Marty asked.

"Motor skills, speech, cognitive ability. These are all things that might have been affected. I say *might have* because, unfortunately, we won't know the extent of the damage until she recovers."

"When can I see her?" Marty asked.

"It will be a while. She needs to rest—six to eight hours minimum. Someone will inform you when you can go in. You're more than welcome to wait here."

"Thank you, Doctor Anderson," I said.

The doctor nodded and walked to the nurse's station.

"Leave, Kane," Marty said.

"Excuse me?"

"You can't do anything here. I'll call you if there are any changes. Find him."

I wasn't going to argue with him. He had a point—I could do nothing at the hospital to help her or find Cross. I walked out the front doors toward the unmarked cruiser I'd come in. I pulled my cell from my pocket. It showed two voicemails and two text messages. I went through them as I walked. The two text messages had come from my sister. She wanted to know what was going on. The first voicemail had come from the captain. He wanted me to call him, no matter how late. I hit the callback button, and he picked up within a few rings.

"How's Samantha?" he asked.

I entered the parking structure and walked toward the car. "She's out of surgery. They can't tell us the extent of the damage for a while."

"Hank said she spoke?"

"Yeah. She recognized her husband. I guess that's a good thing. Anything on Cross?"

"The feds that came in to help are now tracking all credit-card and bank activity from Dan Ellison. They'll be at the station in the morning for a meeting."

"What's going on with Ellison?"

"We dug into him pretty good. He's clean. There's nothing that connects him to Cross. We kicked him loose."

"Okay."

"Do you need a couple days, Kane?"

"No, I'll be there tomorrow morning for the meeting."

"You sure? If you need the time, take it."

"I said I'll be there." I unlocked the cruiser with its keychain fob.

"We'll find him. It's just a matter of time. His photo is everywhere."

"In that matter of time, who knows how many others he'll attack or kill?" I got into the car. "I'm going to drop this car back at the station. I'll see you in the morning."

"When you get back to the station, park the cruiser, get in your car, and leave. Don't go inside. You'll end up sitting there all night, looking over the file. Go home and get some sleep. It's an order."

"Fine. See you tomorrow." I hung up.

I swapped cars at the station and pulled the Mustang into my building's underground parking lot a few minutes later. The elevator had an Out of Order sign taped to it. It was the second time in as many days that it had broken. I walked up the five flights of stairs to my condo and unlocked the door. The jingling of Butch's bell grew louder as he ran to the door. I wasn't in the mood for a leg thrashing. I reached down and picked him up before he began his attack. He seemed surprised. I walked in and kicked the door closed behind me. Butch didn't claw or try to get away. He just stared at me as I carried him to the kitchen. I set him down on the breakfast bar and gave him a pat on the head. "Good cat."

He turned in a circle and ducked his head into me for another pet. *Hmm… Probably should have tried that before.*

I walked room to room in my condo to make sure I was alone. Cross was holed up somewhere. My condo wasn't out of the question for a place he could have chosen. I got back to the kitchen and tossed everything from my pockets onto the counter. The voicemail light on my phone was still flashing from the last message I hadn't listened to. I hit the button to play the message. It was from Callie, reminding me of our date.

Shit. I have to call her to cancel.

I looked at the number she had called me from—Lefty's. I recognized the number from having called in takeout orders in the past. I dialed it. Within five or six rings, their message played with the hours and specials. She was probably busy. On Saturday nights, the place drew a decent crowd. I glanced over at the clock—10:49 p.m. A walk to the bar might clear my head. I'd talk with Callie and explain what was going on. She would understand, I hoped. I changed, grabbed my wallet, and headed out.

The night air was thick with humidity. I walked slowly, thinking only about Sam.

I walked into Lefty's twenty minutes later. As I'd assumed, the place was packed. An end spot at the bar opened, and I took a seat. Callie was working the other end, and another bartender was taking orders over by the pool table. I sat and waited. She spotted me and came over.

"Hey, handsome. Couldn't wait until tomorrow huh? Beer? Food?"

I smiled and thought for a second. I couldn't remember the last time I had eaten, but I didn't have an appetite. "Just a beer, I guess. Do you have a couple minutes to talk?"

She poured me a beer from the tap and set it on a coaster in front of me. She let out a sigh. "That sounds like an *I'm about to bail on tomorrow* talk. Give me a couple minutes to grab some drinks for the guys at the end of the bar. I'm about due for a break here, anyway."

I nodded. She left to do her rounds.

She came back a few minutes later and slid herself in between my chair and the wall. "Okay, talk to me," she said.

I laid out the whole story for her—Cross, him breaking into my house, what he had done to Samantha, everything. She hit me with a barrage of questions. She asked if Samantha was going to be all right. I told her that I didn't know. She asked if I'd be all right. I shrugged. She asked if there was anything she could do. We talked for almost a half hour. She gave me her number in case I just wanted to talk. She wrote it on a napkin and drew a little heart. I jammed it into my pocket. She told me the invitation for dinner was open ended. She understood. Callie gave me a hug and apologized for having to get back to work. I ordered another beer.

Chapter 47

He wasn't planning on running into Kane. Bob had figured that was the last place he'd be tonight though it didn't appear he was there to drink away his sorrows. The lieutenant took small sips from his beer. He seemed to be waiting on something. Bob scooted his chair farther back into the corner and tugged his hat down a little lower. He had buzzed his hair short and cut his beard off. A store up the street provided some clothes that would be more suitable on someone twenty years younger. The tools and lingerie were in a black backpack at the side of his chair. The cop's gun was tucked into his waistband.

A few groups of people sitting between them obscured his view of Kane. Bob made it look as though he was trying to watch the small television at that end of the bar. The woman bartender that had been serving him squeezed herself in next to Kane. She leaned in close and talked to him. They were closer than acquaintances would get. From what Bob could see, she looked concerned. She rubbed

Kane's shoulder. They talked for at least twenty minutes before she left Kane's side and went back to taking orders from around the room. Bob grabbed a beer from the other bartender on her last round through. He needed to pay and leave before he was spotted.

The bartender that had talked to Kane walked up. "Need another beer? Same thing?"

Bob swished the last remaining beer around in the bottle. "I think I'm good. Just the bill, I guess."

She flashed him a smile. "You guess? Or are you sure? Half-price drinks run for another half hour."

Bob smiled back and looked over at Kane. The lieutenant's attention was focused on the television. "You know, what the hell—one more."

"Okay, I'll be right back with your beer."

"Thanks." Bob watched her walk away. The girl rounded the bar and said a few words to Kane. A few minutes later, she came back through the room with a tray, delivering the drinks.

She finished with Bob, dropping off his beer. "There you go, hon. Need anything else?"

"Just the check. Let me pick up the lieutenant's over there, too."

"You know Kane?"

Bob took a pull from his beer and wiped his mouth with the back of his hand. "No. Just recognize him from the television and papers. Seems like a good guy trying to do his part to keep the city safe and all that. Man, that's terrible what that guy the police are after is doing. Have you seen that?"

She nodded. "One second, let me get those tabs." She looked through the receipts from her back pocket. She placed the two bills before him.

"Thanks," Bob said. He totaled them up and handed her thirty dollars.

"Hold on, I'll grab your change," she said.

"Nope, we're all set. The rest is for you." He left her an eight-dollar tip on a twenty-two dollar tab. Bob slammed the beer and stood from his table.

"Oh, thanks. Want me to tell the lieutenant you're picking up his beers?"

He held out a hand to wave her question off. "No, no. It's the least I can do for what he does for the city. No recognition required."

She smiled widely. "Yeah, he's keeping us all safe. Okay, thanks. Have a good night." She left to head back to the bar. As Bob headed out the front door, he saw Kane wave her over.

Is that his girlfriend?

He walked around the corner and up the next street. He stopped in the darkness and waited to see if Kane would come looking for him.

Chapter 48

I sat in a fog, staring at the television above the bar. Callie came to check on me a handful of times. I told her I'd be fine. The last beer I ordered went warm. The thought of me sitting there getting drunk registered in my head as pathetic. I waved Callie over.

"Heading out?" she asked.

"Yeah. Can you close me out?"

"Someone already got your tab."

"Someone got my tab? Who?"

"The guy who sat at the table back there." She pointed toward the back of the bar. "He paid his bill and told me he wanted to get yours too. Said he recognized you from the news. Got up and left a little bit ago."

No one, other than Hank, had ever picked up my bar tab there before—especially because they recognized me as a cop. I spun around in my chair and looked at the door.

"What did he look like?"

She shrugged. "I don't know, just some guy."

"Describe him. Big guy, little guy?"

"Smaller, I guess."

"Hair?"

She shrugged.

"Did he have longer, stringy hair?"

"No."

"Have you seen him in here before?"

"I couldn't say. Maybe?"

"Did he have a beard?"

She shook her head. "A beard?"

I rubbed my face. "Beard?"

"No. Why? What's with all the questions about who picked up your tab?"

"Did he come in after me, or was he already here?"

"He came in an hour or so before you. What is going on with you? I feel like I'm being interrogated."

I let out a breath. "Nothing. I'm sorry."

She grabbed me by my chin and lifted my head. "Are you okay?"

I sat quietly.

A look of concern spread across her face.

"I'm just beat. I need to get home and go to bed. If you see the guy again, tell him I said thanks."

"Yeah, no problem. You want me to get you a cab?"

"Nah, I'm going to hoof it. Try to clear my head some more. Again, I'm sorry." I looked down at the bar.

"Don't worry about me. Remember, you can call me to talk, okay?"

I nodded.

"Okay?" she asked again.

"Okay."

I said my farewell and started the walk home. I wondered if Cross had been at the bar—but why?

It couldn't have been him. You're just being paranoid.

An odd noise behind me caught my attention. I patted my side—no gun. I heard the noise again and turned around. A couple of college kids crossed the street a half a block back. I let out a deep breath. My constant thinking about Cross, mixed with a severe lack of sleep over the last week, was catching up to me.

My walk home ended up being event free. I got back to my condo and climbed the stairs to the fifth floor. My leg was saved from Butch's wrath again when I scooped him up and placed him on the breakfast bar. I looked at my gun sitting in the holster hanging from the barstool. I slid it out and dropped the magazine into my hand. The gun was still loaded. I ejected the bullet in the chamber and reloaded. Then I went room to room, clearing my condo. It was empty, aside from the cat and me.

I made my way out to the patio, slid the door closed behind me, and had a seat. I sat in silence and looked out over the water. The lights from the hospital shone off the bay's surface in the distance. I wondered how Sam was doing. Lately, she had been on my mind more than ever before, since the divorce, and any prior thoughts had usually been filled with anger. The anger was gone. I just wanted her to be all right. I checked the time. My watch read a couple minutes after one o'clock. My bed was calling. I had to get some rest. I decided to stop in at the hospital in the morning to see if someone could give me an update on her condition.

Chapter 49

He watched Kane from the darkness up the street. He was on foot, and Bob contemplated a surprise attack, but that seemed wrong. It didn't fit in with the game the two were playing. After Kane was out of sight, Bob made his way to the alley behind the bar. He waited patiently until a few minutes after three, figuring the staff had to be leaving soon. Three cars sat parked against the side of the building—a newer BMW, a Ford pickup, and an old, beat-up Toyota. Bob sat in the darkness behind a dumpster and watched the back door across the alley. His backpack leaned against the brick wall behind him. In his hands were a syringe filled with five milliliters of Xylazine and the cop's gun. Between the two, he could handle any situation when the staff left.

The back door opened. A man in a white apron walked out and tossed two bags of trash into the dumpster Bob was hiding behind. The garbage bags clanged to the bottom, and the guy flipped the lids closed. Bob crouched close to the wall. The man turned his back and walked toward the pickup truck. He hopped in, fired up the motor, and rolled down the windows. Loud rock music filled the alley. He pulled out and made a right onto the street. *Perfect.* From what he had seen inside, two bartenders remained—both female. He'd caught their names from their name tags. Callie was the dark-haired one talking to Kane. Becky was the shorter, chunkier one.

He waited another ten minutes until the door opened again. Both women filed out at the same time. The girl that had talked to Kane, Callie, stuck a key in the door and locked it. Becky stood and waited. Bob waited too—across the alley, just twenty feet away.

"You have to work tomorrow?" Becky asked.

"Nope. Off day. I was supposed to have a date, but it's not looking that way now."

"Oh yeah, your date with the lieutenant? What happened?"

"Long story." She hit a button on her key fob, and the BMW's lights flashed.

Becky walked toward the beat-up Toyota. "He's a catch, Cal. Don't give up."

Callie laughed. "I don't plan on it. There's just something about him." She dug into her purse. "Dammit, I forgot my phone."

"Want me to wait?" Becky asked.

"Nah, go ahead."

"Okay. See you Monday." She stepped into her car and closed the door.

Callie unlocked the building's back door and headed

inside. Becky started her car.

Bob waited. "Come on, leave," he said under his breath.

The Toyota inched forward and stopped.

"Leave." Bob willed her to pull out.

He waited. Thirty seconds passed. The car hadn't moved. His window was closing. The Toyota's brake lights lit the alley. The transmission clicked down into drive. She pulled forward. Bob scooped up his backpack and stayed low. He rushed to the rear door of the BMW. The Toyota still sat, waiting to turn out. It pulled into the street as Bob pulled the door handle to get into the back of Callie's car. As he closed the door behind himself, he heard the back door of the bar slam shut. The interior light of the car was still on. He glanced over the front seats, and the girl wasn't looking. She stood facing the back door of the bar, locking up. The lights inside the car faded off. Bob lay still.

The door opened, and the interior lights came back on. The girl hopped into the driver's seat and started the car. Bob sprang up and wrapped his left arm around her chin. The syringe in his right hand found the side of her neck. He held her as she struggled. She went unconscious in a matter of seconds. Bob got out and opened the driver's door. He pushed her into the passenger seat and flopped her legs over. Her purse lay at his feet. Bob dug through it, found her wallet, and tossed the bag over his shoulder. He dug through the wallet and found her driver's license. It listed her address out in Tampa Palms. Bob clicked through the prompts on the car's navigation screen and clicked the button that said Go Home. The car mapped the course to the address on her license.

He cranked up the volume on the radio for the twenty-minute drive from the bar to her house. He pulled up to the subdivision. The iron front gates were closed. Over his shoulder, he checked the car's rear window for a gate-entry sticker—nothing. He checked her key chain for a clicker that would open them—again nothing. He found four buttons on the visor and pressed them one after the other. When he reached the fourth button on the visor, the subdivision's gates let out a screech as they parted. He pulled in.

The second street to the right was hers. He followed it to the address and pulled into the driveway. The house was a newer beige two story. In that part of town and that neighborhood, it had to be over a quarter-million dollars. Landscaping lights lined the driveway on both sides. Small shrubs and a handful of palm trees surrounded the small sidewalk leading to the front door. The girl, house, and car didn't fit. Bob wondered if a man was at home.

He went through the buttons on the visor again until the garage door opened. The garage was empty, with no other cars, no work benches, no tool boxes, nor any signs that a man would be present. He pulled the car in, got out, and went to the passenger side. Bob opened the door and unbelted Callie. Her legs, which were resting against the door, flopped out. He'd have to drag her. He pulled her the rest of the way out of the car and did his best to keep her vertical while he hip bumped the passenger door closed. As he stood holding her up in the garage, he noticed a man walking past the front of the house. The guy looked up the driveway at Bob in the garage.

"Too much to drink!" Bob shouted down to him.

The guy let out a chuckle and threw him a wave. "Designated driver, huh?"

Bob waved back and smiled. "Something like that."

The man continued walking. When he was out of sight, Bob let her flop to the ground. He went into the backseat, rummaged through her purse, and pulled out her cell phone. Bob slipped the phone into his pocket and pulled Callie's body through the doorway into the house. He slapped the button on the wall to lower the garage door. Bob found a light switch inside and flicked it on.

"Nice place," he said.

He dragged her out to the living room and dropped her onto the couch. He double-checked the house to make sure they were alone—they were. Bob's stomach rumbled. He headed to the kitchen to raid the refrigerator. He fixed himself a sandwich, grabbed a soda, and went to sit at an unconscious Callie's side. The television remote lay on a cushion by his right hand. He flicked on the TV and found the comedy channel. He laughed at the television as he ate. When he finished, he walked his plate to the kitchen and set it in the sink. Bob slapped his hands together.

"Are you ready for the fun?" he asked.

Callie didn't respond.

Bob had spent the hours lying in wait in the alley planning out their final confrontation. His place in history would be cemented after he was done with the lieutenant.

Bob chose the upstairs bathroom for the location. He rolled Callie from the couch to the floor and began the process of dragging her upstairs. His leg burned with each step. A coughing attack overtook him halfway up. It was worse than the previous ones. He collapsed. Blood spattered the carpet of the stairs. More than a minute passed without him being able to get a breath. His lungs were shutting down, but he only needed a little longer. Bob used the railing to pull himself to his feet. He dragged Callie's body the rest of the way upstairs and flopped her in the bathroom's garden tub. His backpack rested on the counter while Bob dressed Callie in the lingerie.

He stood alongside the tub and balled up the clothing she'd worn. Bob wiped the blood from the side of his mouth. "You look just about ready. Well, two of the players are here. I guess we're ready to call up the third."

He pulled out the girl's cell phone from his pocket. He scrolled the call log. The lieutenant's number showed up. Bob hit Talk.

Chapter 50

My phone vibrated across my nightstand and woke me. My alarm clock read 4:14 a.m. I'd been in bed for three hours—asleep for maybe one. I grabbed my phone and rubbed my eyes. The caller ID showed a number I didn't recognize. I hit Talk. "Lieutenant Kane."

"Hey, Lieutenant! I didn't wake you, did I?"

I scooted up in bed. "Cross."

"Ah, you remembered my voice. How did your ex-wife turn out?"

"You're going to pay for what you did, you piece of shit."

"I kind of had to hurry to get it done. Well, don't leave me hanging. How is she?"

"None of your damn business how she is."

"Did she turn out as good as the other one? Or is she dead?"

I didn't respond. My blood was boiling.

"I guess it doesn't matter."

I balled my bedsheets in my hand and squeezed them in anger. "What do you want, Cross?"

"I just sent you a photo. Let me know when you get it."

I looked at the screen of my phone. The indication for a text message came up, and I clicked it. It was a photo of a half-naked woman lying in a tub. She wore green lingerie. I zoomed in. The girl's hair was covering her face, but I recognized the tattoos. It was Callie.

He laughed into the phone. "Hey Kane, did you enjoy the beers I bought you?"

Realization hit me like a flood. He had been at the bar. He had seen me talking to her. He had her. I sprang from my bed and grabbed the clothes I'd worn to the bar just a few hours earlier. I grabbed the napkin that Callie had written her phone number on. The number was the same as the one he was calling from. "What the hell did you do to her, Cross?"

"Watch that temper, Lieutenant. I haven't done anything yet—just gave her a little something to put her to sleep. She's pretty hot. Is she your girlfriend?"

"No."

"But she wants to be. I heard her talking with her friend at the bar. It would be a shame if something happened to her."

"I swear I'm going to kill you."

He laughed again. "Oh Lieutenant, you and your threats. I told you I haven't started yet."

"What do you want, Cross? Why are you doing this?"

"Oh, I don't know. Fame, recognition, good and evil,

boredom. I'd guess a little bit of a combination of those." He coughed into the phone. "Let's get back to business. I have a challenge for you. Ready to go over the rules?"

"Where are you?"

"Not yet. Rules first."

I sat quietly.

"Come on, Carl. I'm going to tell you where I am this time. This will be easy if you can follow the rules. You ready for them, or what?"

"What are your rules?"

"Good. First, you come alone. Just you. If I spot another cop anywhere, I'm going to drive this ice pick through her eye. Second, you come unarmed. The first glimpse of a gun I see, she gets it. Third, you are on a time limit to get here. You'll have exactly thirty minutes to arrive. A second after, and the fun starts. Clear?"

"Where are you?"

"Are we clear on the rules?"

"Yeah!"

"I'm at her house. Your time has started." He hung up.

I hit the stopwatch on my phone. After a quick stop at my closet safe, I tossed my clothes on and was on my way within two minutes.

I grabbed my wallet and pulled the napkin with her address from within. After I punched it into my car's navigation system, it told me the drive would take twenty-four minutes. I fired her address and a short text message off to Hank, Jones, and the rest of my team. I wasn't going without backup, but he'd kill her if he saw red-and-blues before I got there.

I pulled to the front gates of her neighborhood in less than twenty minutes. They were closed. I backed up. The thought only took a second. I knew what had to be done.

"Sorry, car," I said.

I put the Mustang back into first and slammed the gas pedal to the floor. The gates crashed open, leaving pieces of the front of my limited edition Mustang destroyed and sliding across the pavement. The airbags filled my car with smoke. I jammed the steering wheel airbag out of my way and kept my foot on the gas. I sped past the first street. My GPS showed an arrow to the right in two hundred feet. I slid the car around the corner. Loose pieces of bumper flew into one of the neighbor's yards. The navigation in my car told me the house was approaching on the right. I caught the house number and locked up the brakes.

I got out and rushed to the front door, knowing full well I could be running into a trap. The front door was locked. I put my elbow through the door's glass and reached in to unlock it. After a few seconds of fumbling, I managed to get it open.

I stepped inside. The house was black, aside from a bit of light coming from upstairs. I ran up. The hall spread out left and right. The light was coming from the half-opened door at the end of the hall. I rushed to it and pushed the door the rest of the way open. A master bedroom spread out before me. I spotted more light coming from underneath a closed door at the back of the room. I went to it and kicked it open.

Cross held Callie as a shield in the garden tub. He smiled. His hair and beard were gone. Behind him was a frosted-glass window. To my right were dual sinks and a vanity—a hammer and a spoon sat on the side closer to Cross. A bag of zip ties lay on the counter next to me. To my left was a stand-up shower and toilet. Callie looked unconscious but didn't show any signs that he had hurt her further. I could see both of her hands—she wasn't branded. In Cross's left hand was an ice pick held next to Callie's eye—in his right, a pistol aimed at my head.

Cross rolled his wrist and looked at his watch. "Twenty-eight minutes and change, Lieutenant. You just made it. Good job."

"Put the ice pick down. This is between me and you."

He shook his head. "I think I'll be holding onto it. Tell me, did you follow my other rules? Did you request backup? Did you bring a gun?"

"No."

"I'm not quite ready to take your word for it. Lift up your shirt and spin around."

I pulled up the T-shirt I was wearing and showed him I didn't have anything in my waist. "Satisfied?"

"Pat down your cargo pockets for me too."

I did. They were empty.

"Now, what about calling for backup, Lieutenant?"

"I didn't call anyone."

"Why not? I would have."

"Because I want to be the one who kills you."

"That's not how a police officer should talk. Your job is

to protect and serve. So far, you've been a little lacking in the protection department, though."

"I'll do my service to the community by putting you in the ground."

He smiled widely. "Well, we have a predicament then because I don't plan on dying just yet."

"Put her down and get out of the tub."

"Seems you forgot I am the one holding the gun. I'll be the one giving the orders here. Get on your knees."

I stood my ground.

Cross poked at the corner of Callie's eye with the ice pick. A drip of blood trickled down her cheek.

"Okay, okay." I went to my knees, one at a time.

"Reach up and take the bag of zip ties. Place two around your wrists and pull them tight."

"How am I supposed to do that?"

"Put them around your hands, slide them down to your wrists, and pull them as tight as you can with your teeth."

I did as I was told. I sat kneeling and cuffed in front of him.

"Try to break free from the ties."

I gave it a halfhearted attempt.

"You better try harder!"

I pulled my wrists against them as hard as I could, so the plastic cut into my flesh.

"Good." Cross dropped Callie down into the tub and stood. He held the gun pointed at my head. "You make one fast move, and you're dead." He set the ice pick down and approached. He wrapped another zip tie around my wrists and pulled it tight. Three more zip ties were added around my ankles. Cross walked back to Callie at the tub and stepped in.

I knelt, wrists and ankles bound.

"Now you get to watch the process. Just remember, any sudden moves out of you, and I could slip, and she'll be dead. Well, that and if you make a move, I'll grab this gun here and shoot you. But I don't want to do that. You see, I have plans for you." He placed the gun on the vanity countertop next to him and picked up the spoon, ice pick, and hammer.

I needed to keep his attention focused on me and not Callie. "What plans are those?"

"I'm glad you asked, Carl. You don't mind if I just call you Carl, do you? I think we're to the point where we can be on a first-name basis by now."

I didn't respond.

"First, did you notice that I didn't brand her?"

I nodded.

"I'm going to make you watch the entire process. After I get through with the little bar bitch here, I'm going to inject you with Xylazine and then lobotomize you. Tell me that won't fetch headlines: 'Psycho Surgeon Lobotomizes Cop Hunting Him'. Sounds like Hollywood to me."

I said nothing.

"No response? Really?"

I remained quiet.

"Well, if you got nothing to say, I guess we can just get started, then." He pressed the spoon against her eye.

"Please, Cross. Don't do it."

He ignored me and wiggled the spoon under her eyelid.

I shook my head. "Please! I'm begging you!"

He paused and rolled his eyes at me. "You're begging me? Come on. Have a little respect for yourself." He took the ice pick from the counter.

"Please!" I yelled. I jammed both hands down between my legs. My head touched the floor as I bowed to him.

"Geez. You're pathetic. Are you going to cry next?"

I stuck my hands into the front of my shorts and down into my Ultimate Concealment holster—one of my purchases from the last gun show. It looked like a jock strap with a spot for a pistol that sat in front of my manhood. Then I raised my head from the floor and aimed the gun at his chest.

His eyes caught the gun, and he scrambled for his pistol on the counter. I fired. The bullet caught his left shoulder as he reached his gun. He stumbled in the tub and tripped over Callie's body. He fired off a shot as he fell backward. The bullet hit the ceiling above me. I fired again, catching him dead center in the chest. His backward momentum sent him crashing through the window.

I used the bathroom counter to pull myself to my feet. I rummaged the drawers for anything that would cut the plastic ties. A pair of nail clippers caught my eye, and I snatched them up and quickly freed my hands and legs. I rushed to Callie and checked her pulse—it was strong. A pair of gunshots rang outside in succession. I pulled myself over to the broken window and looked out.

A body was lying on the grass along the side of the house below, but it wasn't Cross.

"Awww," the man said. He rolled backward and curled into the fetal position. It was Hank. "Son of a bitch shot me in the vest. I hit him. He ran," Hank said.

"Which way did he go?" I shouted.

He pointed through the backyard as he tried to get to his feet. "Jones went after him."

"I'll be right down."

I checked Callie's pulse again—still strong. I rushed through the hall, down the stairs, and out the front door. An ambulance pulled to the curb right as I exited the house. The EMTs piled out.

"There's a woman upstairs in the bathroom that needs medical attention. She's been drugged."

One of the EMTs gave me a nod, and they jogged toward the house.

"Where are you going to take her?"

"Tampa General!" he shouted.

Chapter 51

I rushed around the side of Callie's house, looking for Hank. He was gone. I ran in the direction he'd pointed, through Callie's backyard and through the yard behind that. Still no one. In the middle of the next street, I stopped and looked left to right. I couldn't see anyone up or down the block. I continued through the yard in front of me. Someone called my name.

"Kane."

I heard it again.

It was Hank's voice in a hard whisper.

I looked to my right into the next yard. The shadows of two men waved me over. Hank and Jones were standing to the side of a house. I crouched and ran over.

"You okay?" I asked.

"Hit me in the trauma plate; otherwise, I'd still be lying there crying," Hank said.

Jones pointed toward the back of the house kitty-corner to where we stood. "I think he's in the lanai of that house there."

"Think or know?" I asked.

"Someone went in from the outside and ducked into the corner. No lights ever came on."

I nodded and looked to Hank, "You said you shot him?"

"Center mass."

"So did I. He's got to be wearing a vest. Keep it in mind."

"Where did he get a vest?"

I thought about it for a second. "Donner's."

They both nodded.

"Jones, loop around the houses and approach from the other side. I'll take the center. Hank, you take the left side. Stay low—be smart."

Jones disappeared. Hank and I closed in.

"You have body armor?" Hank asked.

I shook my head.

Jones popped out on the right side of the house and took cover to wait for us. Hank and I stayed close to the ground and made our way into the yard behind the lanai where Jones had claimed Cross was. A motion light on the house's back patio flicked on and lit us up like a spotlight. Two shots rang as the light from a muzzle flash appeared inside the lanai. We both dropped to the ground. Another shot sounded, and another flash came from the lanai. The bullet smacked against the back of the house, two feet from my head. We scrambled into the darkness on the side of the house next to Jones. The 10-71 call for a shooting came over the radio. We'd have backup in minutes.

"Hit?" I asked Hank.

"No. You?"

I shook my head.

Behind where Cross was pinned down, the lights in the house flickered on. The house was occupied and they were awake. Cross could turn him being cornered into a hostage situation. I hoped the people ran out their front door as soon as the first shot was fired.

"What the hell are we supposed to do? We don't have a visual, and we can't just fire into the darkness. We can't risk injuring someone inside the house," Jones said.

"Let me think," I said.

"How much ammo you think he has?" Hank asked.

"Ten more bullets if he didn't fire any before the first one at me—maybe an extra clip. He has Donner's Glock."

Four gunshots boomed, and I heard glass shatter. Nothing was hit around us.

"What the hell was that?" Jones asked.

I glanced around the corner of the house. I heard another shot and saw a spark off the patio. The bullet ricocheted into the house next to us. More gunfire came from the lanai aimed into the house—Cross was returning fire. I spun back around the corner.

"What the hell is going on?" Hank asked.

"Damn homeowner is shooting at Cross from inside the house. Cross is returning fire. Hank, get the people out of these houses back here. I don't want a stray bullet catching someone in bed."

Hank rushed off to the front of the houses. Cross was pinned down. He knew we were outside, and now he was taking fire from the homeowner.

I yelled across the yard, "Homeowner, this is the Tampa Police! Stop firing and leave the front of your residence immediately!"

I listened for a response but heard none. I caught the lights of squad cars pulling up to the front of the house. "Jones, call on your radio to get that dumbass out of the house before he shoots one of us or his neighbors."

"Or gets himself killed." Jones made the call and let the other officers know we were in the backyard.

A patrolman made his way along the side of the house. I assumed another was on the other side. I motioned for the officer coming at us to stop. He continued forward.

"Tell them to wait!"

Jones thumbed his lapel mic. "This is Detective Max Jones—hold your positions. Repeat, hold your positions."

The officer stopped. Cross had nowhere to go. Hank came back to my side.

A call came over Jones's radio, an 11-41. The homeowner must have been shot. The *all clear* for the house came a second later. We had officers inside.

"Tell someone to turn on the back lights," I said.

Jones requested it over the radio, and the lanai lit up. I glanced around the corner to get a view but didn't see Cross. A short brick wall and the back of an outdoor brick fireplace stood before a pool and a hot tub. Then I caught movement, the officers inside that lit-up house. The open-concept floor plan and giant glass windows in the back was presenting Cross with a shooting gallery. Cross fired three shots through the house's back patio door at the officers inside. The door cascaded to the ground in a shower of safety glass.

"Shit. Tell them to kill the lights inside and get out of the house. Cross is going to pick them off one by one."

Jones barked out instructions over his radio. The house went black inside. I caught movement in the lanai. Cross was taking cover in the corner behind the fireplace. He had himself a brick bunker. Two shots echoed, and the lanai went dark. Cross had shot out the outdoor lighting.

"Think he'll surrender?" Hank asked.

I cupped my hands around my mouth to carry my voice. "Cross, you're done. We have you on all sides. Give up now before someone else gets hurt."

Bullets slammed into the side of the house next to us.

"Are you dead, Carl?"

"No. You're a lousy shot."

"Stick your head around the corner again and find out."

"Doesn't look like he plans on surrendering, Hank," Jones said.

"How many shots does he have left?" Hank asked.

"I don't know."

"What are we going to do? Wait on SWAT?" Hank asked.

I nodded. "They'll be here soon. Check on it, Jones."

He thumbed his mic. The call came back. They'd be there in ten minutes.

I cupped my hands around my mouth. "SWAT will be here in a few minutes, Cross. What do you think your chances are?"

He didn't fire at us. Cross didn't say a word for almost a minute. "I give up."

"Come on out. No gun. Lay on the grass facedown."

"I'll lay right back here on the patio. You come and get me. Just you. One more cop, and I'm shooting."

"I don't think you have any bullets left."

"Are you willing to bet a life on that?"

Hank swiped at my shoulder. "Wait for SWAT. He's just trying to get you over there to shoot you."

I nodded.

"No deal. We're going to wait for SWAT."

"Fine. More people are going to die."

The patrolman moved closer to the lanai on the side of the house. He was trying to look into the back, to get a visual on Cross.

"Get that guy back!" I yelled.

Jones called to him over the radio. In the middle of Jones's command to the officer, Cross fired off three rounds at the cop, who dropped to the ground and pulled himself back to the side of the house.

"Are you hit?" Jones asked.

The word *shoulder* came over the radio, followed by moans of pain and profanities. Jones put out the call that an officer was down.

"He's got another clip," I said.

Hank shook his head. "Just wait for SWAT."

"He's going to kill one of our guys. Let me try to put an end to this."

"I have to agree with the sergeant here, Lieutenant. Let's

just wait," Jones said.

"Just let me try to talk to him." I turned my head around the corner of the house. "Cross, I'm coming. Throw your gun in the pool."

"Not until I see it's only you."

"Hold on." I lowered my voice to give Hank and Jones their commands. They nodded and disappeared into the night.

"What are you doing, Carl? No tricks."

"I'm not walking up there until you toss the gun."

"I'm not tossing it until you walk up here."

"All right Cross—just remember, I'm a better shot than you. If you fire, I'm putting one between your eyes."

"Fair enough. Come on over."

I crouched and rolled myself around the corner of the house. I could see the short brick wall he was hiding behind. I was confident that if he stood to fire, I'd get a shot off before he did. The back door of the lanai stood a few feet in front of me. I reached out with my left hand. My right kept the barrel of my gun pointed in his direction. I tried glancing into the house to confirm Hank and Jones had made it in—I couldn't tell.

"I'm here. Toss the gun into the pool."

"Just you?"

"Just me."

A splash came from the lit-up pool. It sounded about the size of a gun. I waited for the ripples to subside and looked into the pool. A gun lay at the bottom. I entered the lanai.

"Are you facedown?"

"I'm shot, Carl. Come here, and let's get this over with."

I crouched at the corner of the brick bar and waited, ready to spring into action. Jones and Hank's instructions were to light up the inside of the house and take cover. The light would get his attention, and I could get the drop on him.

"Are you coming or what? I need an ambulance. I'm losing a lot of blood."

"Why would I give a shit if you bled out?" I asked.

He coughed. "Come on, Lieutenant. Think about all the television coverage of my trial if I make it that long."

The lights inside flickered on. I immediately rounded and found Cross, aiming at his forehead. Cross sat hunched in the corner. His left sleeve and left pant leg were soaked in blood. His hands were empty.

"Asshole in the house shot me in the leg. I think it hit an artery."

"Good," I said.

"I got him, though. Put two right in his chest through that window there." He motioned to a sliding glass door that must have led to a bedroom. Shattered glass littered the ground.

"Lay down, Cross. Put your hands behind your back."

He hunched over and moved his hands behind himself. He pulled his right arm from behind his back with a pistol.

"Drop it!"

I heard two shots—one right after the other. A flicker of light came from inside the house. A muzzle flash came from the barrel of Cross's gun. I returned fire, hitting him three times in the chest. It was instinct—the thought of him wearing a bulletproof vest never crossed my mind.

Cross hunched over to the ground. Vest aside, the close range of my shots would have broken his ribs at a minimum. His pistol fell and skidded a few feet away. I went to kick it. Then I felt pain—burning, searing pain from the left side of my head. I reached for it and pulled my hand back—blood. I touched it again. It was hot. Hank and Jones rushed through the back patio doors of the house. Jones pushed Cross over and pulled his hands behind his back. Hank came to me. I touched my head again.

"Put one in him as soon as I saw the gun. He must have gotten the homeowner's weapon somehow," Hank said.

I didn't respond. I poked at my head with my fingers then looked at them.

"Are you hit?" Hank asked.

I still didn't respond.

He grabbed me by the shoulders and turned me so he could see the side of my head.

"Whoa!" He poked at my head with his finger.

"Oww!" I jerked my head away.

"You got a four-inch graze across the side of your head above your ear. It's charred. It's like an inch wide." He looked closer and raised his eyebrows. "It's pretty deep." He headed for Jones and glanced back over his shoulder. "It looks cauterized. You'll be fine."

I touched my head again. If that bullet had been a half inch to the left, I would have been dead. If Hank hadn't shot him when he did, I would have been dead.

Cross lay facedown on the patio's brick pavers. Still alive, he let out a moan. Jones was still pinning him down. I approached.

"I'll let you have the honors." Jones handed me his cuffs and pulled himself to his feet. I took his place and planted my knee into Cross's spine. He flipped his head to the right and moaned from the pain of my weight. The moan turned to a scream when I twisted his right arm behind his back.

Cross spoke, his voice quiet. "Don't let me die yet. I want there to be a trial."

I clicked the right cuff down and twisted his left arm back to link him up. I let out a deep breath when the second cuff clicked. Jones called over his radio that the scene was secure and the paramedics could come.

I stood and looked down at Cross, cuffed at my feet.

He turned his head. Blood bubbled from his mouth. "I don't think I'm going to make it, Carl."

I pulled him to his feet. His knees buckled. I sat him down against the side of the house. "Where are those paramedics?"

"They're coming," Jones said.

We waited. Jones came over to get a look at the side of my head. It was a good couple minutes before the EMTs appeared from the side of the house. They gathered around Cross. He was unconscious.

One of the EMTs looked up at me. "Do you know how many times he's been shot?" Before I had a chance to respond, his expression changed as he noticed the gash running along the side of my head. "Geez, what the hell is that from? We need to get you to the hospital." He stood from Cross and approached. He grabbed my chin and turned my head so he could examine the wound more closely. "Geez," he said again.

"All right, all right." I pushed his hands away. "I'll get myself there and get patched up. Is he going to live?" I jerked my chin at Cross. Two EMTs were at his side. A pool of blood was forming under him.

"I can't say. He looks pretty bad."

"The homeowner? I asked.

"The guy should make it. We have a crew inside attending to him now." The EMT went to assist the others in loading Cross onto a gurney.

"I'll keep an eye on him while they take him in," Jones said.

"Thanks, Jones. We'll meet you at the hospital." I looked at Hank. "Ready?"

"Yeah, I'll drive you," he said.

"I can drive, Hank."

"You're not driving anywhere, and speaking of which, what are you going to drive? I seem to remember seeing a totaled Mustang somewhere."

"Shit." I'd forgotten about my car.

"Just wait here. I'll pick you up out front."

"Fine."

Hank went to get the car. I walked over spent shell casings as I made my way through the lanai toward the door.

Chapter 52

Seventeen shiny staples and numerous stitches later, my head was back together. Eight days of medical leave had been mostly filled staying in at the house, sleeping, and trying to avoid the media when I did leave. I couldn't turn on the television without seeing a report on the case. The media was camping out in front of my condo in hopes of catching a glimpse of me or getting a sound bite. The station had given them a full press release early in the week with all the details of the case. I didn't feel much like adding to it.

Cross, cuffed to the stretcher, had died on the way to the hospital. The blood loss from the multiple bullet wounds was too much. Cross's death didn't bother me. If he'd lived, he would have been put to death by the state after a lengthy trial. From what the captain said, he wouldn't have lived long enough to get through any court proceedings. The captain got his medical records earlier in the week. He'd only had another few months to live, at the most.

The feds had started to dig into his past. They created a preliminary workup on him. It waited for me at work.

I walked through the front doors of the station. It buzzed with officers and detectives working. The elevator took me up to three. I got off and walked toward the captain's office. Patrolmen and detectives stopped me, to offer their congratulations for catching Cross. I nodded but kept quiet. I got to the bullpen, which went dead silent as I walked through. I headed into the captain's office.

"Kane, how you feeling?"

"Fine. Did you go over the feds' report yet?"

Captain Bostok pointed to the chair. "Take a seat."

I slid a chair out and plopped down.

"Just gave it a once-over." He slid a file across his desk. "This one is for you."

I picked up the file and thumbed it open. It was a half inch thick.

"They say this is going to be an ongoing case. They are looking into unsolved homicides that they may be able to attribute to him."

I nodded.

The captain tapped on the side of his head. "How's the noggin?"

"They say I'll live." I turned so he could get a good view.

"You're going to have to grow some hair to cover that."

I shook my head. "Doc says it shouldn't leave that big of a scar."

He chuckled. "Yeah, I bet."

"So when can I come back?"

"As soon as you're medically cleared."

"Okay. I have an appointment to get these staples out tomorrow. I'll see if he'll sign off on me."

The captain crossed his arms over his belly. "Take your time. There's no rush."

"I just want to get back to normal. This sitting-around-at-home business is driving me nuts. I'll be back on Wednesday."

"As long as the doctor gives you the green light."

I slapped the file on Cross against my hand. "I'm going to take this with me to read. My ride is waiting outside."

"No problem."

I stood and headed for the captain's door.

"Kane."

I paused. "Yeah?"

"Good job, Lieutenant."

I nodded and walked out.

I saw Hank sitting at his desk on the phone.

He hung up when he saw me heading over. "Are you back or just visiting?"

"I came to grab the file that the feds put together on Cross. You look at it?"

"Yeah. There's some stuff in there, that's for sure. How's the skull?"

"Staples come out tomorrow. Give me the highlights of what's in the file."

"A lot of stuff about his early years—troubled youth, abusive parents. When Cross was seventeen, his mother committed suicide."

"How?"

"Ketamine overdose."

"Are they thinking it may have not been a suicide?"

"Well, seeing as how she was found dead, lying in bed, wearing green lingerie, there has to be some kind of connection there. Whether he actually did it or not, they don't know."

I nodded.

"Ready for the part that's going to throw you for a loop?"

"I'm listening."

"So, after Cross got out of the military, he tried and failed multiple times to get into law enforcement."

I jerked my head back. "What?"

Hank nodded. "Failed the psych exam. Eight times on record in different cities and states. The feds think there may have even been more that weren't recorded."

"So, he wanted to be a cop? Damn good thing it never happened."

"Yeah, well." Hank held up a finger. "Maybe it would have given him something else to focus his energy on other than floating around from city to city doing odd jobs and…" Hank dug through the file. He pulled out four pieces of paper and slid them over. "This."

They were photos of dead women in lingerie. The backgrounds were different in each photo, yet all the women lay in dirt. Each woman was in a different state of decomposition. Orange date stamps sat at the bottom right corners of two of the pictures. The photos were fifteen and twelve years old. I slid the papers back.

"Where did these come from?" I asked.

"Bank records showed payments to a local storage locker. The originals of those photos were buried among a bunch of junk and old furniture."

"Do we know who they are?"

Hank shook his head. "Feds are going to look into the date-stamped ones and cross-reference his location at the time with missing persons in that area. The two that aren't date stamped, we may never know." Hank pushed himself back from his desk. "Cross is dead—at least there won't be more."

I nodded.

"Want to grab lunch?" Hank asked.

I shook my head. "Can't. Karen didn't pack you one this morning?"

"Nah, I told her I wasn't going to eat that garbage anymore—at home or at work."

I wasn't buying Hank's sudden burst of courage toward his wife. "You're full of it."

"Yeah, I know, but I thought about saying that to her. So why can't you go get something to eat?"

"Got a ride waiting outside—going to head back home, look over this file. Plus, I just ate at Dotana's before I came in."

Hank nodded. "How are Samantha and Callie?"

"Well, I stopped by the hospital a couple of times to check on Samantha. She saw me the second time I went to visit, to tell me she didn't want to see me. It seemed like she blamed me for what had happened to her, which I understand, in a way."

"It's not your fault that she was attacked."

"Either way, she was released to Marty's care the other day. The doctors seem hopeful that she will make a full recovery."

He nodded. "Good, good. What about Callie? What's up with her?"

"She's waiting for me outside. I think they are going to total my car, so I'm without wheels until that gets straightened out. She has been chauffeuring me around the last week."

"Does she remember anything?"

I shook my head. "No recollection. She remembers leaving work then waking up at the hospital."

"It's probably for the best that she doesn't remember."

"I agree."

Hank grinned. "So, you guys have been spending some time together, huh?"

I shrugged. "Yeah, I guess. She's been stopping by and bringing me food every night. We watched a couple movies, talked, and just kind of hung out."

"Does she have a toothbrush there yet?"

I smiled. "Not yet. All right, I'll see you in a couple days. Thanks for saving my life, Quickdraw."

He made a gun with his hand and fired. "No sweat, Kane. Enjoy your next few days off."

I headed down two floors and out the front of the station. Callie was waiting at the curb. The windows in her

BMW were rolled down, the music turned up. I opened the door and hopped in.

"Where to?" she asked.

"I don't know. What do you want to do?"

Callie turned the volume on the radio down. "I took off the next week. When do you have to be back at work?"

"I was thinking a couple days." I shrugged. "Or maybe a little longer. The captain told me to take my time."

"Well, I'm up for anything. You call it." She clicked the car into drive and rubbed my knee.

I sat and thought about it for a few seconds. I tossed the file on Cross into the backseat. "Just drive. We'll see where we end up."

The End

Thank you!

Thanks for reading Malevolent, Book 1 in The Cases of Lieutenant Kane Series. I hope you enjoyed it!

To get all the latest news on upcoming releases, you can sign up for my VIP e-mail list at: http://ehreinhard.com/newsletter/ - Lots of good stuff there… freebies, raffles, sneak peeks, and more.

Reviews help other readers find books. I appreciate all reviews, whether positive or negative. If you have a second to spare, a review would be very welcome.

Now that you've read, Malevolent, the first full-length book in the series, dive in with the rest. The six books in the series (listed in order) are: *Malevolent, Requite, Determinant, Perilous, Progeny*, and *Denouement*. I hope you enjoy them all!

New investigations, new cities, and countless dead bodies.

Hank Rawlings has a new title, Agent. His new job description is straightforward—hunt down serial killers operating in the U.S. and bring them to justice. While the purpose of his position may be simple, capturing those responsible for the ultimate evil against their fellow man is far from it.

The six books in the series (listed in order) are: *Drained, Consumed, Committed, Judged, Mounted,* and *Deserted*. I hope you enjoy them all!

Again, thank you for reading!

Visit the E.H. Reinhard author website at:
http://ehreinhard.com/

See all of E.H. Reinhard's available titles at:
http://ehreinhard.com/available-books/

Made in the USA
Las Vegas, NV
20 March 2025